Ovidia Yu is one of Singapore's best-kr
writers. She has had over thirty plays produced and is the author
of a number of comic mysteries published in Singapore, India,
Japan and America.

She received a Fulbright Scholarship to the University of Iowa's
International Writers Program and has been a writing fellow at the
National University of Singapore.

Also by Ovidia Yu

The Yellow Rambutan Tree Mystery

Ovidia Yu

CONSTABLE

CONSTABLE

First published in Great Britain in 2023 by Constable

3 5 7 9 10 8 6 4 2

A CIP catalogue record for this book
is available from the British Library.

ISBN: 978-1-40871-698-4

Typeset in Contenu by SX Composing DTP, Rayleigh, Essex
Printed and bound in Great Britain by Clays Ltd, Elcograf S.p.A.

Papers used by Constable are from well-managed forests
and other responsible sources.

MIX
Paper from
responsible sources
FSC® C104740

Constable
An imprint of
Little, Brown Book Group
Carmelite House
50 Victoria Embankment
London EC4Y 0DZ

An Hachette UK Company
www.hachette.co.uk

www.littlebrown.co.uk

Dedicated to the Taylors:
Richard and Christine
John and Mary

Author's note

———◆———

I remember several rambutan trees in my grandfather's garden and have happy memories of harvest time – which came all year round.

But these were all red rambutans and when bunches of yellow rambutans were bought or gifted they were always considered special. The thin yellow peels covered with light green hairs were carefully set aside to be dried to be used against fevers, upset stomachs and worms.

The Yellow
Rambutan Tree Mystery

Bad Luck Visitors

———◆———

'Hello! Small Boss Chen! Hello! Small Boss Chen!' It was a
man's voice coming from the front porch of the house.
'Sorry to disturb, Small Boss Chen! Hello!'

The front doors of Chen Mansion were closed and locked
because it was 4 February 1946, the Third Day of the Chinese
New Year.

This was the first Chinese New Year since the Japanese
Occupation had ended and the first two days had been hectic
with visitors allowed for the first time in two years. Food was still
in short supply but everyone scraped together what they could.

To add to the confusion, Uncle Chen's wife, Shen Shen, had
insisted all our servants be sent home to spend the entire fifteen
days of Chinese New Year with their families. Shen Shen had
grown up in a rural area with little public transport, like most of
the servants, and I thought it very good of her to think of them.

Of course Ah Ma had argued: 'This is how it's always been,
what! And on the first two days we're going to have so many
visitors. How will we manage with no servants?'

In the end Ah Ma agreed. I suspect she was glad Shen Shen was standing up to her more. People who say only nice things to your face might be aiming daggers at your back.

Of course, with no servants around, we the family had had to serve our visitors ourselves. Those who came to pay their respects might have felt uncomfortable being offered tea by Small Boss Chen, but Uncle Chen got into it, pressing them to eat more, drink more, to stay for a game of mahjong or join him for a smoke on the porch. He was the life and soul of the party, and I saw the man he'd been before his Japanese detention returning. If Shen Shen had anticipated this, she was brighter than any of us gave her credit for.

And then we'd all come down with sickness. I suspected we'd been poisoned by something made from a carefully hoarded can of imported luncheon meat or sausages.

Even if it hadn't been the Third Day we were in no shape to receive visitors.

In Singapore, you don't have to be Chinese to know that Third Day visits are *pantang*, as my grandmother would say. It's a Malay word that sums up Chinese fears of triggering bad luck better than any Chinese word can. The Third Day is reserved for visiting ancestral graves, meaning any spirits you encounter feel justified in tagging along with you wherever you go – and settling there.

In the pre-war days my grandmother, Chen Tai, had been so concerned about *pantang* that any servants returning from family funerals had had to go through an elaborate washing ritual before they were allowed into the house. She'd only relaxed during the Occupation when Japanese soldiers proved more deadly than jealous spirits.

The Year of the Fire Dog couldn't have started worse for us.

I'd spent most of last night throwing up and I'd heard Shen Shen doing the same. We were the lucky ones. I was more exhausted than sick now. Thanks to my sensitive stomach, I doubted there was anything left inside me to do me harm.

Uncle Chen and Ah Ma were the worst hit. They were so weak and groggy they could barely sip warm water. It was almost as though they had been drugged. I was more worried about my grandmother than I dared admit, even to myself. I'd never seen her so weak. She'd been 'old' as long as I could remember, but now suddenly she was frail. In the irregular pauses between her shallow breaths, I wondered what would happen if she didn't take another.

Even before this latest and worst attack, we'd been having regular bouts of bad digestion. Ah Ma had made the servants scrub out all the cooking pots and utensils with lye, and I'd checked and rechecked our well and water supply. But the eels in the well and the guppies in the dragon pots were alive, so I knew the water wasn't to blame.

My system was always quick to reject what didn't agree with it. I'd found the only thing I could keep down was bananas and I'd been pretty much living off them. Luckily, with all of our banana trees, there was always a bunch hanging up behind the kitchen.

Uncle Chen had never regained his old gusto after being released by the Japanese. Now he was fading even faster than Ah Ma. It was a good thing Shen Shen had stepped up to manage the family business.

'Hello! Small Boss Chen! Hello, please!'

I rolled over and pulled my pillow over my head. I was sleeping on a mattress in my grandmother's room. In the old days this had been so Ah Ma could keep an eye on me, but I'd moved back in so I could keep an eye on her.

Just when I thought our rude visitor had taken the hint and gone away I heard him again: 'Hello! Small Boss Chen!' It didn't sound as if he was giving up any time soon.

Something must be really wrong. Uncle Chen and his friends were a superstitious lot and it would take something major to make one of them violate the Third Day visiting taboo.

I had a sudden flashback to my childhood when men were always hanging around outside the house hoping for work. Uncle Chen shouted at them if he saw them, but he had the servants take them water and food. They would never have dared shout for him like this . . . unless it was something really serious.

I heard Ah Ma turn over and struggle to sit up.

'Don't get up. Why doesn't Shen Shen do something? It's her husband they're looking for and her fault there are no servants around.'

'Shen Shen said she would visit the cemetery,' Ah Ma said. 'I told her she could take the car.' Since Uncle Chen had started fading, Shen Shen had learned to drive Ah Ma's old Armstrong Siddeley tourer to collect rents for her.

'By herself?'

Shen Shen must have felt as lousy as I did, but she was a lot more superstitious. Even if I didn't believe in the old superstitions – thanks to my years at the Mission Centre school, I wasn't sure what I believed in – I was impressed by the power they had to motivate people. The Third Day clearing of the ancestral graveyard was supposed to be a family ceremony so Shen Shen going on her own probably defeated the purpose. But if it kept Ah Ma happy I was content. Ah Ma was in no shape to go out either.

Well, if Shen Shen was out . . .

'Don't get up,' I said again. 'I'll go and see who's at the door.' I rolled over and sat up. 'I told Parshanti I would see her mother today anyway.'

I didn't feel much like going, and if Shen Shen had taken the car to the cemetery, I would have to catch the trolley bus into town – but I'd told Mrs Shankar I'd see her for her to take my measurements.

'Tell whoever it is to come back tomorrow,' Ah Ma said, watching me. 'Bad luck. Don't let them in, no matter what they say. Make sure you lock the door after talking to them. Give them some water, but don't use the good cups.'

'What if it's something very important that Uncle Chen needs to hear about?'

'What can be so important? If you let them in, you let bad luck into the house.'

'Yes, Ah Ma.'

I crawled off my mattress, straightened my cotton housedress and headed up the corridor towards the dim front room of the house – all the shutters were closed.

Squinting against the brightness outside, I recognized the figure on the porch by its size, shape and baldness. 'Uncle Botak?'

Botak Beng looked like a gangster, with his tanned brown skin, his blue, black and red tattoos. He was as large as Uncle

Chen but built like a sailor, with bulging arms, shoulders and thighs. And he had a huge shiny brown dome of a head. I knew he had had no hair since his late teens when he'd been nicknamed 'Botak', meaning bald.

Botak had always managed Uncle Chen's sea transportation needs, which some called smuggling. Botak knew the currents and tides and could predict the weather almost by instinct because he'd worked on the sea for so many years. Like a bird or a fish, he could process information from the wind and the waves and come up with the safest routes. He knew all the best landing spots on the Malayan and Indonesian coastlines. I'd also heard he had 'wives' in all the major port villages in Malacca, Taiping, Surabaya and even Darwin, Australia. All his operations centres were run by his wives and children.

Botak and Uncle Chen had worked together before and during the Japanese Occupation, until Botak started expanding his business after the war. Then Uncle Chen had decided he didn't want his goods carried in the same craft Botak Beng used to transport drugs and women: the risk of attracting official attention was too high.

'You're throwing away good money!' Botak had protested. 'I can't afford to send out boats half loaded and, these days, people will pay anything for American cigarettes and Indian ganja!'

But Uncle Chen, backed or possibly directed by Ah Ma, had maintained that Chen money would stay away from the sex and drugs trades. It didn't make sense to many of Uncle Chen's partners, since the newly re-established British authorities seemed to be closing their eyes to what was going on. They mocked him for not daring to pick up money that was falling out of the sky, and many had gone into business for themselves. But they had remained friends – Botak was among the men who'd come to Chen Mansion to pay their Chinese New Year respects on First Day.

'Miss Chen?' Botak Beng peered at me in the dim interior of the house and gave me the nod – almost bow – of acknowledgement due to my late father's daughter. 'Miss Chen, sorry to disturb your house, ah. I must talk to Small Boss Chen at once. Very urgent, very important.'

I stepped outside and pulled the door shut behind me as I nodded to acknowledge him in return. 'What is so important that you need to visit him today?'

I suspected I knew what the visit was about. The British had just announced an official ban on opium smoking. Choosing to announce it during Chinese New Year was a smart – amounting almost to genius – move on the part of the British officials: it was the only time of year all Chinese businesses were more focused on family than finances.

Botak didn't look like an opium smoker, so it was probably his income he was concerned about. Still, I hadn't thought anyone in the Chinese underworld worried about what our British overlords decreed.

'I must talk to Small Boss Chen.'

'Business should wait until after the Third Day at least,' I said, virtuously superstitious.

'This is not that kind of business,' Botak said. He was fidgeting with something in his pocket. I wondered if it was chewing tobacco or a betel wad. He didn't seem aware that his fingers kept going back to it. 'This is man-to-man business. Very important.'

I hadn't intended to let him in – Uncle Chen was in no condition to see him – but even if I had, his saying it was 'man-to-man business' would have scuppered it. Yes, I was being petty. But when you seldom get to indulge in pettiness you make the most of your chances. I stared at him. You'd think an old boatman like Botak would have pushed me aside but he just stood and looked miserable.

'I didn't come straight from my mother's grave. I went to the temple first. All clean already.' Botak Beng waved his arms, turning his palms up and down as though to show he wasn't carrying evil spirits.

That's when I smelt him.

We think of sweat as water and salt, but what comes out of a body depends on what's inside it. Milk-fed babies smell different from toddlers who have started to eat mashed bananas and mangoes. From the smell coming out of him, I could tell that Botak was sick. I didn't know what was causing it but his body was decaying inside.

'Just say what you need,' I said. 'My uncle can't talk to you now, but if you tell me what's the matter we will try to help you. Never mind *pantang*. You are family to my uncle. What's wrong? Do you need money?'

'No, no,' Botak said. 'I don't need money. *Paiseh, lah.*'

Pantang is anything strictly forbidden by custom or superstition. Asking for money was *paiseh*: embarrassing or shameful, but not *pantang*.

He'd turned away from me in his frustration and– 'Oh! I forgot. I brought mud crabs.'

I saw the metal fish basket containing a hemp sack he'd

dumped at the top of the porch steps. The rough fabric was damp and moving.

'Small ones, but fresh. I just caught them near my place.'

I softened towards him. Uncle Chen was very fond of crabs – and so was I. This might be just the thing to tempt my uncle's feeble appetite. Though it wasn't the season for roe, wild crabs would have tender, sweet flesh. There were crabs in the mangroves near our house too, but I'd not thought to go hunting for them. Was this just an awkwardly delivered gift? Mud crabs wouldn't keep well.

'You want to wait and talk to Shen Shen? She's out now but she'll be home soon.'

All of Uncle Chen's business contacts had been liaising with Shen Shen since Uncle Chen and Ah Ma had been sick. Shen Shen had taken over the routine responsibilities of dealing with tenants. Most other businesses were quiet now as everyone waited to see how the restored British administration would take shape.

'No.' Botak swatted away the idea of talking to Shen Shen. 'No, no. I cannot. No.' For a moment he looked as if he was going to be sick – or cry.

I wavered. What if Botak wanted to tell Uncle Chen he was sick and dying . . . or of some threat to them both?

'Tell me.' I tried to sound gentle and persuasive. 'I promise I won't tell anybody except him.' I doubted he could write so it was no use suggesting he leave a note.

'I must talk to your uncle. Is he angry with me? Is that why he won't see me?'

'No. He cannot see anybody.' Within the fifteen days of the

New Year, I couldn't say that Uncle Chen was sick, too sick to see him, or my words would condemn him to a year of ill health.

Botak checked behind him before he answered. Not just the broad gravel driveway but what could be seen of the road beyond. I wondered who he was worried about.

'Please, *lah*, Lin-Lin,' he said.

The baby name shook me. Uncle Chen had called me 'Lin-Lin' in the old days, before he and Shen Shen had moved out of Chen Mansion to the little shophouse in town. It was only much later that I learned they'd moved out because Shen Shen's family believed my bad-luck presence was preventing them from having children.

'Just ask your uncle if he will see me five minutes. For old times' sake. For your father Big Boss Chen's sake. Big Boss Chen was always good to me. Please, *lah*, Lin-Lin.'

His blunt, brown features were a mix of stubbornness and desperation. I knew Uncle Chen considered Botak Beng 'own people', meaning family. He might actually feel better for seeing Botak. If Botak could be persuaded to stay to eat the crabs he'd brought, Uncle Chen might agree to sit at the table with us. He had been taking his thin rice porridge in the dim stuffiness of his bedroom, with Shen Shen rationing the amount of soy sauce and fermented bean curd he was allowed so he wouldn't vomit again.

'Let me go and see—'

Hope flashed in his face. 'Ask him,' he pleaded.

Just then another voice – a woman's – shouted from the driveway: 'Cooee!'

Botak jumped. For an instant he seemed terrified but once he saw who it was he just looked fed up.

A fair, plump Chinese woman in a tight blue and white spotted Western-style frock was charging towards us. She was vaguely familiar but I couldn't place her.

'Seng Beng!' she called. 'Beng, I told you to wait for me! Why didn't you wait?'

Botak Beng shook his head.

She turned to me. 'Su Lin, right? Sorry, ah, I told this silly man not to come and bother your uncle today. Bad luck. But he wouldn't listen! Men, ah!' She trilled a loud girlish giggle and I recognised her.

It was Fancy Ang. She was the boss aunty who managed prostitutes in a comfort house. I wouldn't judge her for that because she was likely why those girls had survived the war and the Japanese. Still, I was very glad Ah Ma had chosen translation and hairdressing to keep me alive.

Fancy had been pointed out to us as children, either as a danger ('Pray for her but stay away from her!' said the Mission Centre ladies) or with giggles at her clothes and makeup (Mission Centre school classmates).

Fancy Ang was one of the most notorious brothel owners, notorious because she catered to 'high-class' clientele and claimed to provide only 'high-class' girls. Once, a few years before the war, she'd approached my beautiful friend Parshanti, promising she could make good dress money just from going to social dances with British military officers. 'Good money now and even better money later if you're clever and get a rich officer interested in you!'

I wondered who'd been more put out: Parshanti, because she'd been propositioned, or all the other girls in our school, because they hadn't.

More recently, Ah Ma had decided she wasn't going to rent to Fancy any longer for her 'Happy Pleasure' houses. Uncle Chen had objected because Fancy always paid on time and had been renting those properties since long before the war. Besides, he pointed out, Fancy's regular clientele included influential British administrators and planters. But, as always, Ah Ma had prevailed. Her argument was that if the new British regime decided on a morality clean-up, as had happened regularly, that was precisely where they would start. I didn't know where Fancy and her girls had ended up, but she'd clearly survived.

Close up, I saw the once-buxom Fancy Ang had sagged into the soft obesity of malnutrition. Her round face had the look of white silk stockings stretched taut over rocky ground and was several shades lighter than her neck. And she smelt both dangerously chemical and aggressively floral.

'Gong xi fa cai!' Fancy Ang said. 'I hear your Indian friend is getting married to the ang moh doctor. She got baby coming, right?'

'What? No!'

'Whether you want a baby or not, there's no need to get married. Tell her to come and find me at forty-one Desker Road. And you – no job, no husband. You're good with numbers, right? You should come and work for me. I will pay you more than your uncle. And I will teach you more about accounts than your uncle knows! Eh, Botak?' She dug an elbow into him.

I glanced at Botak. He was clearly more than uncomfortable now, furious and miserable. I might have risked letting him in to see Uncle Chen, but not Fancy Ang.

'I'm sorry . . .' I started, but Fancy had picked up the damp, squirming sack and looked inside.

'*Hiyah!* How can you leave them like that?' She thrust it at me. 'Quick, quick! Go and soak them in water!'

I took the sack automatically. It was heavy.

Botak had also brought a white cloth bag of what I suspected were smuggled foodstuffs, but when he held it in my direction Fancy pulled it away from him. He didn't stop her, just turned and checked the driveway again.

'Don't just stand there, girl!' Fancy ordered me. 'Go! Go now!'

'Wait,' Botak said.

'Take your time.' Fancy's push made me stumble. 'We two can talk about the old days, right?'

Even before I was inside the house Fancy's hands were on Botak's upper arms, preventing him from turning away, and she was whispering urgently to him. It didn't sound like words of love, more as if she was trying to talk him into leaving before I bothered Uncle Chen. Well, she didn't have anything to worry about. I wasn't going to disturb my uncle, and not only because he wasn't well. We were already having more than our share of bad luck. Superstition or not, I wasn't going to invite more into our house.

I heard, 'Yes! She said she wants to talk to you! Now!'

So it was trouble with some woman, I thought. I was glad I hadn't given in. Whichever female was giving Botak trouble, it could have nothing to do with Uncle Chen.

I took my time carrying the squirming sack through the house and down to the back kitchen.

Third Day:
Rats Getting Married

———◆———

'Ah Ma, you should be resting. What are you doing up?'

I found Ah Ma in the kitchen, as I should have expected, when I heaved in the sack of crabs. She was still in her sleeping clothes, which she wouldn't have been if the servant girls and the black and white *amah jies* were in the house, fussing over the stove, with bowls and opened packets on the table.

'No, *lah*. You're the one who should be resting. I got some pork belly. I quick-quick make some *chap chye* for you to bring to your friend's house when you go. Who was outside? Are they still there? What did they want?'

On any other day, unexpected visitors wouldn't have been a problem. Like most houses in Singapore, our doors and windows stood open all day to let fresh air in and stuffiness out. This meant animal, insect and human visitors often wandered in and made themselves welcome.

'Tell me what you want to do and I'll do it for you,' I said, without answering her questions. 'You sit down and rest.'

I was small, but my grandmother was smaller. I'd been taller than her since I was twelve years old. Most of the time, her manner generated a larger-than-life personality so you didn't notice how tiny she was.

Now, thanks to this bout of illness, her age and fragility were plain to see. She seemed to have shrunk even smaller, and there was a tremor in the hands moving over the counter.

'Rest for what? If you rest all day you're sure to get sick! Who was outside making so much noise? Did you send them away?'

Ah Ma hated to talk about her health as much as she hated anyone else asking how she was. Some people are afraid to show signs of weakness in front of others in case they're taken advantage of. I suspect it was herself my grandmother was afraid of showing weakness to. As long as she didn't let herself admit how bad things were, she could go on being blind and strong. It comes from a long tradition of women ignoring agonising sores under the beautiful shoes on their tiny bound feet.

'It's Uncle Botak. He brought mud crabs for you and Uncle Chen.'

I put the sack on the kitchen floor. 'I should get some banana cake and pineapple tarts to give back to him in the bag.'

'No, *lah*. Got to wash first. Your uncle can bring some to him next time he visits.' Ah Ma pulled open the sack and we peered in at the crabs Botak had brought. They were a mix, with either large orange pincers or purple ones. Botak had thoughtfully tied the pincers together with raffia so they couldn't tear through the material.

'*Wah*, so many, ah?' Ah Ma sounded impressed, and better disposed towards the badly timed visitor. 'Is Botak still outside? Did he say what he wants?'

'He said he has to talk to Uncle Chen about something very important. But then Fancy Ang turned up. I think she's trying to talk him out of it.'

Ah Ma was poking at the crabs. 'All still alive. Very good. We can steam tonight with fresh chilli, soy sauce and ginger.'

'Ah Ma, did you hear me? Fancy Ang is also here.'

Ah Ma closed the bag and nudged it towards me. 'Put it outside the back door. Leave them in the sack for now but pour some water over them. Don't let them get dry. Whatever business he has with your uncle, Botak shouldn't come to the house on the Third Day. *Pantang*.'

'I know, but—'

'Taste this.' Ah Ma scooped broth out of the pot on the stove. 'Does it taste funny to you?'

'Funny?'

'Shen Shen put in dried *ikan bilis* and dried clams to soak last night. I think she was going to make soup.'

The stock was simmering over the charcoal embers that we kept glowing to dry fish and fruit in the rainy weather we were having. It was good of Shen Shen to prepare the stock, with all she had to do.

'But I think something in it is not very fresh. Maybe we should throw it out and start again. Funny taste, right?'

Ah Ma was very particular about exactly how things should be done, especially in the kitchen. When it came to food, the source of the ingredients and how they were stored was as important as how they were prepared. Unlike the servant girls and me, Shen Shen hadn't been trained by Ah Ma so she sometimes did things differently . . . and Ah Ma always noticed.

'Should it boil for longer? Of course it tastes funny now,' I said. 'Better not to waste it.'

'I can put it in the pig bin and start again,' Ah Ma said. 'Your uncle is so fussy, he won't eat this.'

Uncle Chen wasn't fussy. He just didn't have any appetite. But if Ah Ma was using this as an excuse to steam crabs for him, I wasn't going to stop her. And the pigs, who ate indiscriminately but seldom had fresh stock in their mash, would be happy.

Ah Ma sniffed. 'Why would Botak bring that Fancy here to see your uncle?'

'I don't think he did. I think he was trying to see Uncle Chen and she followed him.'

'If he wants to take one of her girls as his Singapore wife she should let him. Good opportunity for a smart girl . . .' Ah Ma looked at me speculatively.

'Don't even think it,' I said. 'I'm never getting married.'

Ah Ma shrugged. 'Anyway, it's nothing to do with us. Better not tell your uncle Botak came.'

'But the crabs? You'll have to tell Uncle Chen he brought them, won't you?'

'We can steam the crabs in the wok.' Ah Ma sidestepped the question. 'Tomorrow, maybe. We can soak them in the tub overnight. See how your uncle feels. His stomach isn't too good so maybe just use vinegar and ginger. There's no need for anything too fancy.'

Steaming the freshly killed crabs in a simple mix of Chinese wine, vinegar and ginger strips would also avoid having to decide between pepper crab and chilli crab, a choice that triggers more arguments in Singapore families than politics or religion. With no servant girls around and Shen Shen out tending our ancestral spirits, I would probably end up doing the dirty work of crab cleaning. But it would be worth it if it helped Uncle Chen to regain his appetite. And I was partial to tender, sweet crab meat too.

Mud crabs and catfish had always been plentiful in the mangroves, but most people had come to avoid the swamps because the tides often brought bodies dumped by the Japanese. The omnivorous crabs probably grew fat and juicy on all the extra protein and calcium, but finding a crab feeding on a human toe is probably enough to put someone off sucking the meat out of a crab claw for ever.

'That Fancy used to run after both my boys when they were young.' Ah Ma cut into my thoughts. 'Even back then she caused havoc and she never changed. When she got married I knew it wouldn't last. She left her husband's family to live with some *ang moh* officer long before the war. She was supposed to be his housekeeper and instead she had a daughter with him.'

That shone a different light on the objections Ah Ma and Uncle Chen had made when I'd arranged to be housekeeper for Chief Inspector Le Froy – the first police chief to try to make Singapore safe for locals as well as the British – to avoid being married off to one of my uncle's associates. I'd thought they'd just been worried about me working for the police officer who'd routed the toughest gangsters in Singapore – which they probably had. But now I understood their fear that I'd end up working for Fancy. As it was, they had both come to trust and respect Le Froy, who had been good to our family until the war.

It was only now, after the war, that I felt he had betrayed me. I knew my family confidently assumed he would help me find a respectable secretarial post if I asked, but I didn't intend to ask. I didn't need his or anyone else's help.

After all, Ah Ma had made good without taking help from anyone. After my grandfather died, she'd been expected to sell his company or hand over control of his businesses to her brothers or his cousins. However, annoyed by these relatives fighting over property to which she considered they had no right, the young widow had taken control of her husband's affairs. All she had intended, she had once said, was to make sure her two young sons had something to remember their father by. Neither her family nor her in-laws saw it like that. In fact, they saw her business success as an insult to her late husband – it would have been more respectable for her to be overcome by grief than run a black-market empire.

'Luckily I didn't need their help,' Ah Ma had told me. 'Always listen to people, but you don't have to do what they tell you. People can be stupid, even if they mean well. And the stupidest ones always want to tell everybody else what to do.'

My grandmother might not have gone to school, but she was the smartest person I knew. That was why I believed and supported her when she said we had to pull back into 'safe' areas, like housing and business properties. It seemed counter-intuitive: with the British trying to work out how to re-impose control, everything was in upheaval and there was big money to be made if you dared.

...hen had argued that this was the best time to expand. ...eople were doubling and tripling their investments, bringing in scarce goods – food, building materials, home necessities – untaxed.

'It's a family decision,' Ah Ma had said. 'What do you all say?'

Shen Shen had been frustrated that Uncle Chen and I sided with Ah Ma rather than with her. But Ah Ma had promised, 'Once things stabilise we can talk again. But for now, the best thing we can do is stay unnoticed. It's no use making money if new British laws will take it all away.'

Shen Shen had been angry enough to walk out of the house without answering her.

'Shen Shen not back yet?' Ah Ma said, as though reading my mind.

'No. But she'll be here soon. She didn't take Little Ling with her.'

'These days Shen Shen is always going out without Little Ling. As though we don't have enough to do here, we have to look after her daughter. And no servants to help, thanks to that one.'

'Please, *lah*, Ah Ma. You know you and Uncle Chen love looking after Little Ling. When she takes Little Ling out with her, you're not happy. When she leaves Little Ling at home with us, you're not happy.'

Ah Ma made a face at me. 'Just because Shen Shen made that *samfoo* for you, you think everything she does is right. It was my sarong that she cut up!'

'I know, Ah Ma. Thank you for your cloth.' I'd never been very interested in clothes, but I couldn't help smiling at the thought of my Chinese New Year *samfoo*.

This year was the first time since the war started that I'd had 'new' clothes for New Year. Dress fabric was still almost impossible to come by, but Shen Shen had cut up three of Ah Ma's ornate ceremonial batik sarongs and sewn them into *samfoo*s for Little Ling and me. Ah Ma's old sarongs were so well kept that they looked new. The fancy material with its gold highlights gave the short-sleeved top and loose trousers a special-occasion look, but it was still a functional outfit, easier to walk and work in than a fancy *cheongsam* or *nyonya kebaya* and more safely decent than a Western-style frock.

'A surprise gift from a grandmother to her two granddaughters,' Shen Shen had announced.

The only touchy point was that Shen Shen had done the cutting up and sewing without asking Ah Ma. 'But I've never seen you wear those sarongs,' she'd said. 'I thought better to put the cloth to good use before the white ants and silverfish get it.'

Maybe that was wrong of Shen Shen. But when Ah Ma saw how delighted Little Ling and I were by our new outfits, and when she heard the compliments Chinese New Year visitors had paid her on her granddaughters' clothes, she had accepted it. She even said that Shen Shen might have done the right thing by cutting before asking: while it was true that Ah Ma hadn't worn her wedding batiks for years, she might not have agreed to them being cut up.

More importantly, it showed everyone that Shen Shen accepted me, as well as her own daughter, as a granddaughter of Chen Tai. It had taken her a long time to come to that point, and my late mother having been Japanese hadn't helped matters. And perhaps Shen Shen felt she'd paid back Ah Ma for ignoring her expansion plans, so we could put that behind us.

...urse, Ah Ma still grumbled, 'Three beautiful hand-painted sarongs cut up to make *samfoo*s for two small girls. There should have been enough cloth to make at least three if not four *samfoo*s! Are you going to wear your new *samfoo* to town?'

'I may as well.'

Of course I was! Showing it to Parshanti and her mother was the main reason I was going out.

And if Le Froy was back, as I'd heard, it wouldn't hurt if I happened to be wearing my smart new outfit when I ran into him. Le Froy . . . He'd said he would write, then disappeared without a word.

But if he had really come back to Singapore . . .

'I heard your chief inspector came back. If you see him, ask him if he can get you back your job at the police station.' Again Ah Ma displayed her mind-reading talent.

'Ah Ma, I thought you didn't like me working at the Detective Shack.'

'Better than no work, right? Anyway, you might get protection by working for the police.'

I knew Ah Ma was worried about me. Shen Shen had heard rumours in town that I'd been a Japanese collaborator, the lover and/or daughter of Japanese officers, and that the whole Chen family had been involved in profiteering during the Occupation. It was only a matter of time before the police would use this as an excuse to investigate the Chen holdings.

Unfortunately I no longer had any contacts in the police to ask. My former colleagues, Sergeant Prakesh Pillay and Sergeant Ferdinand de Souza, had been transferred upcountry because the new head of the Detective and Intelligence Unit didn't trust locals to police locals.

But my immediate interlocutor was my grandmother, not the police.

'You always told me to stay away from *ang mohs*. Why do you want me to go and ask them for work now?'

'No harm in asking, right?'

No matter what Ah Ma said, I knew I had no chance of getting back my job at the Detective Unit.

'We could have married you to a good man, but you didn't want that. Now you are twenty-six years old, who is going to marry you? I just want you to have someone to look after you when I'm not around any more.'

It was ironic. All my life, as far back as I could remember, I'd wanted to escape from my family, from being the unmarried aunt who did the accounts, helped with children's homework and babysat. With Shen Shen more than capable of all of these things, it seemed I wasn't needed by my family and could do whatever I liked. But instead of enjoying my freedom I felt useless and unwanted. There really wasn't anything else I could do.

My leg and hip ached, as though they were offering me an excuse as to why I wasn't heading for university and a career or a husband and children. But I wouldn't take it.

'I'm going to change and go to see Parshanti,' I said. 'Her mother wants to measure me for my bridesmaid's dress.'

'Before you leave, come back and get some *chap chye* to take for them,' Ah Ma said. 'And don't forget my pineapple tarts. I set aside one tin just for them! Take them some of the good *lap cheong* too.'

The special *lap cheong*, made of duck liver and pig liver, bound with pork blood, had been brought in from Taiwan by one of Uncle Chen's suppliers. Those bunches of rich, hard, dried Chinese sausages were a luxury worth their weight in gold when traded in Chinatown and a sign the war was truly over.

I knew it was also a kind of apology from Ah Ma.

'I will, thanks,' I said.

'Before you leave, make sure you send away those people outside the house. Tell Botak to come back another day without that woman. And, remember, don't tell anybody that your uncle is sick.'

I dressed slowly, hoping that Shen Shen would come home and get rid of Botak and Fancy before I had to. Shen Shen could normally be heard bossing and scolding the servants from morning to night. With no servants in the house, she scolded Uncle Chen and Little Ling. At least she could put that energy to good use on Botak and Fancy.

Dead in a Drain

◆

I was surprised how good I felt when I put on my new *samfoo*. The crisp, freshly ironed cotton made me feel ready for anything. I could almost understand Parshanti's passion for clothes, if this was how they made her feel.

I owed something else to Shen Shen too. Wearing my new *samfoo* on the first two days of Chinese New Year, I saw people gazing at me with admiration and envy instead of the pity or judgement I was used to. Even if they were noticing my clothes instead of me, I preferred it.

I was looking forward to discussing my new discovery with Parshanti and her mother. They'd always seen me as a hopeless case, content to wear old dresses from the Mission Centre and old *samfoo*s cut from Ah Ma's house dresses. I was even looking forward to the bridesmaid's dress that Mrs Shankar was going to make me for Parshanti's wedding . . . if it took place. I'd heard, though not directly from Parshanti, that there were problems.

'Where are you going?' Little Ling asked.

Luckily Little Ling hadn't been ill like the rest of us, but she was lonely and bored without the *amah*s and servant girls who were her usual companions.

'I have to go to town to see my friend.'

'Can I come with you?'

'Not this time.' Even if I'd wanted to take her, Shen Shen didn't like Little Ling spending too much time with me.

'Will you bring me back a present?'

'I'll try.'

There hadn't been any shouting since Fancy had arrived. I opened the front door cautiously, after collecting Ah Ma's *chap chye* and *lap cheong* from the kitchen, and saw that our unwelcome visitors had gone.

Mentally thanking Fancy Ang, I set off to the trolley-bus stop. I was feeling good in my new *samfoo*, my stomach had settled and I was looking forward to seeing Parshanti and maybe . . .

Two houses down, I was distracted by a group of people standing at the side of the road, staring into the storm drain. I heard excited mutterings.

'A body.'

'A dead body!'

'There! That's the woman I saw!'

I saw our neighbour Nasima Mirza, whose house it was. She was with three of her servants and one was pointing at me: 'That's her! I saw her with him! She's a Chinese demon and she killed him and now she's going to kill me!'

Nasima looked apologetically at me. 'Later,' she mouthed, then turned back to the hysterical girl, soothing and calming her. Nasima's servants were not local: they came from a village in Indonesia where she was funding a school in her late sister's name. The girls she brought to Singapore had to learn to read and write as well as do housework. It was pretty much an education in life, like Ah Ma gave her servants, except Nasima's were Muslim and ours were a local mix of Taoist-Buddhist with local superstitions, like Ah Ma.

Nasima and I had become good friends during the Occupation. She loved books and learning as much as I did. She knew a great deal more, though: I'd been educated by the missionary ladies to be a good wife and housekeeper while Nasima had been encouraged to read widely in the extensive library her late father had collected. She'd generously recommended and lent me books, and I'd come to understand how Anglocentric my Mission School education had left me.

I edged over, peered into the drain and reared back in horror.

It was Botak Beng. He was face down, his arms spread out: he reminded me of a huge beached stingray. I couldn't see his face but the figure in the drain was of the same size, same build and same baldness as the man I'd not let into our house.

There was no sign of Fancy. Had she just gone off and left him? I wondered if she had seen what had happened. I could imagine her pushing him, but no more than that. Still, a push might have been enough. And she might have run away in panic . . .

I moved towards Nasima but the wailing servant saw me coming and grabbed at Nasima, pointing at me. I couldn't make out what they were saying in the mix of whispers and shrieks.

Nasima handed the girl to the others and pointed them towards her house. She nodded to me and we moved aside to talk.

'Do you know what happened?' I asked. 'Is she saying I killed him? Why?' Thanks to the nursing experience she'd gained during the war, Nasima wasn't the sort to scream and faint at the sight of a dead man.

'From what I understand, Rosmah saw a man and a woman shouting at each other in the road. Then the woman pushed the man into the drain and ran into your garden through the hole in the fence.'

I guessed Rosmah was the wailing girl.

'What did the woman look like? It wasn't me – I was in the house.' I thought of Fancy. If she'd run back into our garden and was still somewhere nearby . . .

'Was it a heart attack?' a passer-by asked. 'Did he faint?'

Nasima shook her head. 'I don't know,' she said. 'I didn't get a chance to see. All I know is they came to get me because Rosmah was crying.'

'Falling into the drain wouldn't kill him,' I said. 'Could he have hit his head when he fell?' I looked around. 'Could it have been a heart attack? Or a motor-car?' Some of the newly imported vehicles could go up to thirty miles an hour.

'Rosmah didn't see any. She was watching the road for the trolley bus because a friend is coming to see her. She saw the man talking to a woman. She got the impression they were lovers and the man wanted to marry the woman but she wanted him to go away so they were arguing. Then I called her as I had to ask her something. When she went back out she saw the woman running up the road and into your garden. Then she saw a man was in the drain just beyond our gate. She didn't see the woman push him in, just assumed that was what had happened.'

Nasima was waiting for me to say something but I didn't know what she expected of me. I thought Rosmah was 'just assuming' a lot of things, and I wasn't sure I believed her about the woman running into our garden. Very few people knew about the flap in the fence that provided a short-cut to the kitchen, and it was unlikely that Fancy Ang did.

Others were gathering. The milkmen who walked from door to door to provide fresh milk paused with their *kerbau* – buffaloes. Someone was talking about all the evil spirits out on the Third Day: they said the dead man must have made them angry and they had taken revenge. One of the milkmen was telling a long story about a savage red dog that had tried to kill him when he passed what he later learned was a burial site.

I didn't know the milkmen because we didn't use cows' milk. Our milk was delivered by Tamil goat-herders.

Wasn't anyone going to do something about Botak in the drain?

'Are you sure he's dead?' I asked Nasima.

She looked startled. 'He's not moving. Oh, I didn't think– That's terrible! I just assumed–'

Nasima hurried to the side of the drain, shoving the gawpers aside. I followed and saw her trying to climb in but being prevented by Rosmah and the other girls, who pulled her back. They were all wailing now. No one else seemed inclined to do anything.

I steeled myself and edged down the side of the drain on my backside. Botak might have fainted, or tripped and knocked himself unconscious. Even if he'd had a heart attack I might still be able to revive him.

With an effort, I heaved the body onto its back, confirming it was Botak Beng. Even before I could feel for a pulse I knew it was no use. His eyes were open and rolled up in his head and there was foam on his lips. Had he choked on something? I saw a few fine yellowish hairs around his mouth, as though he'd tried to spit out something he'd been chewing.

I gritted my teeth and stuck my fingers into the back of his mouth. If there was something stuck in his throat and I could clear it, there was still the smallest chance I could revive him. If I didn't try now I would always wonder if I could have saved him. There was nothing in his windpipe but I found what seemed to be chewed pulp in his mouth – and more of the yellowish hairs.

What had happened here?

I saw a tiny patch of blood on the front of his shirt, but not enough to have killed him.

Botak was gripping something tightly in one hand – I wondered if it was a wasp that had stung him and triggered a seizure. I prised open his fingers carefully. He was clutching strips of a dried, wrinkled, yellowish vegetable.

'Su Lin! What are you doing in there?' Shen Shen hissed, from above the drain. 'Are you mad? Get back into the house!'

'I was going to town and I saw—'

'If you're going to town then go to town. Get out of there at once! This is nothing to do with us. Don't get involved!'

That was almost exactly what my grandmother would have said. But even as I acknowledged it, I resented hearing her words coming from Shen Shen.

'Su Lin, you must stop shaming the family! Get back to the house! Come on!'

'He came to the house earlier to see Uncle Chen,' I told Shen Shen, once she'd hauled me out. 'With Fancy Ang. He said he wanted to talk to Uncle Chen about something, man-to-man. I saw this only because I was on my way to town.'

'Probably wanted to borrow money,' Shen Shen scoffed.

She was wearing her usual drab grey house *samfoo*, though she must only just have got back from the cemetery.

'You wore that to the cemetery?' I was surprised.

'You think everybody has enough free time to dress up like you, *ah*? Just because you've got new clothes – *hiyah*, it's all crooked at the back. Stand still while I straighten it for you.'

I could tell Shen Shen was keeping something to herself. She had never been very chatty. When she wasn't trying to hide anything, like in the old days when she did the rounds with Uncle Chen, she would hand Ah Ma the list of names and payments. There might have been objections and negotiations, even fights, but we would get the stories from Uncle Chen. He loved to talk. And, consciously or not, he was doing it to keep his mother informed about the people living and working in their properties.

As far as Shen Shen was concerned, nothing needed to be said other than that they'd paid up.

Now, when she claimed there was nothing to say, yet talked on about how I should try to stand up straighter and pull my blouse down to hide my lopsided hips, I could tell she had something on her mind. It made me uncomfortable. Who fusses about clothes with a dead body in the drain next to your house?

I felt she was talking to distract me, like the stranger who makes exaggerated apologies for bumping into you so you don't notice their partner picking your pocket. But what was she trying to hide?

Uncle Chen appeared. He was in his singlet and sarong and hadn't shaved. 'What's happening?'

He looked confused and ill. In a contest between him and Botak Beng, Botak wasn't the one I'd have expected to die first.

Shen Shen grabbed him and pulled him towards the house. 'It's nothing to do with us,' she told him. And to me, over her shoulder, 'If you are going to town, go! Mind your own business. Don't *kaypoh*!'

Shen Shen was even sounding like Ah Ma.

Uncle Chen gave me a wry grimace. His wife was giving me orders: there'd been a time when she'd refused to live under the same roof as me, blaming my 'bad luck' presence for her miscarriages. Thankfully, that had changed once Little Ling was born . . . I realised I hadn't seen Little Ling for a while. 'Little Ling? Where is she?'

'Where is Little Ling?' Uncle Chen stopped too.

'I'll find her,' Shen Shen said. 'Look – the trolley bus is coming. You'd better run if you don't want to wait another hour. Go!'

Changing Landscapes

◆

'May you live in interesting times': that is an ancient Chinese curse. With the war over, I'd hoped things would become dull again.

I managed to get a seat on the bus. The driver waited for me – not entirely out of the goodness of his heart since he'd arrived ahead of schedule. Also, he and the other passengers were staring at the crowd up the road.

'*Simi tai ji ah*?' In Hokkien that means everything from 'What's going on?' to 'Why the fuss?'

I shrugged. Universal language for 'Don't know, don't care.' I'd had enough interactions for one day.

I was shaken, but part of me was surprised that seeing Botak Beng dead hadn't been more of a shock. I was already considering how I would tell Parshanti about it. The Occupation had taught us that after a death the best thing you could do was move on: it was the only thing separating you from the dead, who couldn't. It was futile to ask, 'Why?' because there were no answers. And after what we'd lived through, it was difficult to be shocked by the death of one man, whether from a heart attack or a sudden stroke.

I was glad Shen Shen and Uncle Chen had seen Botak's body. I wouldn't have to break the news to them, which meant it really wasn't my business any more.

Not surprisingly, there were fewer Chinese on the trolley bus today, but still a good number. I focused on wedging my *tingkat* of *chap chye* between my feet and the bag of dried sausages on my lap.

'You look nice,' someone said in Malay.

It was an older woman surrounded by huge bunches of red rambutans. I guessed she was taking them into town to sell. 'Very nice, your *baju*.' She smiled at me and gestured at my *samfoo*.

I found myself smiling back. 'Thank you. You look very nice too.'

I'd treated my new *samfoo* carelessly – was it stained from the drain? – but it still made me feel good. I really should appreciate Shen Shen more than I did. But that felt like reminding myself to be grateful for *kang kong* and tapioca. They had kept us alive during the war but I would never eat them again.

'Try? Very sweet *rambut*!' the woman offered me a stalk with five plump hairy balls.

The driver yelled something about not eating on his bus. The woman shouted back, unabashed, then shoved a stalk at the passenger in front of her, indicating he should take a fruit, then pass it on to the driver. Soon everyone on the bus was sampling her rambutans, including the driver.

She was right about them being sweet: they were fresh and fully ripe. I was hungrier than I'd realised – of course I was! I'd not managed to keep anything down since yesterday's vomiting. Now I felt my body and brain relaxing in anticipation of nourishment. The juicy rambutans were the size of ping-pong balls with fine hairs. Their skin was thin and peeled away easily in strips—

Suddenly I was alert again. There had been a strip of dried yellow rambutan peel in Botak's mouth. But why? And why had he been carrying some in his pocket?

Around me, people were eating and calling compliments. Several, including a couple of bearded *ang moh*s and the driver, bought some from the woman as she walked to the front of the bus at her stop.

'You are a pretty girl.' She put another cluster of fruit on my lap as she passed my seat. 'You should eat more and worry less. Things will go back to normal now.'

Would things go back to how they had been before the war? And did we really want them to? The Japanese had abolished whites-only segregation on buses and in eating places. They had shown us that the European was not all-powerful. And the British had sabotaged their moral authority when they had surrendered us to the Japanese. I couldn't be the only one who felt so.

Now, even as the temporary British Military Administration trumpeted its intention to restore Singapore's pre-war prosperity, we faced food shortages, unemployment and a government that seemed focused only on generating revenue for Britain. But the old system hadn't been all bad. I'd enjoyed my years at school and in the Detective Shack. Despite what I'd told Ah Ma, I couldn't help wondering if Le Froy would return to the local police and if there might be a job for me again.

I didn't want to think about the rumours Shen Shen had heard that Le Froy was bringing a new wife out east. That was why he wasn't moving into the BMA quarters: he was searching for a house for himself and his wife, once he was reinstated. Le Froy hadn't lived in British quarters previously, and he'd sworn that he'd never again work for the British government, which had ignored his warnings about Japan's mounting aggression. Not only that, he felt he'd been let down and used to deceive and betray the people who had trusted him.

In any case, how would such a taciturn antisocial man have found a woman willing to marry him in the relatively short time he'd spent in England? It had taken me years to get to know him just a little.

Then again, I'd neither seen nor heard from him since he'd left, and had no idea how much he might have changed. And the wife he was bringing with him might have been a childhood sweetheart he'd pined for all his life, hence his lack of interest in other women. Perhaps she'd married someone else, who'd no doubt been killed during the war, allowing him to swoop in and comfort her. Or had some woman married him out of pity because he had lost his foot?

That was such a ridiculous reason to marry someone – I already felt indignant on Le Froy's behalf. Such a woman would cripple him further if she insisted on treating him like an invalid. He needed someone who would push him to make the most of himself. Someone who understood that a crippled leg didn't necessarily lead to a crippled life . . .

These were all things that Ah Ma and Le Froy had drummed into me.

Childhood polio might have given me uneven legs and a crooked spine but I wasn't a cripple.

Le Froy had helped me so much, giving me opportunities and the confidence to grasp them. If he'd stayed in Singapore, I could have repaid some of the debt I owed him by reminding him of the lessons he'd taught me.

But he'd returned to England on one of the first repatriation ships. He'd promised to get in touch once he knew where he would end up, but I'd not heard a word from him since.

Whatever he was doing in Singapore, it clearly didn't concern me. Still, I couldn't help wondering, every time I went into town, if I would run into him

Was he really back in Singapore? I couldn't imagine Le Froy in England, which to me was country villages, Agatha Christie and Thomas Hardy, organised gardens growing flowers instead of fruit and vegetables, the people eating roast beef, drinking cows' milk and wearing shoes indoors. The Le Froy I knew drank local *kopi* with his *kaya* toast, had his hair cut by his Indian barber and swore in Hokkien.

My thoughts had so occupied me that we'd already come into the main business district without my noticing. Buildings were decorated Singapore style – remnants of fake holly and pine trees left over from Christmas had been painted, pasted over and otherwise improved with festive red cut-outs and firecrackers for Chinese New Year. Red was everywhere. It wasn't just about good luck: it was fake fire to ward off the monster Nian, the beast that lives under the sea and comes out of its hiding place once a year to kill and eat people and crops unless it's frightened off by firecrackers and other loud noises. Over the fifteen days of New Year there would be lion dancing, drumming and firework displays. The poorer your household, the more desperately you'd try to summon luck and wealth into your home for the coming year.

Today traffic was lighter but still busy. Hawkers were selling everything from drinks and snacks to pots and pans, scrubbing boards, foot massages and good-fortune tokens.

Had I killed Botak by not letting him into the house?

The thought caught me by surprise as I watched the changing landscape and people. What if it had been sunstroke? Not so likely, given the cloudy skies. Or exhaustion and dehydration, which I could have averted by inviting him in and giving him water, a chance to sit down and rest?

I didn't want to think about that.

I also didn't want to think about Le Froy returning, because he hadn't written as he'd promised. And what would he think of me, if he really was back?

It wasn't just Singapore that had changed since the war. I had too. 'Normal life' now seemed unnatural when I felt so different. I didn't even know what I wanted. I'd once been focused on my dream of becoming a lady reporter but, with the war over, the magazines and papers no longer needed women.

At least now I was considered too old to be married off, which wasn't necessarily a bad thing. The current shortage of men – the Japanese had tended to target men and boys – meant that, with my polio limp, I was unlikely to attract a man even if I was ten years younger. Another unpleasant subject. The only thing I could think about safely was Parshanti's problems with her upcoming wedding to Dr Leask.

'Can you believe my father told me I don't have to marry Leasky if I don't want to? That a promise made in the middle of the jungle in the middle of a war doesn't count? And can you believe he said the same thing to Leasky? And that my mother said we should get to know each other in real life before we rush into marriage? We've been together for three years and known each other for ten. Do you think that's rushing? Some people marry off their daughters once they start menstruating. I think my parents want me to wait till I reach menopause!' Parshanti had been so furious when she told me that I'd not dared to tell her I thought it sounded like a good idea. Recently – in addition to spouting medical terms – she'd been so moody and short-tempered it was easy to see why her parents worried that something was wrong.

I got off the trolley bus at the terminus and started to walk down the street. I'd chosen a slightly longer route that took me between Police Headquarters and the Detective Shack, then branched off to the Shankars' shophouse.

No, I wasn't hoping to see Le Froy. I just wanted to pass by the Detective Shack for old times' sake.

And, no, I wasn't very good at lying, not even to myself.

Though imports were still slow, the streets were full of people selling food, lotions and cures they'd grown, brewed or cooked. Of course they would have been there even with plentiful imports: in Singapore, food is art, science and religion. There was haggling and altercation too, of course. If there's anything Singaporeans love almost as much as food it's criticising and complaining. We think of it as quality control.

Walking through the crowd that day, I felt good, despite my uneven gait. If anyone stared, I could tell myself they were admiring the gorgeous gold-on-rose print of my new *samfoo*.

But no one was looking at me: everyone on the pavements and the road was focused on the shouting and commotion in front of the Detective Shack.

Whatever was happening was none of my business so, of course, that was where I headed. There's no better distraction from your own problems than someone else's.

Buaya Curry

—◆—

A couple of *ang moh*s in the khaki shirts and shorts of the local police were yelling at the *makcik* or middle-aged Malay 'aunty' who sold curry over sweet-potato mash from the makeshift food stall she'd set up on the five-foot way. I knew her by sight, though we'd never spoken. Normally she was smiling and joking. She had the kind of clever, happy face that said she made really good curries and the kind of figure that showed she'd eaten a lot of them.

I'd heard her speaking good enough English to sell her food to any *ang moh* who wanted it, but I couldn't walk on and leave an old woman to be shouted at, maybe worse. These *ang moh*s seemed insecure, despite their air of authority, meaning they had only recently arrived from Britain. We'd all learned the difference when Australian soldiers had emerged from months in the Malayan jungles and the offshore islands after the Japanese surrender. Also *ang moh*s, the Australians had smelt – they stank – of diseased dogs and decaying flesh, but were always relaxed and easygoing.

I moved quietly to the curry *makcik*'s side. 'What's happening?' I asked quietly in Malay.

'These men, I don't know what is wrong with them. They ask for curry, so I give them curry. You don't like it, then don't eat it, *lah*. Why would you make so much noise?'

Everyone knew *ang moh*s were funny about food. They ate cow but not horse, pig but not dog. Even more strangely, they were happy to eat chicken legs and wings but not necks and feet, and liked fish fillets but not heads.

The taller *ang moh*, with very short, very dark hair, looked at me suspiciously. 'Move on, girlie. This is none of your business.'

None of the police officers I'd worked with would have called a local woman 'girlie'. I didn't know any of the new men who'd been shipped in since the war ended. They seemed to have little experience of policing or Asia, and this man was on the verge of collapsing from the heat, humidity and stomach bugs.

'My ma don't speak good English,' I said, The mistakes were deliberate. I made sure to look apologetic, scared and protective. The *makcik*, grasping at once what I was doing – she probably understood English as well as they did – played along, clutching my arm and moaning in 'terror'.

It worked. The man relaxed as he accepted I was her daughter. That meant I wasn't some Communist vigilante out to tackle British authority. And since I spoke English – though evidently not well enough to write letters of complaint – I could translate his grievances against the old woman. He didn't know that an old Malay woman in a traditional brown *baju kurung* – a long-sleeved loose blouse over a wrapped sarong – was unlikely to be the mother of a Chinese woman in her special-occasion *samfoo*.

Maybe this was good, though, especially after the savagery of the Japanese: they had tried to pit we Singaporeans, Malay, Chinese, whatever, against each other.

'Fahey! Don't talk to them! It's human meat!' His companion, a fair, plump, sweating man, looked as though he was about to vomit. I hoped not: his belly was of a size that could hold a lot. 'Just bring them in and lock them up and – and– Oh, God. I'm going to throw up!'

'Hold it in, Johnson!' Fahey said. To me he said, loudly and slowly, 'I asked your ma what was in her curry and she said it was human meat.'

The *makcik* grabbed my arm and shook it urgently.'I did not! Yes, I sold them curry. It's not the first time the fat one has eaten my curry. But this one, this is the first time I've seen him. This one, after he'd tasted it, he asked what meat I put in the curry, so I told him. Then he went crazy and started shouting. And the other, the fat one making all the fuss now, he'd already finished most of his while this one was talking. Then he starts saying I'm killing people!'

'She told me the meat in her curry is human,' Fahey repeated.

'Of course it's not! She wouldn't have said that!'

All around us the crowd were whispering excitedly – late arrivals to the show were being filled in on what had happened. Some enterprising soul was taking bets on the outcome. Singaporeans never miss the chance of a little harmless betting.

The *makcik* spoke up: 'I told them *buaya*, from last week. It is not fresh, but it is not yet bad. That's why I put it in the curry.'

'*Buaya!*' Fahey said triumphantly. He had dark hair and his skin was more red than brown, which showed he was a recent arrival. He seemed subordinate to the one named Johnson but gave the impression of being smarter. 'I heard that – did you hear? She said *buaya*! That's what they call us. It means "white man", doesn't it?'

I understood immediately what had happened.

Buaya is the local term for crocodile. Crocodile, like many other wild beasts, had become popular through necessity during the Occupation. Crocodile was a firm white meat, which kept well and tasted of chicken or fish, depending on what it had been eating. But *buaya* was also local slang for a womaniser or flirt, and a general term for Europeans who preyed on local girls.

'Next time tell them it's chicken,' I said to the *makcik*.

'Next time I sell them chicken shit,' she said. 'Next time I spit on it – and charge extra!'

She'd gained confidence from my presence, and the crowd around us was muttering supportively. That wasn't good. No matter how much right you have on your side, the larger the crowd watching, the less chance the authorities will admit it.

'I heard her say "*buaya*",' Fahey said stubbornly. 'No use you getting her to deny it now. I heard her tell you what she said. And I know that's what you call people like us!' His ears were sharper than I'd realised. I made a note to remember that *buaya*s weren't uniformly stupid.

'She gave you meat she saved specially for you,' I said earnestly. 'High-class meat special for *buaya*s because you don't eat snake, rat or squirrel meat. Or bats.'

I watched him process this. There was a good chance it would work: it flattered his vanity while hinting at the horrors on which the rest of us lived.

'What meat is it, then?' the plumper Johnson demanded. 'Not pork. I know people like you don't eat pork. I've been out here a long time, girl. You can't take me in with your nonsense.'

At least he no longer looked like he was going to vomit.

Well, if he'd survived out here for 'a long time' without discovering what *buaya* meant there was no need to enlighten him now.

'It's chicken,' I said. I gave the *makcik* a look telling her to agree or hold her tongue. I didn't care what was in her curry. All I wanted now was to make sure the British policemen didn't care either.

'Chicken!' said the *makcik*, triumphantly, as though she'd just recalled the word. 'Wild jungle chicken. It's tougher than domestic chicken. Jungle chicken! Special for the *buaya*! If they don't want it I'll give to these people!' The onlookers roared with laughter and a couple cheered, making her preen a little. 'Want some more?' she asked the police officers.

'Stop it!' I hissed at her, afraid the officers would see she understood English. 'You want to get into more trouble?'

But we were all right.

'How much did you pay for it?' I asked the plump man, to sweeten the deal.

He told me, then asked, 'Did she overcharge us?'

Of course she did! The crowd muttered when they heard how much the men had paid for the curry. Some were put out that she had taken them for so much, but most were impressed. The only thing that outranks Singaporean respect for food is our respect for money.

'No, sir. I ask because, if you don't like her food, do you want your money back?'

Since he'd almost finished the contents of his tin plate, he couldn't say he hadn't liked it, could he?

'I told you it was chicken,' Johnson said to Fahey. 'I knew these people don't eat pork and there's no beef here. You and your study of local customs and languages!'

I felt a chill inside. So the newly arrived Fahey was interested in local customs and languages. I hoped he hadn't picked up anything incriminating I'd said to the *makcik*. I'd been stupid to assume that, because they were English, they understood only English.

But it was an easy mistake to make. The Dutch, Germans and Russians who came here could speak English as well as their own languages, perhaps because Englishmen stubbornly spoke only English. If you're speaking to an Englishman, though, they don't call it stubbornness: it's principle.

Still, I'd spent enough time working with the former Chief Inspector Thomas Le Froy to know there were exceptions to this rule. Le Froy had spoken Malay and Hokkien fluently, and enough marketplace Bengali, Tamil, Malayalee and Cantonese to have a good idea of what people were talking about when he went under cover.

'You don't like her curry?' I repeated. 'You want your money back? Pass me your plate. I throw it away for you.'

'*Alamak! Tidak!*' My friend the *makcik* jabbed at me in protest but I knew what I was doing.

'All the food here stinks!' Johnson said. But he was holding on to his tin plate. Nothing makes people more determined to hang on to something than being asked to give it up. 'We paid for this.'

He went back to eating. I didn't blame him. The smells coming out of the giant pot of curry were seductive . . . I detected cumin, turmeric and cardamom. All the flavours you'd expect to find in an Indian curry but without the heat of Mrs Shankar's vindaloos. The energy I'd got from the rambutans was fading and I discovered I was hungry.

Mrs Shankar was Scottish by birth, but she'd embraced her husband's culture and cuisine. Even the other Indian women deferred to her suggestions when necessity forced them into making recipe substitutions. Thinking of her reminded me I was due at her home.

Now that the *ang moh*s were eating instead of shouting, the crowd also moved on, some congratulating the *makcik* I heard 'buaya' several times as she told, and they exaggerated, the story. The plump younger man finishing his curry looked pleased,

'If it's good enough for the *buaya*, they all want some, eh? Tell her she should pay us for advertising,' he said. I nodded, apparently shy and overwhelmed by the honour of being spoken to, which was all the payment he deserved.

'Tell her she should cook it for Mrs Jake Evans!' This got a laugh from the crowd.

Mrs Jake Evans, wife of the new acting governor, wasn't popular among the local community. That was nothing new, of course. European women weren't popular. They weren't meant to be. As part of the ruling class, they were to be obeyed. Things had changed now, though. For one thing, there were fewer women than there had been before. For another, they were no longer the invincible ruling class. And fewer servants were willing to work for low pay and insults.

'Come! Try my curry! For you, it's free,' the *makcik* offered. I thanked her and declined: I would be eating at the Shankars tonight and didn't want to risk upsetting my stomach again.

'Or satay?'

'No, thank you. But that's clever.' She had threaded her meat chunks on what looked like steel bicycle spokes instead of the usual *lidi* made from the mid-ribs of coconut fronds.

'They don't catch fire,' she agreed. 'You want some?' She offered to slide the chunks of crocodile into a bowl for me.

'No, thank you,' I said again. 'But it's a very good idea.'

As I walked away I couldn't help wondering if she'd lost the son or husband who'd once prepared her coconut skewers for her – and whether it had been his bicycle that had provided the spokes. I glanced back and saw she had plenty of customers. I hoped that strength in numbers would keep her out of trouble. The only person standing alone was the dark-haired newcomer, Fahey. But he wasn't watching the *makcik* and her happy customers. His eyes were on me. I walked on. With luck I would never see him again.

The Shankars

◆

I heard the Shankars squabbling even before I reached their shophouse. It was nothing new. Parshanti and her mother lived loudly, whether happy or sad, and they had been squabbling over wedding plans ever since they'd been back under one roof. And even that had been a problem.

When they emerged from the 'inside' as the jungle fighters referred to the forests of Peninsula Malaya, Dr Leask and Harry Palin had moved into a set of rented rooms in town. Parshanti had assumed that she would be living there too. 'After all, we're engaged and we've been sharing quarters for the past two years. We're used to living together and Harry won't mind!' Harry, who was the son of a former governor and had trained as a pilot, had become a good friend to all of us.

But the elder Shankars had vetoed the plan. The Scots Presbyterian-reared Mrs Shankar especially had been horrified: 'You're not married yet. You're not supposed to get used to living with a man until after you've been married for years – and even then you should always make sure he doesn't get too used to you or he'll start taking you for granted.'

'Ma, you've been reading too many of those silly women's magazines. Besides Leasky and I have known each other for years. Of course we're used to each other.'

From Parshanti, the jibe about women's magazines was rich. She had always read the romance stories in the magazines her mother accumulated for dress patterns – Mrs Shankar was famous among the expatriate wives for her ability to copy designs from London and Paris.

The front doors to the shop stood open. Even in the cooler months, like February, it's hot in Singapore so doors and windows are left open to invite in fresh air.

I loved Parshanti's tiny Scottish mother and tall Indian father. They'd been part of my life since Parshanti and I were classmates at the Mission Centre school. They'd arranged for me to go to their shophouse in town for lunches instead of heading all the way home to Katong.

In the old days Mrs Shankar had never stood still, not even for two minutes. Now she would freeze and go into a daze just staring at her daughter or her husband. I saw her reach out and touch the sleeve of his shirt or the hem of her skirt as though she needed to persuade herself they were real. Yet almost all the time they were together they were arguing.

'I'll wear something practical,' Parshanti was saying, as I stood in the doorway under the 'Shankar and Sons' sign, letting my eyes adjust to the darker interior.

The 'and Sons' was a lie. They'd only ever had one: Parshanti's brother Vijay. Vijay, like my friend Prakash and many other young men, had been anti-British in the old days, disgusted by how the British treated the rest of us. But, when put to the test, they had fought fiercely with, not against, Britain. And, like too many others, the Shankars' funny, handsome Vijay hadn't returned.

No one in the family said he was dead. Their only comfort was that his body hadn't been found. As long as there was no body and no death on record it was possible that Vijay Shankar would turn up one day, released from detention or rescued from an isolated island or recovered from amnesia.

I could understand that. What I couldn't understand was why Parshanti, who'd been so set on marrying Dr Leask as soon as they came out of the jungle was now contriving as many objections as she could to the wedding. Today it was clothes . . .

Of course, Parshanti talking about clothes was nothing new. In the old days fashion had been her favourite topic of conversation. Only now she wasn't talking about the clothes she dreamed of owning, but the opposite. 'Ma, there's no point wasting your time and ruining your eyes tailoring some fancy dress that I'm only ever going to wear once to church. And if you won't tell that awful Evans woman to get lost, you should be working on her dresses, not mine.'

'Even if she's the governor's wife, you're my only daughter. And it's not just the wedding dress. We have all your going-away clothes to think about. When I think of all the lovely dress materials I'd put by for this day, all gone . . .'

I knew it wasn't just the thought of 'lovely dress materials' that made Mrs Shankar dash a sleeve over her eyes. Parshanti knew it too. She looked away from her mother and caught sight of me standing there. 'Hello, you! You finally got here – we expected you hours ago. Ma's been waiting to measure you for your bridesmaid's dress. I thought you'd changed your mind and were standing us up.'

'There was a dead man in the drain outside our neighbour's house,' I said.

I hadn't meant to tell them about him, at least not straight away. What's more guaranteed to lower spirits when you're planning a wedding than a body in a drain? But it was the first thing that came to mind.

'Heart attack?' Dr Shankar said hopefully, from his chair in the corner. He'd been so left out of the discussion I'd not noticed him. 'Brought on by dehydration, perhaps. Was it an old man? Were his pupils dilated? What was his colour like?'

'Don't know, Uncle Shankar. He wasn't that old,' I said, as I walked over to greet him with a formal bow.

In Singapore, everyone older than you is addressed as 'uncle' or 'aunty' out of respect. Family members have more complicated titles like 'third aunt' or 'husband of the second eldest sister'.

'Hello, Su Lin.' He smiled. 'How are you? How is your grandmother?'

Dr Shankar looked ten or even twenty years older than he had before the Japanese time. I knew he had been a hero during the war. If not for him, so many more would have died, including Prakash and Le Froy, to name only the two most precious to me.

My grandmother would never have forgiven me if I'd told him she and Uncle Chen had been ill over New Year. 'Very well, thank you. She sends you her regards. And she sent you some small snacks.'

'How dreadful, Lin-Lin!' Mrs Shankar reverted to the name she, too, had used for me when I was a little girl, coming to their shophouse with Parshanti after school. She looked happy to see me now and gave me a big hug, even though I'd seen her just last week. 'It must have been such a shock. You're still so thin. We must feed you up!'

'Ah Ma sends you some *kueh kapit* and *kueh bangkit . . .'* I said. Of course I also had the de rigueur tangerines. '. . . and some of her *chap chye* and sausage. I shouldn't come in as it's the Third Day today. I'll just leave them—'

'Don't be silly,' Mrs Shankar said. 'We're not Chinese so we don't have to worry about that. And, anyway, your grandmother's pineapple tarts are sweet enough to take care of any bad luck. Maybe I'll have one now . . .' She ate two as she put some on a saucer for her husband.

Ah Ma's *ong lai* pineapple tarts were famous. Not just because those rich, buttery parcels of tangy pineapple jam were delicious, but because it was whispered that Ah Ma's *ong lei*, believed by the Chinese to herald prosperity if eaten during the New Year, brought real wealth to the households she gave them to.

We'd spent the weeks leading up to New Year preparing all the sweet luck to give away. I just hoped the recipients ended up luckier in the New Year than we had been.

'Who was it?' Parshanti asked. 'What happened to him? How long was he in the drain? Long enough to stink?'

'You can talk about it later,' Mrs Shankar said. 'I've got to get Su Lin's measurements. You like this, Su Lin, don't you? Look how pretty it is!' Mrs Shankar held up a swatch of white fabric patterned almost invisibly with cream roses. 'For the wedding gown. Or this one – it's organza. I think it would go well with a lace fichu.'

'Very nice.' I'd never been interested in dressing up but I found myself exaggerating my enthusiasm to try to make up for the bride's lack of it. 'Very nice – very lacy.'

'Very, very lacy,' Dr Shankar agreed.

Parshanti rolled her eyes.

'Su Lin can tell us about the body while you're measuring her,' Parshanti said. 'You're not going to measure her mouth, are you?'

'If I needed the size of her mouth I'd put it down as half the size of yours!' her mother said. Then she made a strange sound that started as a giggle and ended in a moan.

Mrs Shankar, the most calm and practical of women, suddenly sounded as though she were on the verge of tears. Parshanti stared at her, stunned. She was deeply fond of her mother, despite their skirmishes.

'She used to say that about Vijay,' Dr Shankar said quietly to me.

Ah.

If they knew for sure that Vijay was dead, it would have been the worst kind of pain and loss but they would have grieved and moved on with their lives. As it was, the sliver of hope kept the wound open.

'If only you could wait a little. Your brother will be so disappointed to have missed your wedding.'

'He'd want to take Leasky out and get him drunk. Not a very good idea. Look, Ma, we want a quick, quiet wedding. No need for all this fuss and expense.'

'The Methodist church at Fort Canning should be ready soon. If you wait just a couple of months, perhaps you can get married there, if your father has a word with them.' Mrs Shankar paused wistfully. 'There's an organ – nothing like organ music for a wedding, you know.'

'Ma, it's going to take years to repair. Have you seen the place recently? The Japanese were using it for arms and ammunition storage and they stripped out everything they could melt down for the metal.'

'I don't see why you can't wait a few months,' Mrs Shankar said. 'We want to get to know our girl again, that's all. You've been gone for so long.'

Parshanti, hands behind her back, was curling and uncurling her fingers. In school that had meant 'Help!'

Glancing around in search of something to distract Mrs Shankar, I saw a bundle of olive green striped fabric that had been pushed aside and forgotten. 'What's this cloth going to be? Don't you always say vertical stripes are hard to sew and horizontal stripes are hard to wear?'

'You can say some things till you're blue in the face and still people won't listen. Leave that alone,' Mrs Shankar said. 'It's nothing to do with us.'

'If you're using it, it has to do with us.' Parshanti came over to look, I suspect because of her mother's objection. 'This is quite nice. Wool jersey? It'll be a bit warm for wearing out here. It's for the big-bosomed brigadieress, isn't it? I thought you agreed you weren't going to do any more sewing for her until she paid for all the other dresses. It does drape nicely, though. Look how it falls when I gather it like this ...'

That last comment stopped Mrs Shankar in the act of hustling the cloth away. Mother and daughter had in common their love of fashion and fine fabrics. She ran the cloth through her fingers. 'It is lovely, isn't it? Mrs Evans had this material shipped in from America. She saw a photograph in *Vogue* and wanted a dress just like it. Long and formal enough for dinner parties but soft and comfortable. The problem is . . .'

'You don't have the time to do it?' I suggested.

'I could do it, all right! It's basically a tent dress pulled in with a belt. And perfect on someone like our Shanti. But the lady is . . .'

She didn't have to say any more.

Mrs Shankar's dressmaking skills had always been in demand, not only because she could replicate a pattern so well but because she could tell at a glance whether it would suit a client's figure and how it might be adapted to flatter.

The new brigadier's wife refused to listen to her advice and blamed Mrs Shankar's poor sewing on her 'chunky' appearance in her new outfits. (She looked chunky in her old ones too.) To make things worse, in the six months she'd been in Singapore, she'd ordered and collected eight dresses, all 'urgent' for official occasions and had paid for none. She claimed that the governor's wife shouldn't have to pay for her dresses since her husband didn't pay for his ceremonial sword and uniform. 'As though it makes any difference what she wears. She always looks like an overstuffed sausage!' Parshanti said.

'I see you're socialising again instead of working on my dresses,' trilled a voice.

I jumped, turned and saw a large woman with small brown

eyes and crooked yellow teeth, sweating in a pink floral frock. She must have been on the far side of fifty but dressed and acted aggressively girlishly. This was the first time I was seeing Mrs Brigadier Evans in the flesh, but I knew her at once. I also found myself disliking her, which surprised me until I saw Parshanti scowling at her. I was picking up how my friend felt. But I could also tell Mrs Evans was one of those who believed *she* was made in God's image while *we* were animals.

'Anyway, Mrs Shaker—'

'She's Mrs Shankar,' Parshanti said.

'As I said. Mrs Shaker, I have another little project for you. It's the house servants. They run around in bare feet and in their heathen clothes. It's so terrible and so sad. I was just thinking to myself how those little brown girls would look so much better in white uniforms.' Mrs Evans went to the work table and fingered the materials Mrs Shankar had set aside for Parshanti's wedding dress. 'And I walk in here and find just the thing. Oh, bless me. This is the very stuff that would do for them. The Good Lord provides for those who trust in Him. I want you to make white uniforms for them. Two each, I think – that's six in total. I have such an artistic sensibility and looking at them in their ugliness hurts me. This white cloth will do nicely. Never mind measuring them. They're all about the same size – the size of your servant girl there.' She pointed at me. 'Anyway, they're used to wearing things that don't fit. Charity, you know. Just measure her and make the outfits all the same size. Get them done by next week, will you? And please try to do a better job than you did on my gown. Anyway, I came here because I saw a photograph of Princess Elizabeth in a garden wearing a frock with a ribbon bow in front. I think that would suit me very nicely. I want you to find that photograph and make me a dress like that for next Sunday's garden party.'

'Wouldn't you like to pay for your previous dresses first?' Parshanti asked sweetly. 'I handle the accounts for my mother, you see. And that white fabric is specially imported and very, very expensive.'

'Send the bill to the Government House.' Mrs Evans didn't look at her.

'Oh, no, Mrs Evans,' Mrs Shankar said. 'This cloth is for my daughter Parshanti's— And this girl isn't a servant, she's my daughter's friend, and the cloth, I really can't—'

Parshanti had time to roll her eyes before Mrs Evans turned in our direction.

'So sweet that your little brown daughter has a little yellow friend,' said Mrs Evans. 'Let's make a deal. That's what you people love to do, isn't it? Get a good bargain? I'll let you keep that green striped fabric. Don't think I didn't see you all fingering it. "It won't suit you, madam" is your way of saying, "Give it to me," isn't it? Anyway, you can have it once you've made the white uniforms for my servants.'

'If we can't talk in here let's go for a walk,' Parshanti said loudly. 'I need to get out for a bit.'

'But we haven't settled on Su Lin's dress material and the trimmings,' Mrs Shankar said.

'You already know exactly what you want to do, Ma. Su Lin's not like me. She'll agree to whatever you want and tell you it's lovely. And she'll mean it. Come on, Su Lin, my little yellow friend.'

I followed, stopping to say, 'We'll be going now,' to her mother and to bow to her father, who was discreetly slipping out at the back. It's my upbringing: I can't walk out of a house without saying goodbye any more than I can leave without opening the door.

'I'll see you girls back here for dinner,' Mrs Shankar said. 'Su Lin, you look very nice in that *samfoo*.'

'Thank you, Aunty!'

Parshanti

———◆———

'I can't stand that woman!'

I struggled to keep up with my friend as she stormed away. 'Shouldn't we have stayed? Your mother wanted my measurements.'

'Not with that woman there. Ma won't get anything done until she leaves. I'm surprised she came back. Just last week Mrs Evans was offended because Ma didn't agree to drop everything and become her housekeeper at Government House. Then she said I should work for her, because even though I was half black I could speak enough English to tell the others what to do.'

'What?'

'I swear to you solemnly, Su,' Parshanti said.

She'd stopped walking so I could catch up.

'You're just angry with your mother.'

'No.' Parshanti started walking again but more slowly this time. 'I'm angry with myself for all the time I've wasted on thinking about dressing up when there's so much more to life.'

She sounded as if she meant it. I knew she'd had to adapt to living in the jungle and would need time to adapt back to real life, but I also remembered the old Parshanti. 'Remember you wanted to be a dress designer? If you designed your wedding dress . . .'

Parshanti actually snorted. 'Please don't remind me of what a fool I was. A dress designer! And you were going to be a famous novelist. Like anybody in Singapore would ever need writers and designers! And if they did, they'd import them. It wouldn't be people like us.'

I knew she was right but I didn't want her to be.

'Su, you don't really want to be my bridesmaid, do you?'

True. But even I knew better than to say so to the bride-to-be.

'Who do you want to ask instead?'

'No one! It's Ma who wants a fancy church wedding. And she's the one saying Su Lin will be hurt if you don't ask her to be your bridesmaid.'

'I won't be hurt,' I said. 'But I think your mother's using it as an excuse to give me a new dress.'

'Oh.' Parshanti processed this, then took in my *samfoo*. 'I like what you're wearing today. I haven't seen it before. New for New Year?'

I nodded.

'It's nice.' Parshanti felt the material and lifted my blouse to check the seams. 'This is good cloth, not so nicely sewn up, though. You used an old machine with a blunt needle.'

'I didn't make it. Shen Shen did.'

'Shen Shen?'

'She made one for me and one for Little Ling.'

'Did she?' Parshanti looked surprised. She knew how Shen Shen felt about me. 'I wouldn't trust her if I were you. She's as grabby and more calculating than Mrs Evans, just better at hiding it. Remember all the times she's tried to get you into trouble with your grandmother.'

'She's been doing a lot more at home, even cooking for all of us, not just her, Uncle Chen and Little Ling. And she's been helping Uncle Chen with the accounts.'

'Better double-check them,' Parshanti said.

'It's been hard because people are angry with the family since Ah Ma persuaded Uncle Chen to pull out of opium and comfort houses.'

'I hadn't heard anyone was angry with your family,' Parshanti said.

'Anyway, New Year is all about fresh starts, isn't it? It can't be easy for Shen Shen to have to live with her husband's family now her own family's all gone.'

'That scares me about getting married,' Parshanti said. 'All the things people in different families take for granted without even realising it.'

We weren't talking about Shen Shen any more. 'You're worried about fitting in with Dr Leask's family?' I knew next to nothing about them.

Before the war, Gordon Leask had come out east as a fresh graduate to be the resident doctor at the St Andrew's medical dispensary. Dr Shankar, Parshanti's father, had helped him settle in and the two had become fast friends.

As a European, Dr Leask didn't face the prejudice Dr Shankar had to put up with. Though a graduate of the Imperial College School of Medicine and King's College, London, Dr Shankar couldn't practise medicine in Singapore because Europeans didn't trust an Indian doctor and Asians didn't trust Western medicine. That was how Dr Shankar had ended up running Shankar & Sons Pharmaceuticals and Photographic Prints. He had asked Dr Leask to keep an eye on Parshanti when he and his wife were imprisoned by the Japanese.

'I've never met any of his family,' Parshanti mused. 'They'll probably hate me and he'll be miserable.'

'Your parents like him, don't they?' I knew they did.

'They get along better with him than they do with me! Su, I don't even fit into my own family any more. I can't get used to my mother bossing me about all the time. She treats me like an infant.'

I knew what she meant. You can't put the chicken back into the egg. At the same time I saw Dr and Mrs Shankar's point of view. Their precious little girl was back with them and they wanted never to let her out of their sight again.

'In the jungle we knew we could be dead tomorrow. No point in making long-term plans when there may be no tomorrow.'

'But what if there is a tomorrow? And you're not ready?'

'You don't understand,' Parshanti said. 'You're like my mother. She obviously thinks the only reason I want to get the wedding over with is sexual intercourse. But she can't make herself say the words, so she dances around the subject saying there's a lot more to marriage than I know. I can't stand it when people who've had sex can't even say the word "sex".'

'So you and Dr Leask don't have sexual intercourse?' I gave the words the same emphasis she had.

'Well, we—' Parshanti stopped. 'When you say the words it sounds funny. Well, yes, and we know we're meant to be together for ever because who else would take either one of us? But there's a huge difference between ending up with the man who just happens to be there and one who makes the effort to come back.'

'What are you talking about?'

'Don't be coy. We all know Le Froy's back. Why didn't you tell me?'

'I didn't know!'

'Oh, sure. Mrs Evans is worried he's after her husband's job. But if Le Froy's not with the police any more, why can't he be the new acting governor? It seems anyone can. Evans was only a clerk in Government House before he ran away to Australia. They promoted him to brigadier because it sounds better.'

'Have you seen Le Froy?' I was torn between not wanting to talk about him and desperate to know what he was up to.

'Not yet. But he came round to talk to Leasky and Harry while I was at my parents' place.' Parshanti perked up when Le Froy was the subject. It was easier to talk to her when she was moody. 'So what have you and Le Froy discussed so far? Can you persuade him to come over for dinner? Ma and Pa would love to see him again.'

'I haven't seen the chief inspector,' I said stiffly. He wasn't chief inspector any more, of course, but I found it more difficult to make myself say 'Le Froy' out loud than 'sexual intercourse'. 'I didn't even know he was back. He's nothing to do with me.'

'Oh, you're such a goose!' Parshanti said impatiently. 'You can tell me! I know the man came back for you! Is he having trouble getting to the point? That's the problem with men. The ones who feel don't talk and those who talk don't feel. Oh, I swear I'm so

64

jealous of you. And I'll never forgive you if you let him go after he travelled millions of miles of ocean to come back to you.'

'Less than seven thousand nautical miles, actually.'

'You know what I mean.'

'I do know what you mean and you're wrong.'

'You can't bluff me, Su. I know you.'

It was no use arguing with Parshanti. For her, arguments were contests and, as with mahjong tiles, the facts didn't matter as much as what you could get someone to believe.

'No, you don't. Not if you think I'm lying.'

'Why won't you tell me the truth about you and Le Froy? You know I won't say anything.'

'There's nothing to tell! It makes me uncomfortable when you assume Le Froy's back because of me. It's not true.'

Parshanti was more than surprised: she looked shocked. And she must have been because, for once, she had nothing to say.

I'd said what I wanted to. I waited.

'I thought you were just being coy about it. Everyone knows that's why he's back. He doesn't have an official appointment or anything. I just don't understand why you don't trust me enough to tell me.'

I waited some more.

'Su Lin, are you serious?'

I suddenly felt tearful. I hadn't realised Le Froy's return was so much discussed. Even allowing for Parshanti's exaggerations, this meant I'd not been the only one who'd wondered if it was possible that—

But I would never let on. Le Froy had promised nothing. I had only myself to blame if I was disappointed.

'You know what I missed most of all?' Parshanti slipped her arm through mine and started walking again. Caught up in the conversation, I hadn't noticed we'd stopped in the middle of the five-foot way.

'Talking nonsense to you,' she went on. 'All those afternoons when we were supposed to be doing our homework and you were memorising grammar rules and capital cities and scolding me for reading the ladies' magazines. While we were in the jungle camp that side of me never had a chance to come out. The chaps were good to me. They always made sure I had the best of whatever food and water there was. I felt like a parasite. Especially at first. I was always getting rashes or fevers. Leasky was using up his medical supplies on me and it seemed such a waste because I was useless. There were times when I felt I should have stayed and let the Japanese do what they wanted with me.'

'Oh, no!' I said. 'You don't know how bad it was for the girls they took to the comfort houses. And it would have been even worse in prison.'

'Leasky said I was his morale booster,' Parshanti said, as though I hadn't spoken. 'He said he wouldn't have been able to keep doing what he did for the resistance if not for me. But he kept going because I needed him. And he was right. I wouldn't have survived without him. But now there's nothing to struggle against, it's like we don't even know each other.'

'That's because you don't know each other in normal life,' I said. 'In normal life he's just this friend of your father's who sometimes st-st-st-stammers when he's talking to you. Maybe you should go on a date with him and count how many sentences you can get him to say to you without stammering.'

'Su! Don't be mean! He doesn't stammer with me any more.'

But at least she was laughing. I'd missed that. But I also needed her to listen to me. 'I'm serious, Shanti. The war is over. The Japanese have gone. The people we had to be while they were here are gone too. You need to get to know him all over again.'

'We can't just pretend the last three years didn't happen.'

'We're not pretending. We're moving on, deciding which parts of us we want to bring with us into the future. Shanti, you love him, don't you? You're just feeling funny because all your life you've been fighting against your parents to get what you want, and if you don't have to fight anyone to be with him, it's like you're doing what someone else wants so it must be wrong. Is that right? Well, I think having you back alive is so big for them that right now you could marry a monkey and they'd be happy.'

'I know,' Parshanti said.

I took a deep breath. 'Sorry, I know it's not my business but I have to say I hope you won't go through with marrying somebody just because everybody expects you to.'

It was so important that I stopped walking: I had to focus on what I wanted to say. Parshanti stopped too, staring at me. We were blocking the walkway but people grumbled and pushed past us, as smoothly as fish swirling around rocks in the river.

'What are you talking about, Su?'

Parshanti was one of the few people I dared to speak my mind to. 'If you've changed your mind you should say so. Never mind all the plans. It'll be much more difficult to get out of it if you go through with the marriage. That's when it becomes a legal contract.'

'What a horrible thing to say!' She didn't sound as if she appreciated my frankness. 'How can you say something like that? Do you think I shouldn't marry Leasky?'

'I think you should if you want to.'

'What makes you think I don't? Did he say something to you?'

'No! I've not even talked to him, except at your place.'

'Then why are you talking rubbish?'

'Okay, sorry, forget it.'

'No, Su. You brought it up. You've heard something about him, haven't you? Believe me, I've heard all the stories. He told me everything, if you want to know. Whatever reasons you've got for me not marrying him, the man has already used them to try to put me off. So, why do you think I shouldn't marry him?'

She wasn't going to like it. But I wasn't going to like myself if I didn't say it. 'I'll tell you after you tell me why you're getting married. You're acting as if you don't want to be.'

'I do want to get married. Leasky and I, we're as good as married. We swore to each other that if anything happened to either of us we'd watch out for the other's parents even. That was real. What my mother's planning is like playing dress-up.'

'Shanti, darling Shanti, you've been planning your glorious wedding day for as long as I can remember. Right down to designing your wedding gown, your going-away dress, your bouquet and the flowers in the church. And you always said you wanted to get married in the Wesley chapel at Fort Canning because of the stained-glass windows and the Hammond organ. You've been saying that since you were ten years old! It was going to be the most wonderful day of your life. And now all your mother wants is to make it special for you and it's like you can't stand talking about it. I hope you still want to marry Dr Leask. I like him and I like how he looks at you. But if you're having doubts, better you let everyone know now rather than later.'

Parshanti took a deep breath. 'You see too much. No, I'm not at all keen on the wedding. Don't look at me like that, Lin-Lin. You're worse than Ma.'

'Does Dr Leask know?'

'Of course! He probably knew before I did. When I was making all those plans right down to the last detail about getting married, the one thing I didn't plan was the man I was going to marry. The most important piece was missing.'

'You were always falling in love,' I reminded her.

She grimaced. 'I thought I was. But I didn't even know what I was looking for until I found him. And now that I have, none of the rest matters. That's why all the fuss feels so stupid. I'm not that silly girl any more. Whether we sign a contract at the Register of Marriages or swear to have and to hold in front of the bishop makes no difference. We know we're meant to be together and we want to be together. What's wrong, Lin-Lin?'

'I think I'm jealous.' I sniffed and wiped tears on my sleeve. 'I think that's wonderful. But—'

Parshanti twisted her mouth, 'But what?'

'The big wedding will make your parents happy. They've been so worried about you.'

'So you're saying I should just make them happy all my life? It's not like this is the only life I'm ever going to have!'

'Your mother's been looking forward to you getting married—'

'Yes, I know. But I can't just do it for her!'

'Is it Dr Leask? He doesn't want a big wedding? Or doesn't he want a wedding?'

For a moment I thought she was going to slap me. She thought so too. But she rolled her eyes and hugged me instead. 'I can't explain it, but he's the right one, okay?'

I felt her tears on my neck and I knew things would be all right between her and Dr Leask.

We started walking again, slowly.

'Anyway, tell me about that dead man you saw.'

'On the bus I remembered something weird. He had half-chewed yellow rambutan skins in his mouth. I didn't know what it was at first, until I saw the yellow hairs.'

'People don't chew rambutan skins or seeds. They're poisonous. Are you saying he committed suicide?'

'I don't think they're that poisonous. It would be a very slow way to kill yourself,' I said.

'But are you sure he was really dead?' Parshanti asked. 'Maybe he was in shock or something. Perhaps he fainted or tripped and fell into the drain. And all the people passing by thought he was dead so they just left him there until he really was dead.'

Assault by Flirting

———◆———

'Hey there, girls. Who's really dead?'

We turned round, startled. We'd reached the junction of Robinson Road, near to where I'd seen the *makcik* earlier. She had gone but three *ang mohs*, who were smoking in the shade of the building, had heard us. One was familiar – the plump, fair police officer I'd seen eating *buaya* curry, the one named Johnson.

'Hey! Missy Short Hair! Watch where you're going!'

Parshanti was tall and slim, with honey-brown skin and dark brown eyes. The long hair that had once fallen in waves to below her waist was short, almost like a boy's, but she was, if anything, even more beautiful now. A graceful strength and energy seemed to shimmer about her. She caught people's attention without meaning to and that wasn't always a good thing.

'Ignore them.' Parshanti pulled me on, 'Tell me how you knew he was dead. Do you know who he was?'

I nodded. 'A friend of my uncle's. He came to see Uncle Chen but he was asleep so he left.'

'The man went to your house today? He's not Chinese, then?'

'He is! Was, I mean.'

'So that's probably why he's dead. The spirits got him for breaking your Third Day taboo!' She laughed. I didn't. 'Anyway, you can't be sure he's dead. Maybe he was just drunk, and after you left he woke up and climbed out of the drain.'

'I'm sure he was dead,' I said. 'I climbed into the drain and made sure.'

As we walked down the five-foot way side by side, Parshanti automatically matched her stride to mine so I wouldn't have to hurry and stumble. Even if we weren't completely comfortable with each other yet, the physical habits came back as though we'd never stopped spending all our free afternoons together.

'Should we get back to your place?' I asked Parshanti.

'I'm not going back while that woman is there. I really hate Ma going on her knees to rich *ang moh* women.'

'Pinning hems?'

'Don't be so literal, Su.'

'It's like a surgeon lancing boils on a man's bottom. A job, not a humiliation. She's got a skill they need and she's helping them.'

'Still, most of them give her more respect than— Oh!'

Parshanti bumped into someone and almost fell.

'Hey! Missy Short Hair! Watch where you're going!'

She had walked right into Johnson. I suspected it wasn't entirely her fault. In fact, it wasn't our fault at all. The three men must have run down the road to get around us and now they were standing across the five-foot way. We couldn't have passed them without bumping into one.

Johnson was leering at Parshanti while the others laughed. Surely it was too early for them to be drunk. Unless it was the heat. Only Johnson wore the khaki shorts and shirt that indicated he was a police officer. The others seemed to be more recent arrivals, like Fahey, who was 'interested in languages'. He wasn't with them.

'Hey, sweetheart. Talk about being impossible to miss, eh?' Johnson put an arm around Parshanti and squeezed her against him. She struggled but his hand, clamped on her far shoulder, locked her in place.

'Let her go!' I said.

'Look! This one's jealous! Sorry, sweetheart, I saw her first. I heard you give group discounts to soldiers so how about a special deal for us?'

'Please, oh, please, let her go!' I yanked at Parshanti's hands, trying to pull her loose, which just made Johnson and his friends laugh louder.

Johnson smelt of stale sweat and badly washed clothes. When he batted me away with his free arm the stench made me wince.

'Come on, fellows!' Johnson shouted at the others. 'Party time! Whoever gets that wildcat off us can keep her!'

'Don't touch her!' Parshanti spat, struggling with renewed vigour.

Johnson seemed to think it was a huge joke and tickled her with his free hand, making her swear at him.

Some passers-by stopped to watch but stayed at a safe distance. No one wanted to get involved with the police for no reason, though they made clear what they thought of the *ang mohs*. I heard '*Buaya*' several times, accompanied by disgusted looks.

It was enough for Johnson's friends.

'Put her down, Johnson.'

'Come on, let's go.'

Johnson just laughed. He was enjoying himself even more now he had an audience. I could tell from the way he stood, his stocky legs apart, swinging Parshanti around so the crowd gathering could see her struggling to get away from him. He was the kind of man who'd bullied other students at school, then spent the rest of his life trying to recapture the feeling.

In the east, where he was treated as a superior being, he must have felt he'd won the jackpot. Except his friends had backed away from him and the angry crowd was closing in, muttering in Malay, Hokkien, Teochew and Cantonese that he should let the girl go and stop being so stupid.

'Just having a bit of fun,' Johnson said. 'Come on!' Confident as he was, he didn't want his friends to leave.

Someone in the crowd jeered. Someone else booed and threw a rock. More people threw rocks and someone spat. The mood was turning ugly and even Johnson finally saw this.

Before he moved I knew he was going to do something reckless. He might have grabbed Parshanti as a dare, but he wasn't going to back down publicly, letting himself be bested by a couple of girls.

'I'm going to have to arrest you two girls for a breach of the peace.'

Still maintaining his grip on Parshanti, he grasped my arm and yanked me off balance. I fell, but he dragged me along the pavement on my knees, not giving me the chance to get back to my feet.

'Come on!' he shouted to his friends. 'We'll work out what kind of penalty they'll have to pay if they don't want to spend the night in the lock-up.'

Johnson grinned as his two mates came after us. He was comfortable again. I suspected this was something he'd done before. All I knew was that I had to make sure we didn't end up going wherever he wanted to take us. I squatted and braced myself on the ground, halting him.

'Hey!' he said. He pulled my arm but, crouched on the ground, I was a deadweight.

I needed to help Parshanti get away from him, even though she'd spent months in the jungle toughening up. She was the one he was interested in. Over the eighteen years we'd grown up together it had always been Parshanti who'd caught men's attention while I kept her safe from them.

Johnson let go of my arm and reached into a pocket.

I heard a distinct metallic click as he pulled something out and I knew, before I saw it, that he was holding a pocket knife.

My body reacted before I could think what to do. I sank back from my squat to sit on the ground. As Johnson turned towards Parshanti holding the knife I kicked at his legs. Mine may not be the same length but they made contact at the same time, catching him just below the knees. If I'd damaged either of them we wouldn't have to worry about him for a while. But although he let go of Parshanti as he stumbled, I hadn't brought him down. He growled as he turned back to me.

I made sure he could see I looked scared, so that he'd think I'd fallen and kicked him by accident. There was no point in making him angry. Not while he still had a knife.

He smirked, 'So you like to play rough, little wildcat?'

He reached for me again, and Parshanti was on him. I didn't see what she did but he yelled and lost his balance. I thought he was going to land on me, but before he could, Parshanti had darted round and kneed him in the face so that he fell backwards.

I gaped. Parshanti had fought back? She never had before. She must have learned the skills in the jungle. I was so taken aback I just sat there.

'Are you all right, Su Lin?'

'What did you do?'

She helped me to my feet. 'Let's go.'

'I'm hurt!' Johnson sounded shocked. His face was covered with blood. Nosebleed, I guessed. It looked even worse after he'd wiped it on his sleeves, smearing his shirt. It wouldn't have worried anyone who's ever worked with or cared for young children, but his two mates were aghast. The gaggle of local onlookers fell silent and started to step away from the drama. Even if it wasn't a life-threatening injury, it was British blood, and the British had a way of rounding up and blaming everyone in the vicinity.

'That bitch broke my nose!'

'Go and cry to your mummy,' Parshanti said.

I was beginning to see exactly how much Parshanti had changed. 'Come on!' I started to walk, trying to drag her with me.

'Stop them! Those girls attacked us! They're Communist spies! Stop them!'

The onlookers parted before us. Some touched us as we passed, muttering protection blessings.

'Good kick!' several said to Parshanti.

If we could just get away, the chances were that the men would let it drop. They wouldn't want it to get around that they'd been beaten by a couple of girls they'd been pestering.

But, unfortunately for us, the two men with Johnson grabbed us.

'Station,' Johnson said. He was holding an already bloody handkerchief to his nose. 'Fahey can lock them up. Give him something to do.'

'Okay,' Parshanti said to me, 'you win. I'd rather be looking at dress patterns.'

Back in the Detective Shack

———◆———

We ended up being strong-armed into the Detective Shack, across the road from the main police headquarters building. This was where I'd worked as Chief Inspector Le Froy's secretarial assistant and cultural liaison when he'd set up Singapore's Detective and Intelligence Unit.

'I can walk by myself!' Parshanti shook off the hand on her arm and climbed the familiar two steps. She'd often come over to visit me in my room on the second floor of the little brick building. I'd done the cleaning and coffee-making as well as the typing and filing. Maybe that was why we weren't as scared as they might have expected us to be.

Also, after the calculated cruelty of the Japanese, it was hard to take British authority seriously.

'Harry!'

Harry Palin was coming out as we got to the door. His years in the jungle had left him lean and brown as a local, but there was no disguising his thick reddish brown hair. He'd changed, though. The old Harry would have charged over and pulled the men off us. 'Please don't—' I wanted to ask him to stay calm and not escalate this, but I didn't need to. Our eyes met and locked yet he continued on his way. But he must have turned because he followed us in.

'Where's he gone?' Parshanti gasped, looking around wildly.

I shushed her. To anyone in the office, he'd come in with us but to the men who'd brought us, Harry had just stepped out and was returning. Once inside he bent over a desk as though he was filling in a form and instantly faded into the background against the wall where a painting of his father, Sir Henry Palin, had once hung. Now it bore a large photograph of Brigadier Jacob 'Jake' Evans, the former Customs official who was now the new acting governor of Singapore.

I was impressed. I wanted to tell Harry everything was all right, but I honestly didn't know that it was.

'Johnson – sir – what happened to you? What are you doing with these girls?'

Just my luck. It was the dark-haired man whose sharp ears had picked up the word '*buaya*'. And from the way he looked at me I suspected he recognised me.

Fahey was wearing nothing but a thin cotton singlet over his stiffly starched khaki shorts. 'Where's your shirt?' I exclaimed.

Looking back it's funny how shocked I felt. I hadn't understood how thoroughly the British had drummed their standards into us.

Fahey's face went red as he grabbed the shirt hanging over the back of his chair and put it on as his colleagues laughed.

The others in the room also looked like recent arrivals, which made sense. Most of the *ang mohs* who'd been stationed out east when the war started were long overdue for home leave.

'They were talking about killing a man. I heard them. That lame one was telling her friend she knew he was really dead because she'd made sure of it. And then they attacked us. Out of the blue! Like those suicidal Japs.'

'No!' I said.

'You didn't say you killed a man?' Fahey asked me.

'I saw a dead man this morning,' I said, 'on the way to town. I was telling my friend about it.'

'Why tell her?' Johnson said. 'Chances are she killed him! Be careful – that one's a real wildcat! Deal with them, Fahey. I'm going to get this seen to. The slut broke my nose!'

Fahey pulled a notepad towards him, gesturing Parshanti and me to the stools in front of his desk. 'Tell me about the dead man. Who was it? Where did you see him? What killed him?'

'In the storm drain near my house. He was Botak – I mean his name was Ho Seng Beng. I don't know what killed him. I think maybe he choked. I found something in his mouth when I tried to see if he was breathing.'

Fahey got up and went over to one of the filing cabinets.

Harry had come to stand beside me at the desk. 'That's Botak Beng. He can't be dead,' he said.

'Ho Seng Beng, alias Botak. Smuggling operations. Closely connected with the Chen family network,' Fahey read, from the file he'd collected. I recognised it as one of Le Froy's. He looked at Harry. 'Palin, he's the one you've been looking for. You say he ran off with your sister?'

'What? Dee-Dee?' I turned to Harry. 'No! He wouldn't! Why didn't you say something?'

'That's not what happened,' Parshanti said.

This drew Fahey's attention to her. 'You're the Shankar girl. You came out of the jungle with Palin here and his Communist friends, didn't you?'

I sensed it was Harry, rather than Parshanti, the officer was trying to provoke an answer from. But instead of explaining, Harry Palin, who was clearly not the friend I'd thought he was, turned away and walked out of the Detective Shack.

'Harry?' Parshanti said, but he didn't stop.

I didn't know which of us he was avoiding, so I was piqued on behalf of us both. On Fahey's behalf too. 'Respect the khaki,' Le Froy had always said. It was what the uniform stood for that counted, not the man inside it. Harry shouldn't have walked out on an officer in the middle of an interview.

But Harry Palin had never been one to respect authority. His father, the former governor, had been a planter and Harry had been living out east since he was a child. I believed he was a good person because I'd seen how much he cared for his sister, Dee-Dee. Deborah 'Dee-Dee' Palin had survived a terrible attack of fever when she was seven years old and had remained at the mental age of seven. She'd been known locally as the Palin *sor nui*, or silly child, a term of affection rather than contempt.

'You're limping,' Fahey said, once Harry was gone. 'Did they hurt you?'

'No, sir. I had polio when I was a child. I'm not hurt.'

'You speak English very well,' Fahey said. 'Are you a spy?'

'No, sir. I studied English at the Mission Centre school.' That was true, though my fluency came from listening to Ah Ma's shortwave radio and translating the nightly BBC news programmes into Hokkien and Malay for her. Ah Ma believed in knowing her enemies, but in me the British radio programmes had fostered a love of the English language.

'I know who you are now,' Fahey said. He sounded pleased with himself. 'You're the English-educated granddaughter of the Chen family. The old woman's favourite. She crippled you so you couldn't marry and planted you in the police to keep her warned of raids. And your uncle is behind all the illegal betting and money-lending.'

'Su Lin was working here, in the Detective Unit, before the war,' Parshanti said. 'She was Chief Inspector Le Froy's secretarial assistant and cultural liaison.'

Fahey nodded. I could tell this wasn't news to him. 'And you, Parshanti Shankar, you're one of those who spent the war hiding in the forest.'

I didn't like the way he studied her, taking her in from the short curled hair on her head to her dark red peep-toe slingback shoes. The shoes, which she loved despite her attempts to eschew fashion, had been shipped in by her father and were decorated with bows and perforated patterns.

'I was,' Parshanti said calmly. 'Both my parents were interned by the Japanese. It was safer in the jungle.'

'I've heard most of the jungle fighters were in the Communist Party. Told by the Chinese Communists to run and hide in the jungle instead of trying to block the Japanese Army's advance.'

'We also had Europeans and anti-Japanese locals who didn't run away,' Parshanti said, 'and Allied soldiers parachuted in with arms and supplies sent by Lord Mountbatten's South East Asia Command.'

'So you played Robin Hood in the jungle for two years,' his eyes went to her feet again, 'if not in those shoes.'

Was the man flirting?

'Not in these shoes,' Parshanti agreed. 'It was two and a half, almost three years. And I wasn't playing Robin Hood. I was watching for downed British and American aircraft.'

'You brought down planes? What planes?'

'Of course not. We tried to get to the crash sites first when reconnaissance patrols and cargo planes were shot down,' Parshanti said, 'so the Japs wouldn't get the survivors.'

'You did, did you?'

I felt sick. Parshanti was on their radar for her time spent in the jungle and I'd given them an excuse to question her. If I had to choose between boorish (Johnson) and slimy (Fahey), I'd go for boorish any time. It was easy to make such men feel clever and act stupid but Fahey might actually be clever.

'What's happening here?'

It was a polite, cultured and wonderfully familiar voice.

I spun round and saw Le Froy, with Harry Palin behind him. So that was why Harry had darted off. I took back every one of the barbs I'd mentally fired in his direction when he'd disappeared.

Le Froy

'Chief Inspector!' Parshanti gave a little gasp and nudged me hard, a huge grin on her face. I didn't have enough brain space to deal with her while I was taking him in.

Le Froy was still clean-shaven and his hair – more grey and silver than I remembered it – was crew cut in the way his Indian barber had kept it. He was painfully thin, and the skin that had been once been taut and dark as a coolie's now hung loose and pale.

He nodded to Parshanti and me, barely glancing at us. He was handling his prosthetic foot pretty well. I doubt anyone who didn't know him as well as I did would notice his frustration with himself.

'Chief Inspector.' Fahey echoed Parshanti's words in a very different tone.

Chief Inspector Thomas Francis Le Froy had once struck fear into the hearts of all the gangsters and gamblers in Singapore, including those protected by my grandmother and Uncle Chen.

'Just Le Froy.'

I'd worked out exactly how I would behave if I ever met Le Froy again. I would be friendly, of course. I wasn't going to let anyone think I'd been hurt or angry by his leaving without saying goodbye. But I wouldn't be over-friendly or familiar.

Not like when I'd met Miss Forsyth, a former Mission Centre school teacher. She'd been in an ambulance when she saw me on the five-foot way straight after the Japanese surrender. She had shrieked to the driver to stop and jumped out while the vehicle was still moving. Miss Forsyth hadn't been a favourite teacher, calling us her 'little brown cherubs' and not allowing us to read anything in her English lessons other than the King James Bible and her precious copy of *The Velveteen Rabbit*. But I'd found myself in tears as she held me tight while weeping and thanking God that I was alive.

When someone has a good heart, you can forgive them almost anything.

But Le Froy was a different matter. He'd been an employer, not a teacher. I'd come to think of him as a mentor or *sifu* like the rest of the team working under him in the Detective Unit. And he'd left without any word of when or if he would return.

It hadn't been a problem for my former colleagues, Prakesh Pillay and Ferdinand de Souza. They had their police certificates. But the only employment record I had on the books was as 'domestic assistant'. Le Froy had never updated the first contract I'd signed with him. So how had I been drawing my salary?

'Miss Chen, good to see you again.'

I reminded myself he'd left without saying a word. I reminded myself not to fawn all over him. But I felt tears in my eyes. I was so glad to see him alive.

'You know this Chink slut?' Johnson reappeared and sneered at Le Froy. There was still blood on his shirt but he seemed to have forgotten his nose was broken. 'She's being charged with assaulting the police.'

'She's former staff,' Le Froy said mildly. 'Here.'

'Well, she's not staff now!'

'Miss Chen was telling us about a murder she witnessed,' Fahey said. 'One Botak Beng.'

'The smuggler?' Clearly Le Froy knew of Botak.

'If he was a damned smuggler, someone just saved us the trouble of putting him behind bars. But that doesn't explain what you're doing here,' Johnson said to him. 'We can get rid of difficult locals ourselves. Not to mention vigilantes like these.'

I could see I was on the verge of being charged, probably with being a vigilante and a Communist, because Johnson wanted to provoke Le Froy. Maybe Harry hadn't done us any favours by bringing him in.

'What about this murder?' Le Froy asked me.

'I didn't actually see it,' I said. 'And it wasn't a murder, just a dead man in the drain when I was walking to the trolley bus. I was telling Parshanti what I saw when these men started shouting at us and grabbing us.'

Johnson changed his story. 'Fact is, these two are shameless prostitutes. They approached and solicited us on the street in broad daylight.'

Fahey seemed to be taking it all in. Writing it down, even. This pleased Johnson, who kept going: 'They're probably thieves too. Pickpockets. Lots of people have reported things missing, just from walking down the street. They'll have a cache of stolen property somewhere. We should keep them here, search their quarters.'

'Who, sir?' Fahey paused, pen uplifted.

'Who what?'

'Who reported things missing? I'll look up the reports.'

'Lots of people. There aren't any reports. They reported to me and that's good enough.'

'Give me one name.'

'Why the blazes should I?'

'So that I can fill in this report, sir,' Fahey said. 'Brigadier Evans asked to have everything documented, sir.'

'Brigadier Evans,' Johnson said. 'Put that down on your blasted report.'

'And what did Brigadier Evans report missing?'

Johnson glared at him. Fahey gazed back mildly, pen in hand.

'Just write the damned report. I'm swearing to it, and that's good enough for anybody!'

'Which version of events are you swearing to, sir? That you arrested these girls for murdering a man, that these girls attacked you and broke your nose, or that these girls are prostitutes and pickpockets? Sir?'

Parshanti looked shocked, then grinned. I was glad she was going to marry Dr Leask because the old Parshanti would have fallen in love with Fahey for that.

'Do your job, Sergeant,' Johnson said. 'I'm going to the hospital.'

The two men who'd been with him when he came in followed him out.

'Trainees?' Le Froy asked.

OVIDIA YU

'Friends,' Fahey said. 'We've only got budget for one sergeant, and that's me. And we don't pay me enough. It's an honour to meet you, sir. I've heard a lot about you.'

It wasn't surprising. Le Froy was a legend in the Crown Colonies. He spoke fluent Hokkien and Malay: in the old days he'd tracked loan sharks disguised as a rickshaw-puller and infiltrated gambling dens as a Chinese drains inspector. He'd been a real-life hero, a combination of Douglas Fairbanks and John Barrymore.

Now I saw him close up, he looked older and tired, and he smelt different, as though the different food he'd been eating had changed the composition of his body. Or maybe because, as he'd once told me, people didn't sweat enough during the British winter so never flushed out the waste in their systems through their pores.

'Miss Chen worked for me and I trusted her completely,' Le Froy said. 'And I would stake my reputation on Miss Shankar being innocent of solicitation, pickpocketing and murder.'

Fahey nodded. But 'What do you know about the dead smuggler, sir?'

'No one knows anything just now. Will the body be examined?'

'Yes.' Fahey made a note.

'There's no point in speculating till we have the facts.'

I realised they'd been looking for Botak Beng before his death. That must have been why he was so furtive at the house. He knew he was being hunted by the authorities. I felt sorry for him. I wished he'd told me, though I didn't know what I would have done with the information.

I hadn't mentioned that Botak had tried to visit Uncle Chen at Chen Mansion, but I didn't want to prolong our stay at the station. After all, Botak hadn't come into the house.

'Well,' Fahey said, 'why don't you all get out of here before the boss comes back?'

'Thank you,' Le Froy said.

'Don't,' Fahey said. 'I'm probably going to say you made me.'

'I could bust your nose, too, to make it convincing,' Parshanti offered. Was the old Parshanti back and flirting? 'Thank you.' Yes, she was.

Fahey gave an awkward laugh. 'No, thanks. I'll manage.' And it was working.

Parshanti started for the door.

'Wait,' I said. 'Chief—' Le Froy looked at me but I had nothing to say. Or, rather, I had so much to say that I couldn't get anything out.

'Come to my parents' place for dinner,' Parshanti said. 'They'll never forgive me once they hear I saw you and didn't drag you round to visit them.'

Le Froy glanced over his shoulder. Fahey was watching us.

'Su Lin will be there. I'll tell Ma you'll come when you've finished here?'

Le Froy looked at me, then nodded. 'If it's not too much trouble. I'd like to pay my respects to your father.'

Dr Shankar had amputated Le Froy's foot while they were in prison. It had probably saved his life.

'Brigadier Evans would like a word with you. He's expecting you this evening, sir,' Fahey said.

'Brigadier Evans expects a lot,' Le Froy said lightly.

'You can come and search our house,' Parshanti said to Fahey, 'but I won't ask you to dinner.'

'Why did you do that?' I managed to wait till we were safely out of sight of the Detective Shack before I turned on Parshanti.

'Why did I do what?' She seemed genuinely confused. 'I thought you'd be happy to see him. Anyway, it's true. Ma and Pa will want to see him. Especially when they find out those stupid police let us go thanks to Le Froy.'

'Why did you hit that stupid man?'

She was staring at me as if she didn't know me. 'I was trying to help you. He was dragging you away!'

'He was just trying to provoke you into following him. He wasn't interested in me.'

Parshanti rolled her eyes and started walking. Her generous mouth, usually so quick to smile, was in a grim, straight line.

'How are you going to help anybody if you get yourself arrested?'

'Su, wake up. If they want to arrest us or shoot us, they'll just go ahead.'

I stood still, watching her, till she turned and said, 'What are you waiting for?'

'I don't want to stay for dinner. I need to tell my grandmother what people are saying about her.'

That stopped her.

'Oh, Su, please! Your grandmother probably already knows! Anyway, what's she going to do tonight?'

Harry appeared from an alley and joined us. 'Just wanted to make sure he got you out.'

'Thanks,' I said.

He raised his eyebrows at me.

'For getting Le Froy.'

Harry shrugged. He'd never been much of a talker but this was ridiculous.

'Harry's got a standing invitation to have dinner with us but he never turns up,' Parshanti said.

'I have things to do,' Harry said.

Suddenly I didn't want to let him disappear again. 'Please tell me what happened to Dee-Dee.'

He hesitated. 'Yes. But not now.' He walked away, head down.

Things weren't easy, but maybe they wouldn't be so bad after all. We were all working out where we fitted into this new post-war world. And Le Froy was back in Singapore.

Mrs Evans

'The Home Office isn't beyond sending spies, you know. Now the war is over, they've got them all over the place with nothing to do but make trouble for hardworking men just trying to do their jobs.'

'Your mother has a client with her,' I said.

Arriving back at the Shankars, I wanted to get upstairs to the privacy of Parshanti's room but we couldn't walk in while Mrs Shankar was seeing a client.

'It's only Mrs Evans,' Parshanti said. 'Still here. She keeps hanging around because she has no one else to bully and Ma won't send her away.'

'Maybe we should wait,' I said. 'Or go round to the back.'

The concrete spiral staircase at the back of the shophouse was used by the night-soil collectors and led up to every floor.

'Door's locked and the key's in my room,' Parshanti said. She squared her shoulders, ran a hand through her hair and stepped into the house. 'Hello, Ma.'

'Here are the girls, back at last!' Mrs Shankar said. I thought she looked relieved to see Parshanti. Had she thought she wouldn't come back? Then I realised we'd been gone almost three hours after leaving for our 'short walk'.

'Come, come, dear Su Lin. I really must measure you for your bridesmaid's dress.'

Mrs Shankar and I pretended not to hear Parshanti's snort.

'Is this the crippled girl they're all talking about?' Mrs Evans was paying more attention to me than she had earlier. 'Now that the man's crippled too, it's rather like poetic justice, isn't it?'

Mrs Shankar looked embarrassed but Mrs Evans was taking me in with her bulging eyes. 'I wanted to have a good look at the girl,' she said. 'I've heard so many rumours. She's no beauty, is she?'

There were crumbs around Mrs Evans's mouth. She'd been sitting in the Shankars' house, eating Ah Ma's pineapple tarts, while Parshanti and I were trying not to get arrested.

Making pineapple tarts was tedious, hot work: peeling, coring and slant carving the eyes out of our home-grown pineapples, cutting them into chunks to simmer with cane sugar and *gula* – a darker sweetener made from the sap of palm trees – vanilla pods, cloves and star anise. I'd resented the time it took for as long as I could remember. But at least at the end of all the work you had the tarts to show for it. I had nothing to show for the hours we'd spent being harassed in the Detective Shack.

'So sorry to keep you for so long, Mrs Evans,' Mrs Shankar said. 'Now you've met our Su Lin, I'm sure you'll want to be on your way.' So Mrs Evans had stayed expressly to look me over. And even now that she'd seen me, she showed no inclination to take Mrs Shankar's hint and leave.

'You and your husband must be so busy since you're both so important,' Parshanti said. 'Won't he be worried with you gone for so long?'

Mrs Evans laughed. 'Oh, no. He says he just has to keep the natives quiet and happy so they don't make trouble.'

Parshanti's eye-roll and snort were too much for even the oblivious Mrs Evans to ignore. Mrs Shankar hurried to reclaim her attention. 'Do you hear that, girls? Stay happy and don't make trouble!'

I heard real fear behind her mock ferocity and Parshanti must have, too, because she didn't say any more.

It made no difference that Mrs Evans was still there, jabbering away in her vulgar-genteel way. Parshanti and Mrs Shankar were still watching out for each other and that was good.

I saw from the state of Mrs Evans's clothes that she'd been eating the *kueh bangkit* or tapioca cookies I'd brought too. Those little white cookies were my favourites, a delicious melt-in-the-mouth snack. Literally – you pushed one into your mouth and it dissolved on your tongue. Ah Ma's secret was that you had to use coconut cream, not coconut milk, because the extra liquid in the milk would make them too dense and heavy. People traditionally place them on altars as offerings because the departed can use them as currency in the afterlife.

Mrs Evans had eaten so many *kueh bangkit* that her lap and the front of her dress were covered with a fine dusting of white powder. I felt sorry for Mrs Shankar. Usually when a guest who drops in between meals is offered a second snack they know it's high time to leave. Mrs Evans had clearly had no qualms about accepting and swallowing everything she was offered.

Maybe we'd had a better time with Johnson than Mrs Shankar had had with Mrs Evans.

'We invited that man to stay in Government House, you know. It's a huge place, with guest rooms. We could easily have put him up for a week or two. I told Jake to let him know he was welcome. Jake didn't like the idea at first, then said it was much better to have the man somewhere you can keep an eye on him. I thought it was all settled. But we're not good enough for your Mr Le Froy apparently. I suppose once someone's gone native, like that man has, it's hard to live in a civilised way again, eh? So. Where is he living? I suppose you're playing housekeeper for him again, are you?'

I defended myself against Mrs Evans's coy innuendos by keeping my earnest blank expression and pretending I didn't understand.

Mrs Evans nudged me and nodded towards Parshanti. 'That girl's so pretty, isn't she? She's got no manners and no style – such a waste. I could have got her a good place in Government House if only she kept a civil tongue in her head. But there you are. With looks like hers she knows she's got all the men falling for her so she can't be bothered with other women. You hate her, don't you? Be honest, I can see it in your face.'

I was certainly feeling the pleasure of hating someone, but it wasn't Parshanti.

There was no way to be both truthful and polite so I said nothing.

'I thought you said the cripple understands English?' Mrs Evans said to Mrs Shankar.

She said something else to me in a language I didn't understand, and glared at me when I genuinely didn't understand her.

Later I learned Mrs Evans had spent some of her childhood in colonial India. As a result, whenever she met an Asian who didn't speak English she talked Hindustani at them, as though all non-English-speaking Asians belonged to the same herd and spoke the same language.

'I'm so fed up with all the bureaucrats trying to make trouble for my husband. Especially when it comes to the Detective Unit. That's why I'm sure Le Froy's behind it. No one else really cares who heads what as long as the natives are kept in order. That's why I know personal reasons brought him back.'

Again she looked at me. Again I looked blank.

Parshanti yawned hugely and peered obviously at the clock on the wall. Mrs Shankar looked miserable. Dr Shankar was nowhere to be seen.

'That man Le Froy is fond of his toddy, isn't he? I've heard it's what he missed most at home in England. That's the only other reason I can think of that would bring him all the way out here where he's not wanted.'

Toddy, or *kallu*, is a drink made from the fermented sap of coconut-palm flowers. It looks like boiled barley water, with the same white cloudiness, but has a slightly sour alcoholic fizz over its natural sweetness. Drunk at room temperature, it's a cure-all: it's claimed to cool you down when you're too hot yet will warm you up when your blood is cold. The sap is very sweet and 'mild as mother's milk' when it's first tapped, but once it's fermented in the sun it becomes 'a man's drink' – alcoholic.

And, of course, it being popular with local coolies, it's despised by the Europeans who don't see its similarity to their imported brandy and whisky.

'I've never seen Chief Inspector Le Froy drinking toddy,' I said.

Mrs Evans glowed in triumph. She'd broken my silence. 'You'd say anything to defend him, wouldn't you?' she said. 'That man's not the chief inspector any more. He may think he can just walk back into the office and get his job back, but that's not how it's going to be. Did he tell you the real reason he came back?'

'No, ma'am. Just now when we saw him in the police station, that was the first I knew of him being back.'

That wasn't strictly true. But it was the first time I'd seen him and everything else was hearsay.

'What were you doing in the police station?' Mrs Shankar asked.

'Le Froy's got a nerve, coming back when everyone knows it was his fault that the Japs could just waltz in and take over,' Mrs Evans said. 'If you ask me, all the people who were in charge here should be shot. My son Robert says that if he'd been in charge of defending Singapore—'

'Your son was in Singapore. He didn't defend anything. I heard he ran away with you and your husband, didn't he?' Parshanti spoke up. 'Your government was calling for reinforcements to defend the island but you paid for yourself and your able-bodied son to be smuggled by boat to Australia. Le Froy stayed to defend us and didn't leave until the Japanese surrendered.'

'My husband says Le Froy came here without official approval. I don't know what he's trying to do, but they're already on to him. My husband won't appoint him to anything. I don't know what he expects. Look at him! He's moved into a local house with some local woman instead of accepting our hospitality. He has no respect for authority. Plus he's probably picked up all kinds of local diseases and juju. The locals already have a new head detective and they're very happy with him.'

'What were you girls doing in the police station?' Mrs Shankar had asked the question several times but we hadn't been able to answer until Mrs Evans stopped for breath.

'Oh, some idiot policeman tried to arrest us.' Parshanti ran a hand through her short curly hair and smiled at Mrs Evans.

'Arrest you for what?' her mother demanded.

'Oh, for laughing at him when he tried to flirt with us. And pushing him away when he put his hands all over us.' She shuddered and grimaced. 'He pushed Su Lin to the ground and dragged her around. Then he got scared because people were shouting at him to let us go. So he arrested us for making him look bad. Le Froy came and talked them into letting us go. Apparently it's not against the law to be mistaken for a prostitute by the new chief detective when you're walking down the road in broad daylight.'

'What? Su Lin, are you all right?' Mrs Shankar was clearly shocked. 'They didn't really arrest you?'

'I'm all right,' I said. 'To be fair, Fahey was only trying to do his job when he was told we were disturbing the peace. That was a lie. We weren't disturbing anybody until that bully Johnson disturbed us by grabbing Parshanti and putting his hands all over her. I'm not sorry he's got a bloody nose.'

Mrs Evans gave a squawk and stood up, barely pausing to look around for her gigantic handbag.

Parshanti picked it up and shook it. It rattled. 'What did you steal from my mother this time?' she wondered.

'Mind your own business, you rude hussy!' Mrs Evans snapped. 'Your mother has a right to contribute what she likes to Government House.'

Parshanti sank into a chair and laughed. 'Her face! What did she make you give her this time?'

Mrs Shankar brushed off her question.

'I don't understand,' I said. 'Is she going after Le Froy? We said he was at the Detective Shack. Is she going to look for him there?'

'Robert Johnson is her son,' Mrs Shankar explained.

'The horrible Johnson?' I saw the familial similarity, now that I knew the connection. And I wasn't just thinking of appearances.

'Previous marriage.' Now Parshanti was rolling her eyes at me. 'Come on, you must have heard her talking about him. My son this, my son that . . .'

Now it made complete sense to me that Robert Johnson had been brought in to head the Detective Unit.

'Nepotism.' Parshanti read my mind. 'Another revered British tradition. Along with appointing the greatest fools to the highest places. You see why we all hope Le Froy's back to kick Evans out?'

I understood why Mrs Shankar worried about Parshanti. But I could also see sense in what Parshanti had said.

'It's difficult to settle down in an unfamiliar place,' Mrs Shankar said. 'I've heard the women cleaning and cooking at Government House say the governor has a bad temper and takes it out on his wife and her son. Then Mrs Evans has her own tantrums and accuses people of deliberately not speaking English, not cooking proper English food and being dirty. It's not easy.'

The most important thing about religious beliefs is respecting other people's. But Mrs Evans believed her god was superior to everyone else's and had made her superior to anyone who was not British.

Dinner at the Shankars'

———◆———

I needn't have worried about Parshanti inviting Le Froy to dinner. Mrs Shankar was only too happy to have more people crowding into the back room because they hadn't seen Le Froy since his return.

She measured me quickly and efficiently for my bridesmaid's dress, told me my *samfoo* fabric was lovely but the seams weren't going to hold, and if I didn't do something about the raw edges they would fray. Then she swept us into dinner preparations and soon had Parshanti and me cooking like demons.

It was almost like the old days. Even Parshanti seemed to enjoy peeling and chopping, with her mother shouting instructions at us, and Dr Shankar setting the table with eating and serving utensils. Dr Leask would be coming too, and Harry had been invited, but as Parshanti said, 'Harry's always invited but he never comes.'

It was almost like the old days.

I let Ah Ma know I was having dinner in town but, in spite of pressing invitations from Parshanti and her mother, I would

not be staying the night. Sharing food is one of the best ways
of spending time with others, especially after you've survived
scarcity and there's finally enough food for all. But the other
guests didn't arrive by 6 p.m. which was the normal dinner time
at the Shankars' and back at Chen Mansion too. We waited
dinner till seven thirty when Mrs Shankar decided we would
eat: 'The men won't mind. They have only themselves to blame
if they're late.'

I could see she was worried about Dr Shankar, although he
was sitting quietly in his corner as usual.

We were halfway through the meal when Le Froy arrived
with Dr Leask.

Mrs Shankar threw herself at him, like a tornado, flinging
her arms around him and kissing him on both cheeks, 'I knew
you were alive and back here, but I've learned never to count on
anyone until I see them for myself.'

Dr Shankar was quieter but just as emotional. 'It's good to
see you, sir.'

'It's thanks to you I'm here,' Le Froy said. 'Please, don't stand.'

'You really don't hold it against me?' Dr Shankar was talking
about the foot he had amputated. Even though he'd made the
best decision, I knew he tormented himself wondering what
more he might have done to save Le Froy's foot.

'You saved my life,' Le Froy said. 'I hope you don't regret that!'

'You sit here,' Mrs Shankar took over, 'next to Su Lin. Leask,
you know where your usual seat is. Sit. Where are you staying?
I'm trying to get Su Lin to stay the night, but she insists on going
all the way home. If you can run her back I'll be so much easier
in my mind. Do you have a motor-car yet?'

'I've arranged to have the use of a vehicle. I'll take Su Lin safely home,' Le Froy said.

'I hope they brought you back to replace that lascivious fool Johnson,' Parshanti said. 'He grabbed me today, right there on Robinson Road in the middle of the day. And then tried to get Su and me arrested for disturbing the peace.'

'What?' Dr Leask sounded horrified but Parshanti patted his hand.

'Don't worry. The man's still alive with all his parts intact. I remembered what you said.'

'I'm not here to replace anyone,' Le Froy said. 'I'm no longer with the police, pensioned out with disability. Anyway, everything's run by the Military Authority now.'

'Most of the British MA people out here are just trying to get rich before they get demobbed,' Parshanti said. 'Right?'

Dr Leask nodded obediently. 'What's the mood on the ground in England now?' he asked.

'Everyone held up superbly during the war. We're at our best in a crisis, especially when we're the noble underdogs. The problem is, when you're not under threat, you realise how much is wrong with the British system. And the fog in London. I'd forgotten that thick, stinking fog.'

Mrs Shankar produced several covered dishes she'd held back, and even Dr Shankar ate, though he was more interested in examining Le Froy's prosthetic foot.

Dr Shankar had always been interested in prosthetics. He'd come up with several devices for me to wear to compensate for my misshapen leg and alleviate the pain in my back it caused. Now he was full of questions about Le Froy's back. ('Any aching?

Ah, that's to be expected. Try not to compensate with your stride or you may strain your back.')

He was almost his old self again.

I saw Mrs Shankar watching them intently. She noticed me looking and gave me a wry smile as she shook her head, laughing at herself. I knew she wasn't interested in Le Froy's missing foot but in anything that would catch Dr Shankar's attention and bring him back to life.

'If you're staying, will you join the police again? The men in charge now think all locals are criminals. Or animals,' Parshanti said.

I wanted the answer to that too.

'All the good people are leaving or have gone,' Dr Shankar said. 'It's not safe here any more. I want Leask and Parshanti to move to the UK after they're married and take my wife with them. Can you recommend a good post for Leask?'

It was clearly a subject that had come up before. Clear, too, that his wife and daughter didn't agree with him.

Le Froy held up his hands to indicate surrender: he wasn't going to get involved.

'Mrs Evans already told us you weren't back officially,' Parshanti said. 'She thinks you came back because of Su Lin. We thought so too. What I'd like to know is why everyone seems to know this except Su Lin?'

'The UK isn't all bad.' I saw that Dr Leask's way of handling Parshanti was not to hear her. 'Back me up here, Le Froy. People there are insular and they believe the wild stories they're told. Once they get to know Parshanti they'll love her like I do. I'm not saying I want to move to the UK for good, but I really want to take my girl to Aberdeen to meet my parents, especially my mother.'

'I told you–' Parshanti started.

'I'm not saying we should live there. Just pay a visit. I'd like you to see where I grew up. Your parents already know what it's like.'

'I know the food there is truly horrible,' Dr Shankar said, 'they have this boiled chicken–'

'Like with chicken rice?' I liked chicken rice.

'Not anything remotely like chicken rice. With a pathetic sauce made of stale flour and metallic water. Bland boiled chicken, eaten with bland white sauce. What I would have given for a good chicken curry or a Hainanese chicken rice! I would have done better as a hawker than a doctor there.'

'Depends where you go. There are good and bad restaurants and cooks, same as anywhere else,' Mrs Shankar corrected. 'Depends what you're willing to pay.'

'The street food here is cheap and good,' her husband countered, 'almost as good as yours,' which made her smile.

'I thought you'd be here much sooner,' Parshanti said to her husband-to-be.

'Sorry. Nothing serious at the hospital but small things take time. We could really use some help there.'

Parshanti and her mother glanced at Dr Shankar, but he didn't take the hint.

'Did you hear anything more about what happened to Botak Beng?' I asked, more to change the subject than anything else.

Leask brightened, 'Murder,' he said. 'Definitely murder. The man was stabbed.'

'He can't have been,' I said. 'It was a heart attack or he choked. Didn't I tell you he fell into the drain?'

'Don't look at me,' Parshanti said. 'You should ask Leasky. He's the one who says it was murder.'

'There was nobody near him!'

As the words left my mouth I remembered the spot of blood on the front of Botak's shirt. I thought then that he must have ... No, he wouldn't have been able to stab himself so cleanly by falling forwards.

'It was definitely murder,' Dr Leask said.

'Ssh!' Mrs Shankar said. 'Not in here. Don't say anything. Bad luck!' So much for her not worrying about Chinese taboos. But in that, too, she was totally local. Superstitions and taboos, like most other religious caveats, were just a way to justify doing what you wanted.

'He wasn't found immediately, was he? They were told nobody saw it happen,' Le Froy said.

'A neighbour's servant found him. Remember Nasima? He was still warm, can't have been dead very long.'

I didn't mention that the girl also claimed to have seen me with him.

'Anyway, they think it's just another gang killing,' Dr Leask said. 'Nothing for us to worry about.'

'Nobody here is worried,' Parshanti said laconically. 'The only thing people around here really worry about is how expensive lace ribbon is and whether black or green cardamom seeds are better for promoting fertility.'

Dr Leask looked surprised but Mrs Shankar pressed her lips

together as though she was holding back words that were trying to force their way out.

Maybe if they all said what they needed to say, I thought, they could have one big blow-up and get over it. But this wasn't my family or my business. And even if a good run of diarrhoea solves someone's stomach problems, you're never going to be thanked for provoking it.

Which made me realise, to my surprise, that everything I'd eaten had stayed down. My stomach had finally settled.

'Though I hear they're also looking into an anonymous tip-off that the man was killed for trying to break away from the Chen cartel and threatening to expose the Chens for processing and distributing opium,' Leask said.

'Maybe he was hit by a motor-car that didn't stop. Those things are dangerous,' Dr Shankar said. 'I remember in the old days motor-cars had to have a man walking ahead carrying a red flag. And they couldn't go faster than two miles an hour. Things don't always change for the better.'

'That was repealed in 1896,' Leask said, as helpful as he was irrelevant. I could see why Parshanti found him irritating at times.

'They're also looking at Harry Palin because he was hunting Botak Beng all over town. Apparently he accused Botak of trafficking his sister to Australia or Indonesia.'

'What? Harry?'

'He arranged for Botak to get Dee-Dee out just before the Japanese came. Apparently she vanished after the boat reached Australia.'

'So he really wasn't poisoned?' I said, remembering the rambutan skin in his mouth.

'Stabbed right through the heart. Got the right ventricle. Something long, sharp and probably metallic, like an ice pick. Death would have been almost immediate. He might have had time to give you the killer's name if you were standing beside him. But the only person there would have been the killer.'

At times like this Dr Leask reminded me of Dr Shankar.

'How?'

It was Dr Shankar who answered: 'The heart is very close to the surface. You only have to go two to three inches in if you get between the ribs.'

'The killer went in just below the sternum,' Dr Leask indicated the spot on his own breastbone, 'upwards towards the left shoulder blade. Not a very tall person, I'd say. The victim didn't see it coming. No defensive marks on him.' He leaned forward with a conspiratorial wink. 'It seems Brigadier Evans had business dealings with the dead man. If you ask me, some government officials didn't like the acting governor dealing with a gangster and got rid of him.'

I didn't agree. If strangers from the government had stabbed him they would not have got away unseen. No, if Botak Beng had been murdered, someone familiar with our neighbourhood had done it.

'The man had money on him, so it wasn't a robbery. But you know what's strange? There were strips of dried rambutan skin in his pockets.'

'Yellow rambutan?' I asked.

Leask looked surprised and disappointed. 'Yes, as a matter of fact. Not as strange as I thought, apparently.'

'Tea?' Mrs Shankar offered, into the silence. 'I have some

Earl Grey. I was saving it for the—' She stopped, looking at Parshanti.

'If you were saving it for the wedding, better give some to the inspector now,' Dr Leask said. 'I doubt anyone will be able to appreciate delicate flavours with all the excitement. Don't you think so?' He looked affectionately at Parshanti but she seemed not to notice.

'I'm not an inspector any more,' Le Froy said. 'And I never was much of a tea drinker.'

'I'll make his coffee,' I said. 'If I may, Mrs Shankar?'

I wanted to get away for a bit, to think myself calm. But, also, I knew how Le Froy liked his coffee.

In the old days he'd always depended on cheap local coffee to keep him going. The type that hawkers made from wok-fried beans, thick with lard, sugar and cloves, then coarsely ground.

'Is there enough for me too?' Dr Shankar asked.

'Of course,' I said. 'Dr Leask, sir?'

'No, of course not. He drinks his coffee English-style. Like my mother. And you don't have to call him "sir",' Parshanti told me.

I used Mrs Shankar's little granite mortar to grind the toasted beans, crushing them just enough to release their oily strength, enjoying the heady fragrance that arose when I poured hot water over them and stirred. It would take five minutes to reach the strength Le Froy preferred.

Then I poured the thick black oily mixture of coffee grounds and water through a cloth, then did it again, dividing the mixture carefully between the two pots. This would both cool and froth the brew.

Parshanti came to help me, packing sugar into a clean kitchen cloth stretched loosely over another pot.

'I used to cook for them too, you know,' she said, 'when we were in the jungle.' Then she leaned in close to me and hissed, 'You know why he wants to take you home, don't you? He's going to make you an offer! *The* offer!'

'Don't be silly,' I said. 'You don't know what you're talking about.'

'Of course he is. Why do you think he's bothering to borrow a car and everything? He wants to talk to you in private. No – don't interrupt. Just listen to me. All I'm asking you, begging you, Su Lin, if you've ever considered me a friend or taken my word on anything, all I want you to promise is that, whatever he says, you don't say no immediately. Okay? Will you do that?'

'Not immediately. Does that mean I can count to ten then say no?'

'Not immediately meaning you tell me about it first. Then if you still want to say no, after hearing me call you an idiot for twenty-four hours, you can.'

'Just take them their coffee, okay?'

It was so good to hear him say, 'Oh, God, I've missed the coffee here!'

I didn't let myself wonder what else he might have missed.

In Le Froy's Car

— ◆ —

'Better than talking in public.' Le Froy unlocked his car. I nodded, sliding into the passenger seat.

Le Froy started the engine and turned on the lights. He expertly navigated the uneven roads, not even swearing at the bomb damage, like the trolley-bus drivers always did.

It was nice being in a private car again, moving through the darkness with the dry snugness of seeing but not feeling the light drizzle on the windscreen and windows. These days, only Shen Shen used my grandmother's old car, when she took Little Ling with her to collect rents or went shopping. Shen Shen didn't like Little Ling to go on the buses or any public transport.

'There's something I want to talk to you about,' Le Froy said.

My breath caught. Had Parshanti been right? What was I going to say? More importantly, what was he going to say?

What Le Froy said was, 'Could that man's death have something to do with your uncle? Botak and your uncle Chen were having problems, right?'

What? It took me a second to process what he was saying.

Botak Beng's death seemed a lifetime ago, instead of just that morning.

'No, they weren't. Botak came to visit him on the First Day.' I certainly wasn't going to mention that Botak had been desperate to see Uncle Chen just before he died.

'Your uncle Chen has been cutting ties with his former connections. Botak was one of them.'

'The police were looking for Botak,' I countered. 'Maybe they found him and killed him.'

'Why would they?'

'You know what the police here are like. He was a local.' I didn't believe it, but if Le Froy was going to question me like a police detective that was how I would treat him.

'Botak Beng probably had warehouses full of reasons to avoid the police. He might have talked to me in the old days, but now ...' He shook his head. 'Anyway, they're going to investigate your grandmother and uncle.'

'What? Why?'

'Fahey believes the Chens control most of the black market around here.'

'Who told him that?'

'He warned me. He was concerned for me, an old retiree being taken for a ride by a couple of young girls working for the local smuggling and gambling monopoly.'

'Fahey's only just got here. Where did he get crazy ideas like that?'

Le Froy had the grace to look abashed. 'There might have been notes in the detective archives.'

'You put in your records that Ah Ma and Uncle Chen go around killing their friends?'

'I put down the facts I had at the time. Your family was involved in smuggling and protection rackets and worked closely with Ho Seng Beng. Fahey's reaching his own conclusions.'

'He's an aggressive pig. Does he know you wrote most of the reports he's warning you about?'

'I don't think this generation cares who wrote what. They just take what they want to believe and throw out the rest.'

Le Froy was famous for putting out of business most of the criminal gangs and triads terrorising Singapore. Ah Ma and Uncle Chen hadn't involved themselves in 'criminal' activities so much as working outside, beyond and beneath the law. They took care of things that slipped between the cracks. My grandmother wasn't a moneylender or a loan shark. She did favours and helped people, and when they could, they paid her back.

Le Froy had observed but left them alone.

And now, thanks to Le Froy, Fahey was going after them.

'He's also looking at Harry Palin.' Le Froy changed the subject. 'Harry's been going around trying to track down the man and making threats against him.'

'It's about his sister Dee-Dee, isn't it?' According to Parshanti earlier, Harry had managed to send her to safety in Australia before the Japanese landed. But although he had had confirmation that she was on the cargo boat Botak had organised, Dee-Dee had vanished once it docked in Darwin.

'I don't think Fahey's taking it that seriously. But Harry's been causing such a stir that they can't ignore him.'

Le Froy drove carefully, but I knew him well enough to tell when he was holding something back. 'All right. What is it?'

OVIDIA YU

'What was Botak Beng doing so near to your house on the Third Day?' Le Froy had spent enough time in Singapore to understand the visiting taboo. 'Is it possible he was there to attempt a coup and take over your uncle's business?'

'That's mad!' I said. 'Anyway, he brought crabs for my uncle. He wouldn't have gone hunting for mud crabs if he meant to kill Uncle Chen.'

Le Froy was silent, but I heard the unspoken accusation.

'I didn't mention that earlier because it's not relevant. I can't expect someone who's never hunted mud crabs in the mangroves to understand.' I thought of Botak in the coolness of the mangrove swamps with his feet in the thick, warm mud. 'It's not something you do if you've got a coup planned. It's messy.'

'Is there anything else you haven't told Fahey?'

'No,' I lied. There was really no point in mentioning Fancy Ang.

We drove on in silence for a while. I wished Parshanti was there, so she could see how absurdly wrong she was about Le Froy's intentions.

'Where are you staying?' I asked. 'Are you back in the Emerald Hill house?' Unlike most other colonial administrators who lived in the huge black-and-white mansions outside the city, Le Froy had lived in a traditional Peranakan-style terrace house surrounded by local families. 'Mrs Evans sounded very offended that you turned down her offer of a bunk at Government House.'

'Oh dear.'

Given my brief encounters with Mrs Evans I wasn't equipped to judge her. But his tone made me laugh.

'Evans is doing his best,' he went on, 'but it's a hell of a job.

The Home Office is pushing the BMA to increase revenue from the colonies. And they can't even think of rebuilding here until Britain's been dealt with.'

There was no answering that.

'So where are you staying? A hotel?' I couldn't imagine Le Froy staying in the Farquhar, or the colonial administration allowing him to rent a bed in a coolie house.

'I'm renting a couple of rooms.' Le Froy changed the subject. 'Fahey's not a bad sort. You can't expect too much of a new police sergeant.'

'Prakesh and Ferdie were new sergeants when I met them and they were never this idiotic. Fahey can't be very bright if he's relying on ten-year-old records.'

'But he understands the need for thoroughness and is willing to learn.'

I remembered Johnson mocking Fahey's interest in local culture and language. 'The man isn't a puppet,' I said.

'I'd say that alone is enough to recommend him. He's still young. Given half a chance he could make something of the job.'

'Rather than going around bullying an old woman,' I said.

'Fahey? What old woman?'

'Well, more Johnson. But he was there and didn't stop him. And he started it, with his "*Buaya* meat is human meat"!'

'Cik Cahaya? On Robinson Road?'

I was surprised. 'Maybe – I don't know her name. You know her?'

'Cik Cahaya isn't a victim except by intention. Looking like a victim is one of her strengths. She's my landlady, incidentally.'

'Your landlady?'

'Cik Cahaya was one of my friendly sources of information for years and she had rooms she wanted to rent, so it was an ideal arrangement for us both when I had to come back for a while.'

'I see.'

What I saw was that Le Froy had been communicating with his former informers, letting them know he was returning to Singapore, without bothering to get in touch with me.

It was his turn to look as though he was hearing words I hadn't said. That's the difficulty of knowing someone too well. You hear what you expect them to say rather than their actual words.

But I had missed even this. We'd always worked well together as a team because, while we filled in the gaps in each other's experience, we thought the same way about many things.

Le Froy stopped the car before the mosque at the end of the road. It was where he'd dropped me off in the old days if I didn't want to be seen from the house getting out of a car. Not that it had ever made any real difference: that was what neighbours and street hawkers were for.

'Thanks for the lift,' I said. I pulled up the door lock.

'Thanks for risking your life with a crippled old driver.'

His tone stopped me. I worked out patterns to understand things. That was what helped me pick up languages and skills, like adapting recipes and organising files. And I recognised a pattern here that I'd never seen in Le Froy before.

'Why have you given up?' I said.

Le Froy was clearly taken aback. 'Given up? I just showed I can still drive with this thing.' He kicked his prosthetic foot against the floor of the car. 'Damned gears.'

'You once told me the only thing that made me a cripple was my brain. You hired me for the Detective Unit when I was already crippled. What's changed?'

The shame on his face hurt more than any anger.

'I didn't know what I was talking about. I was a fool back then. I apologise for everything. When you're the one who's useless, you see things differently.'

He was feeling sorry for himself. He was where I'd been before he took me into the Detective Unit and trained me to see myself as a valuable asset.

But he wasn't a fool. I'd met a great many fools, including the Christian ladies who came to the Mission Centre school and told me either that it was God's will I was a cripple, or that I would be healed if only I had enough faith, so evidently I didn't.

Le Froy was still a European, so I couldn't tell him I thought he was being more of a fool for feeling sorry for himself. But Le Froy had taught me to use my language skills and local networks to solve crimes and he'd offered me his arm in support over difficult ground, both literally and figuratively. Didn't I owe him as much?

'You didn't come all the way back to Singapore just to show you can change gear with a wooden foot.'

'All right. I do have a reason for coming back to Singapore but I can't discuss it. I'm on the hunt for something they don't want to make an official fuss about.'

Somehow being right didn't feel as good as I'd expected. In fact, it felt horrible.

Now I could say, 'See? I was right!' to Parshanti, Mrs Evans and Ah Ma, though I didn't foresee myself bringing up the subject.

'And what's happened to you? I thought you were dead or married off. That was the only reason I could think of.'

I stared. Le Froy was looking at me accusingly.

'Reason for what?'

'For you not answering any of my letters. At least you could have written to say no.'

'No to what? What letters? I didn't get any letters from you. You never wrote at all after you left.'

'I did. Many letters.'

'You wrote many letters?' In all the years I'd known Le Froy I'd never seen him write a letter.

'One long letter. With all the options laid out. Then the rest said things like "Did you get the letter?" or "Tell me if you didn't get the letter dated whenever because if not I'll write out all the options again even though that would be tough because I didn't use a carbon" – like you always said I should if it was anything important. I know. I agree. I just didn't – and I said time was running out if we didn't want to miss admissions for this year. Which we have.'

'I didn't get any of those letters,' I said.

I could see he thought I was lying. Well, I thought he was lying . . . except not really. Le Froy wouldn't lie about writing. He'd just not write and not say anything. So?

'The post office?' I said.

'More likely the damned postmen,' Le Froy said. He'd come to the same conclusion about me. I might not tell the whole truth, but he knew I wouldn't lie unless it was necessary or profitable.

I took a deep breath and felt something shift in my core as my world clicked back into alignment.

'You've been sick too, haven't you?' Le Froy said. 'You've lost weight.'

'Some kind of stomach bug. I couldn't keep down anything I ate. It hit all of us after the first two days of visitors.'

'You were all right tonight.'

I'd noticed that too.

'Could be something in the water or cooking pots poisoning you,' Le Froy said.

'Or maybe I'm over it,' I said. 'I thought I looked quite good today. Don't you think my new *samfoo* looks nice?'

Unlike Parshanti and her mother, Le Froy didn't seem impressed. He didn't even see it was a hint for him to compliment my outfit. 'I'll try to get you some milk powder. You missed the early admissions, and that's too bad. But there's always next year.'

'I don't know what you're talking about. What were all those letters about?'

'Studying back in Britain. You want to become a journalist, right?'

So it was an offer – just not one I or Parshanti had anticipated. 'I'm twenty-six years old. Too old for silly dreams.'

'One day you'll look back at this and realise how young twenty-six is. So what are you going to do now?'

I shrugged. What could I do?

'I remember you wanting to be a lady reporter. When you were having a tough time with anything, you'd say, "I can write about this one day."'

I remembered those dreams. They seemed so naïve and out of reach now: I was older and more aware of all the barriers in place. I wasn't even sure if such an occupation existed any more. I had thought I would write reports on the threat of war that would never become war. And then war had come upon us and done its worst.

I was sixteen when I met Thomas Francis Le Froy for the first time. That was ten years ago. On the surface a lot had changed, but beneath it we were still much the same. Still, the things that changed drastically around us forced us to evolve in relation to them.

Now I was no longer a student hoping to go to university and avoiding being married off. Now it was unlikely I could marry even if I wanted to: the best of the men of my generation had been killed in the war. I might seem to be the same person in the same place, but I was several years older and several years more disillusioned. And that made all the difference. I didn't want to be ungrateful, but I wasn't sure what I had to be grateful for.

'We were good at solving stuff,' I said. 'Before you give up and retire to feel sorry for yourself, can you help me find out what happened to Botak Beng?'

'I'm sorry about your uncle's friend but I really don't have anything to do with the police—'

Shen Shen

———◆———

I walked around the house to the back, my mind playing through everything that had happened. The doors at the front would be locked and bolted by now. As I limped along the familiar trail through the dark I knew it wasn't finding out what had happened to Botak that was making me excited. And if I was feeling good because I was excited to have seen Le Froy again, that was wrong. I couldn't use Uncle Chen's dead friend as an excuse to work with Le Froy again. He wasn't even a policeman any more.

But what if I was feeling good because I was tapping into the problem-solving, analytical part of myself I hadn't used for so long? Perhaps . . . But that was still a lousy reason and a transparent excuse to spend more time with Le Froy.

And Le Froy would be the first to know it.

But what about the letters he'd said he'd written since returning to England?

Was that true? Or did he just write one long letter that got lost? Postal services weren't very reliable. Sometimes letters arrived months late after being lost or rerouted. The post office could easily have lost one letter. But that wasn't the Le Froy I knew. If he didn't get a response to his first letter (written without a carbon copy) he would have followed up. Once a month at least. The same went for the postman. He might have lost one letter, but not all of them.

I felt a chill. Someone was monitoring and confiscating our mail. That seemed certain. I just didn't know whether it was Le Froy or the Chen family they were monitoring. But who was behind it?

If Le Froy believed me, and by now I was sure he did, he would arrive at the same conclusion, and he was better placed to find out. I started walking again.

Robert Johnson was a loud, aggressive bully but I couldn't see him having the patience or the tenacity to have our mail searched. Then I thought of Fahey. He had known about Botak. He'd been going through Le Froy's files. Whoever was monitoring us, it couldn't have been a coincidence that Botak had been killed after he'd tried to see Uncle Chen. What had he wanted to warn Uncle Chen about? And who had stopped him?

'Su Lin? So late, *ah*, you?'

I jumped. Shen Shen had startled me when she stepped out of the darkness beyond the open kitchen and the main house. 'Why are you outside here alone? Somebody killed Botak Beng. They might still be around.'

She must have been squatting in the tiny triangle of space between the wood pile, the charcoal bins and the far wall of the kitchen. I would have walked past her if she hadn't spoken to me.

'Why are you talking nonsense? What's wrong with you?' Shen Shen sounded angry. But that was nothing new. She had been bad-tempered since the mountains of Japanese-issued banana notes she'd accumulated during the Occupation had been declared worthless by the returning British. That's what happens when you adapt too soon to systems that don't last. I couldn't blame people who believed in 'wait and see' any more. In fact, I think I'd joined them.

'Nothing's wrong. I'm fine. What are you doing outside so late?'

'Work, *lor.*' Shen Shen held out a grimy basket. I saw she was sorting charcoal chips for the claypot stoves by what little light came from the kerosene lamp in the kitchen.

Over a low fire, metal skewers of split fish were slowly drying and smoking. It was the best way of preserving fish that were too small to eat but too large to ferment. It was a task the servant girls usually took care of and was sometimes delegated to Little Ling. I remembered how proud I'd been as a child when I'd graduated to 'really helping'. Now we used the modern hygienic metal skewers instead of the sharpened wood or bamboo sticks that needed to be constantly soaked in water so they wouldn't catch fire.

'Can I help?' I was tired but felt I had to offer.

'No need. How is your stomach? Yesterday you were vomiting so much. Maybe you're pregnant.' I knew she didn't believe that or she would have said it to Ah Ma, not to me.

But I'd heard Shen Shen vomiting in the outhouse. Was she trying to hint that she was pregnant? This was so different from Shen Shen's previous pregnancies, and when she finally had Little Ling. Then Uncle Chen, Ah Ma and the servants had been obsessed with what she ate and what she couldn't keep down.

Now they were barely interested. I didn't know whether it was because they were too ill themselves to notice or because they hadn't realised she might be expecting another child.

'You should get more rest,' I said.

'Did you have a good time going to town to play cops and robbers? You should have stayed here if you wanted to see the police.'

'Why? What happened here?' I stopped and turned back to her.

'You know what. Your uncle's friend died. Then your uncle got up and went outside while the police were there, saying his old friend was dead. So, of course, they asked him questions. Your Ah Ma told them we thought he was in his room sleeping. So the police wanted to know if he often leaves the house without us knowing. They asked him whether he and Botak had had a fight, but your uncle was so confused he couldn't even say no.'

'Anybody can see Uncle Chen is in no shape to fight anybody.'

'Anyway, the police asked him questions,' Shen Shen said. 'If they ask you, you'd better not say Botak came to the house to see him. They will use it as an excuse to make trouble for him. Just say you don't know who Botak was or what he was doing here. If you keep your mouth shut and don't stir up trouble, the police will forget about it.'

'How do you know?'

'The woman whose sister cleans the police station says they think Botak was a gangster killed by other gangsters. Nothing to do with us. They won't bother with it.'

I guessed Shen Shen was scared her husband would get dragged in for questioning again. I could understand that. Uncle

Chen hadn't been his old self since the Japanese had taken him in, and Shen Shen had borne the brunt of that. However curt and abrupt she was with him, Shen Shen always put him and his needs first. Like Ah Ma said, that was why she'd chosen Shen Shen as a wife for Uncle Chen – so he would have someone to watch out for him when she was gone.

It seemed like we'd traded places since I'd come back to live at home. I was the one without any future while Shen Shen was busy in the house as well as running Ah Ma and Uncle Chen's business.

'You must be so happy that your policeman is back,' Shen Shen said.

I recognised her tone. It was how she'd always talked to me in the old days, back when she'd still hoped to make Uncle Chen persuade Ah Ma to rid the Chen family of bad luck by sending me away. She'd stopped when Ah Ma and Uncle Chen had made clear they weren't getting rid of me and instead set up a shophouse in town for her and Uncle Chen. They'd moved back into Chen Mansion when Little Ling was born.

Lately, though, it was the tone she used with Little Ling or the servants when she was preparing to accuse them of hiding a bowl they'd broken or sneaking leftover food for the stray cats. She usually managed to get a confession out of them too, whether or not they were guilty.

'He's not my policeman. He's not even in the police any more.'

'Did he tell you anything about that dead man?'

'They found dried rambutan skins in his pocket.'

'Rambutan skins? Don't talk nonsense. Why would Botak have rambutan skins in his pocket? Those people are mad, *lah*!'

I wanted to argue. Especially as I'd found and identified the hairs from the skins and the police were good enough at grabbing credit without me helping them. But it wasn't something I wanted to discuss yet. Already I regretted mentioning it.

If I knew her, and I did, she was trying to work out if Le Froy had brought me home so she could make a fuss about it to Ah Ma.

'Anyway, what are you doing? Is the kitchen out of charcoal?' I was sure it wasn't. The servants would have made sure we were stocked up with everything before they left, eager for their *ang pows* and to avoid any possibility of a scolding on their return after Chinese New Year. 'I'll help you finish and then we can sleep.'

'That Muslim girl from up the road came here looking for you.'

'Nasima? It was her servant who found Botak. The girl said she saw a woman run into our garden. Could it have been Fancy?'

'You shouldn't mix with Nasima. She's not our sort of person.'

'She's my friend.'

'You should stay away from her. Her kind will try to use you.'

I didn't agree with her. But I was never one to take on someone else's problems and prejudices if I didn't have to. At least her tone had returned to the normal one she used to complain about our non-Chinese neighbours.

I decided I must have startled her when I suddenly appeared out of the dark. People tend to get angry easily when startled. 'Did I scare you? I'm sorry,' I said belatedly.

She shrugged it off. 'Anyway, why does she have so many girls at her place? What if she makes you join them? She might say that unless you go to live with her and do her wicked things she'll tell the police you killed Botak. What if she and her girls killed Botak?'

I realised what should have been obvious. Shen Shen was scared but not of me. That's why she was acting so oddly. People get scared just as animals do. They will attack the nearest thing to them. And why not? A friend of her husband had been found dead outside her home. Who wouldn't be frightened?

An old memory surfaced. As a child I'd once seen Botak with terrible lacerations across his arms and face. I thought he'd been in a fight and asked Ah Ma if Uncle Botak had killed anyone. She laughed and told me that Botak was stupid enough to rescue a pregnant cat that had got stuck in a pipe. The memory made me want even more to find out what had happened to him. 'Botak wasn't so bad,' I said. 'Uncle Chen liked him and he was always respectful to Ah Ma. I hope they find out what happened to him.'

'Do you want something to eat?'

'No. I've had dinner. A lot.'

It was true. After an episode of nausea on the trolley bus en route to town, I'd not had any problems with my stomach. I hadn't felt sick all evening. Maybe the excitement of everything that had happened had pushed it out of my mind. Or maybe it was Mrs Shankar's cooking? Or—

'Tomorrow we should scrub out the rice pots and the wok,' I said, 'in case there's germs or something poisonous in them making us all sick.'

The Japanese had tried poisoning locals to save bullets. It hadn't worked because people took too long to die, but who knew what might have been left in the soil or storage bins?

'You know, my own mother wished I had never been born. In fact, she tried to abort me,' Shen Shen said.

'Oh?' I said, instead of 'Why are you telling me now?'

'When your Ah Ma chose me to marry your uncle Chen, it was the first good thing that had ever happened to me in my whole life. I will never forget that. You mustn't think my cooking is making your family sick.'

'I didn't say that!' I said. 'That isn't what I meant. Just maybe a change of food helps. Parshanti's mother gave me some for all of us.' I showed her what Mrs Shankar had packed for me to bring home.

'I don't think your uncle and grandmother can eat funny Indian food.' Shen Shen dismissed the carefully packed delicacies without looking at them. 'Your uncle can only eat white porridge with a bit of soy sauce and he can't even finish that. Ah Ma couldn't eat any.'

'I should ask Dr Shankar to come and see them,' I said.

'No!'

'It's all right. He'll come as a friend and he won't charge us.' Dr Shankar would refuse to take money but, of course, I would find a way to make it up to him.

'No, no, no. These Western-trained doctors don't know how to treat people like us. They want to shut you in a hospital and cut you up. Your Ah Ma already asked somebody from the temple to come. Don't make them angry by going to a Western doctor.'

This was another fight I didn't intend to have with her. But I would remember to mention it to Dr Shankar. I wondered if it could be the lingering effects of malnutrition or something gone bad in the tinned food the troops had treated us to in exchange for fresh catfish and barramundi from the mangrove swamps.

'Let me finish sorting the charcoal. You go in and rest,' I suggested.

'No, *lah*, no need.'

Shen Shen got to her feet, stopping as a wave of nausea hit her. I saw her grimace and wait for it to pass.

'Are you sure you're all right?'

'*Yah lah, yah lah*, don't fuss.'

That explained what she'd been doing outside by herself in the dark. She'd probably decided to work on the charcoal till she was sure her own nausea had passed.

'There's some cake.' I dug one of the bundles out of Mrs Shankar's cotton bag. 'She sent it especially for Little Ling. She knows she likes cake.'

Cake might not have been the best suggestion for nausea, but I knew Shen Shen had a sweet tooth. I saw her struggle. Her automatic response was to reject anything alien with 'No need' or 'I don't want it.' But she loved Little Ling and Little Ling loved cake almost as much as Shen Shen did.

Especially Western-style cake made with imported sugar, which was what I was holding out to her. Shen Shen took the bundle. But just so I didn't imagine she'd accepted a favour from me, she threw out her own distraction. 'The real police are going to come for you again. Don't say I never warn you, *ah*.'

'What?'

How had Shen Shen found out so quickly about my encounter with the police? I'd hoped to keep it quiet from Ah Ma since she didn't go much to town, these days. And I'd hoped it would be something the police would also prefer smoothed over. 'How did you know? What did they tell you?'

'Your good friend Nasima next door told them,' Shen Shen said.

'Told them what?'

'Her servant. She said when she was on her way home she saw a skinny Chinese woman quarrelling with Botak. And then the woman ran past her and into our house. That was before Botak was found dead. The girl said she heard them shouting but didn't hear any more after the woman ran away. She told the police she thinks the skinny Chinese woman killed Botak.'

'And the police think it's me? They came here?'

'No. Your good friend Nasima next door came to warn you the police think it was you and might be coming to question you. I don't know why you want to befriend people like that. If she's so worried about you, why talk to the police in the first place?'

Late as it was, I got Shen Shen to tell me exactly what had transpired. She broke off bits of Mrs Shankar's excellent fennel-seed cake and nibbled them as she told me how Nasima-next-door had come looking for me.

Nasima's servant, I guessed she was the one I'd seen crying by the drain, had calmed down and described seeing a thin Chinese woman arguing with a large bald man on her way out of the house. She hadn't paid much attention because she'd been hurrying out on an errand before she went to meet her friends who worked nearby.

It was on her way home that she'd found the body of the big bald man. It was only much later, after Nasima had calmed her down, that the girl told her about the woman she had seen him with. The other girls hadn't noticed anything, meaning the pair had to have come out of the Mirzas' home or ours. The house between the two had been damaged in the fire at the Mirzas' and hadn't been repaired yet.

'So you must stop running around alone in the middle of the night like some low-class loose woman or people will say all kinds of things about you. If you get yourself murdered, what will people say about your family?'

'I was quite safe. Le Froy drove me home.' I was proud of how casually and evenly I threw out his name as I walked up the steps to the back of the house.

If Shen Shen was pregnant again, we had to make allowances for her. It would be good for Little Ling to have a baby brother or sister. I would do my best, though I hoped Shen Shen wouldn't scratch me, like that cat had scratched Botak.

Getting ready for bed in the dark, Ah Ma stirred. 'You're back?' she said. 'What's wrong?' She could always tell when I was focused on something. 'What are you up to now?'

'I want to find out what happened to Uncle Botak,' I said, 'because I didn't let him into our house. Maybe that's why he's dead.'

'Go to sleep. Tomorrow you still won't have let him into our house and he'll still be dead. Rest first, then we'll see.'

Fourth Day:
Kitchen God's Birthday

◆

I woke the next morning from confused dreams of the dead man begging me to let him in before he was killed. That was a good sign – I'd slept deeply enough to dream weird dreams.

The next good sign was that Ah Ma was up and her facecloth was spread out to air next to her thin blanket. I found her in the kitchen, cooking rice porridge. 'I'm steaming some fish,' she said. 'Good that you got back safely last night. Have you eaten yet?'

Of course I hadn't. She knew as well as I did that I'd only just woken. The meaning behind her routine question? 'I see you and I'm happy to see you because I care about you.'

'Ah Ma, did you sleep well? Have you eaten yet?' I asked in return. It was a language I knew well, even if it irritated me at times.

'Have a drink. Sit.' Ah Ma pushed me to a stool at the table across from Shen Shen and Little Ling and poured me a glass of boiled barley water.

Lukewarm, of course. My grandmother thought cold drinks were dangerous all the time, but especially in the mornings.

'Let me help you. Look, Ah Ma, Shen Shen already made breakfast.'

'No. I must do it myself.'

'Why, Ah Ma?'

'Today, the Fourth Day, is the kitchen god's birthday.'

'I know it's the kitchen god's birthday,' Shen Shen said. 'I already made special food. See?'

'This is my kitchen so today I must make the food myself. Today I will offer plain rice *congee* to the kitchen god. I don't want to eat anything that he doesn't accept.'

Ah Ma looked tired and unwell as she pushed aside the food Shen Shen had prepared and set out so carefully on the table.

Shen Shen looked hurt and I could understand that. She must have got up early to make breakfast, even after being up so late last night. I wondered if Ah Ma's mind was weakening. But, in her way, Ah Ma was very spiritual. She believed in ghosts or, rather, in spirits and a kind of karma.

According to the old stories, all the kitchen gods (or the one big kitchen god who rules over all kitchens, depending on which version you've heard) return to Heaven to celebrate Chinese New Year with the Jade Emperor. The Fourth Day is when each kitchen god returns to the kitchen for which he's responsible. It's customary to provide food and sweets to welcome him back so that your kitchen will be accident-free for the rest of the year.

'Plain rice porridge,' Shen Shen said. 'The granddaughter of the Chen family is eating plain rice porridge during New Year. No wonder people think this family is getting weak.'

Slowly and carefully, Ah Ma stirred her porridge and checked the fish steaming in the double boiler.

I was so glad to see her moving around instead of lying in bed that I was happy to wait. To my grandmother, offerings to the ancestors and at the shrines of the unknown dead were all part of the same business. In return these spirits protected her family from potential danger and put her in the path of potential blessings. I wondered whether she would consider Le Froy's return as a potential danger or a potential blessing.

As though she was sensing my thoughts Ah Ma said, 'So you saw your *ang moh* policeman yesterday.'

Maybe her spirits had told her. More likely it had been Shen Shen.

'Her *ang moh* policeman brought her home in his car last night,' Shen Shen said.

Yes. 'He gave me a lift home.'

'Is he going to be working here again?' Ah Ma asked. 'Will he be taking over and be the one in charge?'

In some ways Ah Ma was like Le Froy – they had both predicted the direction in which the power balance was shifting before war broke out. Ah Ma had sent me to learn Japanese long before anyone thought Japan would win, let alone move beyond, their war with China. And then she'd apprenticed me to a Japanese hairdresser, so that when Singapore was occupied I had tacit protection from the many Japanese spies whose heads I'd massaged when they were in Singapore posing as sales representatives and travelling photographers.

Le Froy had been mocked for warning the Home Office in London of the surge in covert Japanese activity during the eighteen months preceding Japan's declaration of war. You'd think the Home Office would have more respect for him now. Wouldn't they want to put someone who knew the region in charge? No. Instead they'd retired him.

'Did you bring me any presents from town?' Little Ling asked. 'Any sweets?'

The cake? I looked at Shen Shen but she turned away.

'Sorry, I didn't,' I said. 'Next time, okay?'

Little Ling pouted. Then, 'Su Lin likes the *ang moh* policeman,' she said. 'Look at her face. She looks like Papa looking at Mama! Goo-goo eyes!'

I wanted to strangle the little monster. Next time I went to town I wouldn't bring back any cake for her.

'He's *ang moh*,' Ah Ma said, as though that settled everything. For her it did. And she expected the same to apply to me.

'He'd heard about Uncle Chen's friend dying outside our house.'

'That man wasn't your uncle's friend,' Shen Shen said. 'He was just a former employee. He probably came to try to borrow money. Anyway, your grandmother and your uncle don't want to have anything to do with people like him any more.'

It was true that Ah Ma's recent moves to legalise all the properties and businesses had shown me how close to the edge of 'illegal' things had been run. Given how arbitrary the authorities were, it was impossible for a local business to operate a hundred per cent legally all the time. But at least the most obviously illegal or unjust issues had been cleaned up.

'They were long-standing friends. They grew up together in the old *kampung*,' Ah Ma said. 'I remember when his mother was so angry with him about her yellow rambutan tree, he begged to come and stay in our house because he was scared of her.'

'What?' I said.

'Don't say that! You mustn't say that!' Shen Shen said. 'If they come asking questions, you must all say you don't know him. You never had anything to do with him. Don't you understand? They're going after people from the old gangs and people like you, Niau Chen. They'll be coming after your properties next. The *ang mohs* are no better than the Japanese. All they want is to take, take, take! Unless you do something they'll take over everything we've got.'

I was surprised to hear Shen Shen addressing Ah Ma as 'Niau Chen' or Mother-in-law Chen. That was the right term, but it sounded strange because Shen Shen had been calling her 'Ah Ma', which covered 'Ma' and 'Granny', like the rest of us. It was also the first time I'd heard Shen Shen admit she knew anything about her husband's family business.

Ah Ma didn't seem surprised. 'If that's what they want to do with their time, let them try, *lah*.' She put a dish of steamed pomfret on the table in front of us. It was beautiful, topped with shredded ginger, spring onion and coriander. It smelt heavenly too, with the slightest fragrance of Chinese wine.

'Little Ling doesn't like fish,' Shen Shen said. 'She finds it too fishy. Right?'

Little Ling didn't answer. She watched as Ah Ma carefully carved out a spoonful of the tender, juicy flesh and put it in the little porcelain offering bowl with a generous scoop of its broth. Only when that was on the altar next to the matching bowl of white porridge, with the joss sticks lit, did she return to the table with our bowls.

'*Wah*, you're cooking fish but never called me, *ah?*' Uncle Chen appeared in the kitchen.

'Sit! Sit!' Ah Ma's face lit up. I saw her perform a quick – but deep and grateful – bow in the direction of the altar as she hurried to get another bowl of porridge for Uncle Chen. I was shocked by how old and frail he looked. But at least he was up and ready to eat. I sort of bowed – nodded – towards the altar too. We could do with a fresh start to the year and I was grateful to any gods who could help with that.

I loved my grandmother and I owed her so much. I would look after Ah Ma for the rest of her life, of course. And then I would try to be a good spinster aunt to Little Ling and any other children Shen Shen and Uncle Chen produced. It didn't seem likely there would be more – since Uncle Chen had returned from his imprisonment by the Japanese, Shen Shen had spent her nights on a mattress in Little Ling's room. She said it was because Uncle Chen's nightmares woke and frightened his daughter.

'More like they frighten her,' Ah Ma grumbled. 'He's the one she should be looking after.'

Anyway, my life here was comfortably mapped out. Why wasn't I comfortable about living it?

'I thought you didn't feel like eating,' Shen Shen said, as Uncle Chen took his seat at the head of the table. 'If you told me you wanted to eat fish I would have cooked it for you.'

'Never mind who cooks, *lah*. We have food. Everybody can eat,' Ah Ma said.

Shen Shen mock-whispered loudly to Little Ling, 'Ah Ma thinks the food your mama makes isn't good enough for your baba!'

'Can I have more fish?' Little Ling asked. 'Mama?'

'Isn't that right, Su Lin?' Shen Shen turned to me.

Experience had taught me not to respond to such statements. If I took it up with Ah Ma, Shen Shen would laugh and say, 'Joking only, *lah*!' but if I laughed she'd grumble that I didn't appreciate all the hours she spent cooking for the family.

Instead I sidestepped: 'You know how superstitious she is. It's her kitchen. Of course she needs to prepare food herself for the kitchen god.'

But Shen Shen hadn't finished. 'I've been drying *kembong* and *selar* I brought back because you all say you don't feel like eating fish. Then you go out and buy fish.'

'From the Mirza house,' Ah Ma explained. 'Nasima had extra so she sent some over for us. She was looking for you,' Ah Ma nodded to me, 'but I told her you were still asleep. If you go over to see her later, thank her.'

I'd go over later to find out what Nasima wanted.

'What pretty flowers, Little Ling,' I said to her. She had put a spray of blue morning glories in a glass on the table. We called them *bunga kembang seri pagi*, literally 'the flower that opens in the morning'.

'Can I use them to make cakes?' Little Ling asked.

'No! No! No!' Ah Ma said. 'You cannot, cannot, cannot! This flower is poisonous. The seeds are even more poisonous. You are thinking of the *bunga telang*, the blue sweet pea flower we use for colouring drinks and rice cakes. You mustn't mix up the two. If you eat the seeds of this one, you will be ill, maybe die. And have very funny dreams.'

The simply steamed fish was so good with plain rice porridge, especially after the rich fare of New Year and our days of food poisoning.

'I was telling Su Lin that you and her father were friends with Seng Beng in the old days. Before he was *botak*,' Ah Ma said.

"I know that he's dead,' Uncle Chen said. 'Very sad.' He put his spoon down.

Shen Shen glared at Ah Ma. 'Why did you have to upset him?'

'Maybe it was a heart attack,' Uncle Chen said. 'We're all getting older.'

'The police say he was killed,' I said.

'It's those new *ang moh* soldiers,' Uncle Chen said. 'Those new *ang moh* policemen. They're catching and killing people for being Communists or gangsters. Must be them who killed Botak.'

'The police are trying to find out who did it,' I said.

'People are saying he was most likely killed by the vigilantes,' Shen Shen said, 'the MPAJA. That's what they're saying at the morning stall.'

The 'morning stall' was at the end of the track leading to where the small fishing boats docked. Any fish not worth transporting into town were sold or bartered there to people living in the area. It stayed open for less than an hour, just until all the fish and seafood were gone.

'Why would the MPAJA kill him?'

The Malayan People's Anti-Japanese Army had been the biggest group of anti-Occupation fighters, mostly made up of

139

Chinese guerrillas. They'd protected a lot of people, saved many lives. They were well trained but non-English speaking, which meant that, though most locals trusted them, the British didn't.

'It must be the police,' Uncle Chen said. 'They think he was a gangster. Because of his tattoos.'

'Was he?' I asked.

'In the old days they were all gangsters,' Ah Ma said. 'If you're not a soldier or a policeman they call you a gangster. To them everybody's a gangster. Botak was a sweet boy.'

'Sweet?' I remembered his scars and tattoos.

'He had muscles, but no brains. But he was a good boy if he found a good boss. He was very good at doing what he was told.'

I remembered how Botak had dismissed the idea of talking to Shen Shen. 'Did you and Uncle Botak have a fight?' I asked her.

'What kind of question is that? How dare you say such things to me? Did you hear the words your granddaughter threw at me?'

Ah Ma and Uncle Chen seemed more shocked by her reaction than my words.

'Su Lin?' Ah Ma said. 'Why did you ask if they'd had a fight?'

'Only because when I told him Shen Shen would be home soon, that he should wait and talk to her instead of Uncle Chen, he said, "Cannot, *lah*," as if he didn't want to talk to her.'

Uncle Chen laughed. 'That Botak! He always thought women don't know anything. Shen Shen's better at collecting money than any man.'

'Anyway, the police will go after everyone they think was in the gang with him,' Shen Shen said. 'People are saying they think he came here looking for Small Boss Chen and Small Boss Chen killed him.'

Despite his enormous size, Uncle Chen was 'Small Boss' because my late father was still 'Big Boss Chen' to those who remembered the Chen brothers.

'What?' Uncle Chen stared at her.

'I'm only telling you what people are saying.'

'People say all kinds of rubbish,' Ah Ma said, topping up Uncle Chen's porridge and putting more chunks of fish onto his side plate. 'But you stay at home for now. Forget about the rents. We can collect late this month. New Year gives us that chance.'

'I can go,' I said. 'I want to go into town anyway.'

I wanted to make sure Harry Palin was all right, now I knew he had been hunting for Botak Beng. Although I didn't really believe it, a small part of me worried that Harry might have found him. If they'd struggled and Botak had fallen into the drain and landed on something sharp, Harry might not even know he'd killed him.

'I'll go,' Shen Shen said decisively. 'Su Lin just wants to hang around her *ang moh* policeman. Anyway, I've got to take Little Ling to buy new shoes for school.'

I saw Shen Shen wanted to get away from the house for a bit too. Going to town was the perfect escape, but it had to be a duty, so it didn't come across as fun with her daughter.

I knew monthly rent-collecting excursions could be fun because Ah Ma used to take me with her when I was around Little Ling's age. The tenants would usually give us drinks and sweet snacks so it was more like a social visit. If there was any difficulty Ah Ma would ask, 'So, wait until when?' and occasionally there would be whispered conferrals. But most of the time it was fun.

'And, Su Lin, you'd better stay away from those Muslim people. Don't blame me if they get you arrested.'

I thought of Fahey taking our names and winced. 'Ah Ma, Dr and Mrs Shankar send you their respects. May I invite them for dinner one day?'

What I really wanted was for Dr Shankar to take a professional look at Ah Ma and Uncle Chen.

'No!' Shen Shen said. 'Why must you invite strange people over when everybody is so tired? Are you trying to upset your uncle? Or are you just looking for an excuse to bring your policeman here?'

'Maybe not now,' Ah Ma said. 'No need to upset anyone.'

I didn't think it was Uncle Chen she was referring to.

'You won't be satisfied until they come and drag your uncle off to prison.' Shen Shen yanked Little Ling off her stool so roughly that the child cried. 'You'll end up selling yourself on Desker Road, you and all your non-Chinese friends. Stop making so much noise, Little Ling. I've got to get you cleaned up.'

They left – Little Ling in tears, Shen Shen in a huff.

'No need to say anything to your *ang moh* policeman,' Ah Ma said. 'We haven't worked with Botak for a long time. This has nothing to do with us. No point giving them the wrong idea.'

But Uncle Chen said, 'Is your policeman going to try to find out who killed Botak?'

'I want to find out,' I said. I wasn't playing detective but I wanted to know what had happened. 'Do you remember the time Uncle Botak came to see you with scratches all over him? I asked you if he had killed somebody and you told me he'd rescued a cat.'

Remembering Botak Beng

◆

'He *kenah* scratched all over!' Uncle Chen shook his head and laughed. '*Kenah*' was untranslatable Singlish shorthand for being subjected to something painful or embarrassing. 'Your father took one look at him and said, "You've got a girlfriend, *ah*?" But it was this skinny old cat. It got stuck somewhere and there was barbed wire and he *kenah* scratched by the cat and the barbed wire, *aiyoh*. But he got the silly cat out. And the cat, from attacking him became like his second mother. If you shouted at Botak, the cat would hiss at you and chase you away.'

'I wonder if the police went to talk to Uncle Botak's family,' I said.

'His mother died years ago,' Ah Ma said. 'He had no more family down here.'

'He wasn't married? Nasima said Botak was talking to the woman like he wanted to marry her. I forgot with everything else going on. Do you know who Botak could have been wanting to marry? Would he have told you?'

That would explain his awkwardness with me and his unwillingness to discuss anything with Shen Shen.

'Hah! Only if he wanted to marry you!' Uncle Chen said. 'Though that would explain the crabs he gave us. But no, *lah*. Botak never said anything to anybody when he married any of his wives.'

'Any of his wives?'

'Not here. Here he had his old mother so he never got himself a Singapore wife. Up north in Malaya and down south in Indonesia. Botak Beng was good at choosing wives. Smart but not too greedy. Strong and not too pretty. His wives took care of his business when he was travelling,' Ah Ma said. 'Three wives, three different families in three different towns. He liked children. He took good care of his wives.'

'Those poor women.' I'd not thought of Botak Beng as a player with multiple families.

'Yes,' Ah Ma said. 'These days it isn't easy to find men who are still good to you after you give them children and get fat. But Botak was always good to his women. All of them always had rainproof roofs and full rice bins. And Botak had first-month celebrations for all their new babies, the girls as well as the boys. The mothers received the same food allowance for his daughters as for his sons. He was a good man. If Botak wanted to marry you I would have said yes.'

If *Botak* was Ah Ma's idea of a good husband for me . . .

'*Aiyoh*, those poor women and their poor children. Who's going to take care of them now?'

'They will be all right, *lah*,' Uncle Chen said. 'Botak knew he could go at any time. He always told us, "A wife is like a boat.

First, you've got to choose a good one. Then, if you take care of it, it will take care of you. Otherwise you will both sink!"'

'Marriage is like any other partnership,' Ah Ma said. I had to wonder if she was regretting the loss of Botak as a potential son-in-law. 'If the partners involved are satisfied and work together well, nothing else matters. But down here in Singapore, Botak was a good son to his ma. He was the only son she had left so he stayed with her until she died. That woman could be fierce. *Aiyoh*, she almost killed him over the yellow rambutan tree.'

'What happened?' I remembered the yellow rambutan skin in Botak's mouth. 'What yellow rambutan tree?'

'You should remember that old tree,' Ah Ma said to Uncle Chen. Uncle Chen ran a hand over his backside and winced. Ah Ma shook her head at him. 'There was a yellow rambutan tree on Botak's mother's property. Your father and uncle used to run wild over there. In the old days, it was all still jungle.'

'Botak was already going *botak*,' Uncle Chen said, 'so he started shaving his head. And he was already transporting stuff. Remember the gebang palm seeds we used to bring home for you? We didn't find them. Botak got them from Indonesian fishermen in exchange for betel chews that your father made me fold. Even before he had his own boats Botak was transporting things for people.'

'Why would Uncle Chen remember that tree?'

'We thought we were doing her a good deed,' Uncle Chen said. He sounded grouchy but remembering made him smile. 'Madam Ho – Botak's ma – had the old house right at the end of the road by the river. In those days she had two rambutan trees in her garden. One produced the sweetest yellow fruit you ever tasted. The other never had any. One day we boys cut down the barren tree and planted several saplings. We thought we were helping her, but the other tree stopped fruiting, and none of the trees fruited again.'

'Why?' I asked.

'Madam Ho blamed us for making the tree spirits angry. She made us put offerings there and apologise to them. And she caned all three of us,' Uncle Chen rubbed his bottom again, 'and buried the bloody cane where the tree had been. After that two of the trees produced fruit but only red rambutans, even the tree that once produced the sweetest yellow rambutans. And they were never again as sweet as before.'

'Male trees don't produce fruit, but females won't bear fruit unless there's a male tree nearby.' I'd read about some, if not all, trees being male and female like animals. From Ah Ma's story, I worked out that the wrong male trees were planted so the fruit was red. The female trees produced the fruit but the males – and the type of male – made a difference too. Like Botak had made a difference in the lives of those women now widowed.

'Where was the yellow rambutan tree?' I asked, remembering the dried skin I'd found.

'All long gone,' Uncle Chen said. 'You know where they built the Kallang airport? That was where they used to live until all the property was taken over by the government.'

I knew those old *attap* houses built along clay and stone roads that were treacherous bogs during the monsoon season. The old *kampong attap* houses would be pulled down and rebuilt as people married, moved out or needed to expand sleeping space as their families grew. When they died there were no disputes over who inherited the house because it would be pulled apart and built anew.

'Look for the lane between the fifth and sixth milestones. That was how they gave directions if anybody needed to find them by the road,' Uncle Chen said. 'But most people would come by sea or down the river. A kuning rambutan tree like that would be worth something nowadays. Not as common as the red ones. Some people believe they're lucky and use the seeds and skins for medicines.'

'There was what looked like rambutan skin in his mouth,' I said. 'Do people chew it? Did Botak?' I didn't mention I'd found it.

'Rambutan skin can be medicinal,' Ah Ma said. 'But I never heard of people chewing it. Usually the leaves are used because if you take too much of the skin and seed it can be poisonous. Better to leave that to the traditional-medicine herbalists.'

'You can tell it's not safe to eat because monkeys, chickens and goats don't eat rambutan skins,' Uncle Chen said. 'The yellow-hair skins are supposed to be more poisonous than the red. Botak's ma used to boil the seeds to make candles and soap when there was no pork fat. And when she was boiling it down she used to warn us to stay away because the stuff is dangerous. Botak was always hungry and would try to eat anything.'

'He wasn't very clever,' Ah Ma said. 'He couldn't write his name properly. Whenever he needed to apply for licences or permits, anything in writing, he would come and look for your pa. Your pa was always the smart one,' this with a fond nod at me.

I listened intently. I would replay it in my mind later, as I did any scrap of information about either of my parents.

'But even your pa couldn't beat Botak when it came to scrounging and scavenging,' Uncle Chen said. 'Botak was like a rat, very good at finding ways into places and getting things out without being caught.'

'Stealing, you mean,' Ah Ma said.

Uncle Chen waved this away. 'Botak and I were the same age and we both looked up to your pa, Su Lin. If we could do anything to impress him it was a big deal. But even your pa couldn't find things the way Botak did. If Botak liked what he saw, he took it. If somebody said, "Oi, you! What are you doing?" Botak would say, "Can I take this?" and sometimes people let him! If not, well, he'd go somewhere else and try again. He never felt hurt. He said he was too stupid for that. Later he got women in the same way. They all wanted to look after him and help him. Botak's businesses were all managed by his women. Three wives in different locations to manage his shipping orders and distribution. Their families helped him too. How to find employees so loyal?'

'They think Botak was smuggling stuff and working with you,' I said. 'The police have been looking for him for some time. Yesterday when he came here looking for you I saw he was worried about something but he refused to say what it was. I'm very sorry I didn't invite him in to wait to talk to you.'

Uncle Chen would have done anything he could to save his friend's life, but I knew he wouldn't hold it against me.

'Is that what your *ang moh* policeman told you?' Ah Ma asked. 'What did you tell him?'

'Nothing. He's not with the police any more but I heard they'd been looking for Botak. They also wondered whether Uncle Chen and Botak had had a fight because Botak wanted to stop working for him. I'm just telling you what they said.'

Uncle Chen snorted at the impossibility of this.

'Botak would never betray your uncle even if he wasn't happy with him. He would see it as betraying your father too,' Ah Ma said. 'His death wasn't your fault. You couldn't let him in. People should know better than to visit on the Third Day. Look how much bad luck Botak brought!'

'I just wish he'd told me why he'd come,' I said, 'but Uncle Botak always treated me like a little girl.' It was petty of me to resent that – but if he'd said something he might still have been alive.

'It was his way of protecting you. He was giving you respect as the daughter of Big Boss Chen. He treated me as an old woman long before I was old because I was the mother of Big Boss Chen,' Ah Ma said.

'And I was Baby Brother of Big Boss Chen.' Uncle Chen emptied a bottle of wok-roasted peanuts into a bowl that he pushed to the centre of the table. Sitting around the table talking, we were almost holding a wake for Botak. And it felt right to remember the man as well as to try to understand what had happened to him.

'We used to dig up wild peanuts and eat them raw. Botak was always the best at finding them.'

'He was doing transport for the Japanese, wasn't he?' I'd guessed that was how he'd survived the Occupation. It was another reason I'd been uncomfortable with him. 'Could someone have killed him because of that?'

'Nobody alive here now can say we didn't work with the Japanese,' Uncle Chen said. 'Who can be bothered to go and kill him for that? We all needed what he brought in. Transport, smuggling, same thing. The only difference is who's paying you and who you have to pay.'

Maybe I should have been shocked but I wasn't.

'Fancy Ang was here too. She was all over him but I don't think he was interested.'

'Fancy is not his type,' Ah Ma said. It clearly wasn't news to her. 'I wonder who's going to manage his business here now.'

I went out to wash myself. Shen Shen and Little Ling had left in the car and it was my turn to scoop clean fresh rainwater from the giant red clay dragon pot in the zinc-walled cubicle at the back of the house. Even when it didn't rain we had a tap and running water to fill it. Things had changed so much since the days when every drop for washing or cooking had to be hauled out of the well.

Other things had changed too. My father and Uncle Chen had grown up in this house without a father, and I'd grown up without either of my parents. Ah Ma had been there for all of us, making sure we were fed and safe. But now Little Ling was growing up with both of her parents. It was her childhood and future I wanted to protect. She was a clever child and I hoped she would have opportunities I'd missed out on. That meant persuading Uncle Chen and Shen Shen to let her continue studying, even to go to university some day, if she got the chance …

I was startled out of my thoughts when someone banged on the flimsy wall of the cubicle, setting off the zinc cacophony. 'What?'

'Police are here, hurry up! Put on some clothes and come out before they barge in and get you!' Ah Ma said.

'Police?' My thoughts went instantly to Le Froy. He'd said he would give me time to consider his offer . . . He hadn't said how much time, but this was ridiculous.

'Not your policeman. Another one. Different one. Young one.'

Now I thought of Robert Johnson and my heart sank. Was this about the *buaya* curry or Parshanti? And how had he found me?

Either way his questions were best faced with clothes on, so I got dressed.

Fahey at Chen Mansion

At least it wasn't Johnson. It was the slim, dark-haired detective sergeant who was interested in local culture and languages: Mike Fahey.

I saw him looking around the formal living room, taking in his surroundings. It was an uncomfortable space reserved to impress less welcome guests, full of ornately carved teak and marble furniture inlaid with mother-of-pearl and ivory, and crowded with wall hangings, jade carvings and gold pots. Ah Ma must have brought him there to wait – a glass of F&N orangeade was sweating on a lace coaster on one of the tiger-clawed wooden side tables – but there was no sign of her or of Uncle Chen.

Chen Mansion had been in the family since my grandparents' time. My late grandfather had built it out of the proceeds from rubber tyres and 'business' – in other words tax-free imports and exports, or, in yet another word, smuggling. But it was my grandmother who had expanded it into an empire of loan and rental businesses after he had died.

But that was before Fahey's time and none of his business.

He was looking around the room as if he was assessing how much the furniture was worth.

I stepped through the door. 'Hello,' I said.

Fahey spun away from the wall hanging he'd been examining. '*Buaya* curry is no more made of *buaya* than *roti* John is made of Johns,' he said.

'What?'

'"John" is what the locals call British soldiers. Informal but more respectful than "*buaya*". "*Roti*" means bread, so *roti* Johns are bread for johns, French-loaf type bread stuffed with fried egg and sometimes luncheon meat. They're so-called because the hawkers shout, "John! *Roti!* John!"'

Whatever I thought of the man, I was impressed he'd dug that out.

'That old *makcik* who's not really your mother lives near there and you live out here in this house . . .'

'How can I help you?'

'Officially I'm here to see Chen Tou Seng. Your uncle? And ask him a few questions about the unnatural death that took place outside here yesterday.'

I nodded.

'But I thought I'd speak to you first. In case I need a translator.'

I nodded again. Why say more than I had to?

'This is a very impressive house. Chen Mansion you call it, yes? So you're like the local Mafia?'

I shrugged.

'I suppose you've heard the man who died outside here yesterday was stabbed through the heart with a sharp stick. Something like a bayonet – an instrument like a long nail or a metal satay stick.'

I'd already heard this directly from Leask but it caught my attention now. I came closer to him. 'Have you found it?'

Fahey smiled. He'd scored a point in getting me to talk and we both knew it.

'I didn't have anything to do with what happened to that man,' I said. 'I don't know anything about it.'

So Botak had been furtive because he knew he was being hunted by the authorities. But why were they still so interested in him now he was dead?

'But your family has – had – connections with him. Mr Ho Seng Beng was their main connection with unofficial sea trade.'

'You mean smuggling?' When you're on an island, unless you're flying goods in – which would be impossibly expensive – everything has to come by sea.

'Not just what you would think of as smuggling. Before the war he was transporting explosives and information for the Japanese—'

'What? No! My uncle can't have known about that.'

'Mr Beng – Botak – was working for your uncle,' Fahey said. 'Your uncle would have known even if you didn't.'

'Working with rather than working for,' I corrected. 'My uncle worked with a lot of people. And Botak – Mr Ho – probably worked with a lot of other people too.'

I could guess this was more information he'd taken from Le Froy's notes on pre-war Singapore. Damn Le Froy and his putting down everything 'just in case'.

For years he and many of his colleagues in the police believed Uncle Chen controlled the Singapore black market. It was ridiculous, of course. By their definition, 'black market' covered everything that didn't pay exorbitant taxes to the British government. The Chen family dealt in trade and property and, like everyone else, didn't believe in paying anything we didn't have to.

'Do you want to speak to my uncle? He isn't feeling well right now.'

'The Japanese?'

'He survived the Japanese. But now he's sick. So is my grandmother. I don't know what's causing it. I thought it might be the water supply so I've even been boiling the water for washing-up.'

He waved that away. 'I know who you are. You were working for Le Froy, weren't you?'

That was open, official information. I was on the record at the Detective Unit where I'd been drawing a salary as an official interpreter and for local liaison duties.

'I was working for the local police department,' I said. 'I'm not working anywhere now. The Detective Unit no longer employs locals.'

'Johnson's a fool,' Fahey said. 'What I want to know is, what are you trying to do now? What does Le Froy want?'

'You seem to think you know. In your opinion, why did Le Froy come back?'

'Maybe he wants to take control of the Detective Unit again.'

'What? He never wanted the job in the first place. He likes detecting, not managing other people.'

'A lot of men feel like that while they're in the force. But then they find retirement doesn't suit them and they miss it. They miss being in charge and running things.'

'Did Robert Johnson say Brigadier Evans told him that?'

'It's a well-known fact.'

I would have bet anything that Johnson had told him so too. 'A fact doesn't become well known just because you say it is.'

Well, I couldn't blame Fahey for siding with the man who was essentially head detective of the island. But then he surprised me.

I studied him: he was sweating, as he had been before, but it wasn't so bad in this cool, dark, high-ceilinged room. And I realised he was studying me too. Fahey seemed torn between not wanting to speak ill of a colleague and wanting to set me right.

'Maybe you should have some of your drink.'

He finished the glass in one. The British desire to help the world see things from the British point of view won.

'Sometimes what would be seen as ignorance and incompetence at home is indulged as eccentricity out east. As if it doesn't matter because no one who matters comes here. At least, not without enough warning to put on a good show. Never mind that it exposes British administration as a joke. But it doesn't matter to the men in charge because they'll blame their staff and the local people and leave it at that.

'I know I lack seniority and experience. I only got the post because there were no other men on the ground here when they needed to fill it. And I thought I'd be able to train under Inspector Le Froy. I'd heard about him, of course. I read some of the papers he wrote on working within local hierarchies. Then I came out here and found he's not only retired but under some kind of unspecified cloud.'

'That was good of you.' I meant it too.

'But his files were still here, so I read everything I could get my hands on. And I remembered the brigadier said my lack of experience didn't matter because he wanted me as new blood, without connections to the local gangs. He said my not knowing anyone here made me a better choice for the position.'

'Brigadier Evans told you Chief Inspector Le Froy has connections to local gangs?'

'He's not the chief inspector any more. No, Brigadier Evans didn't say he did. He just said I didn't.'

The implication seemed blatantly obvious to me. 'You should have been a lawyer,' I told Fahey. He seemed uncertain as to how he should take that. Maybe the man really was a gormless bookworm.

'I found out that Le Froy had extensive documents on your family's business dealings. And he started to take notes on you. Then it stopped, so suddenly that it makes me think he just tore out the pages. So I'm thinking you and he came to some arrangement.'

I thought I knew what he was talking about. 'Are you accusing Chief Inspector Le Froy of taking bribes from the Chen family?'

'The former chief inspector,' Fahey said. 'You are an informer for him. You traded for your family's protection from prosecution. And in return you gave him information to rid you of your competitors. It would have been a good deal for both sides.'

I shook my head. It was no use protesting this wasn't true, and I managed not to laugh and call him stupid. He would believe what he wanted to believe. But, to my surprise, he didn't push it.

'Look, I'm not trying to dig up any past dirt. If your man wants his job back, that's fine with me. This isn't where I want to be. But I'm not going to be kicked out of the back door for doing a bad job. I know all about the great advantage of partnering with the Chen family. You don't have to worry about guarantees and collateral because they own every other building and business in the poorer parts of town. And they have people everywhere. At least that was how it was then.'

'How do you know all this?'

'I went through the files.'

'You got all that from Le Froy's files?' I said. Part of me wanted to laugh but another part was horrified. Of course Le Froy's notes had been placed with the rest of the files in the Dungeon, the former cell for drunks in which I had set up the system for the Detective Unit. 'And you think he's trying to get his old job back?' The sudden change of direction had startled me out of my polite discretion.

Fahey seemed not to notice. 'I don't know what he's trying to do. All I know is they tell me he's gone and suddenly he turns up. Why else would he have returned if he doesn't want his old job back?'

I'd been wondering the same thing. 'I don't know why he's here, but I'm quite sure Le Froy doesn't want his old job back.'

'Of course he does. Anyway, Johnson – he's the first to say he's only here till something better turns up, but he wants to move up, not be moved out. And he thinks Le Froy wants his job. Why else would he be here putting up with the heat, the humidity, the sun, the mosquitoes?'

His manner was more that of a homesick young man at his wits' end than an authority figure.

'Why don't you ask him?'

This might have been taken for insolence but he snapped back, 'Why don't you?' Then he shook his head and laughed. The sudden release of tension made me laugh too. We were probably about the same age and in any other circumstance – or any other world – we might have been friends.

'Sorry,' he said. 'I meant just to come and say hello, see if I could work something out – oh, nothing.'

He turned to leave but this time I stopped him. 'Really, why not just ask Le Froy? He likes you, you know.'

'No, he doesn't.'

'He said you could make something of the job.'

I saw Fahey struggle not to look pleased. 'That's like saying I'll never amount to anything more, isn't it?'

'Do you think it's an insult?'

'No. Dr Leask thinks well of you,' he said. 'He said you helped the police solve several cases because you know the people and places here better than any of our men do.'

'Before the war,' I said. 'Before you decided local people couldn't be trusted in the police force.'

'Anyway, Brigadier Evans wants the police to find out who's responsible for that smuggler's death,' Fahey said. 'Some cargo belonging to him has gone missing so now he's got men combing the island for this smuggler's hideout, throwing all the manpower he can get at finding it because he reckons that whoever killed Botak Beng did it to get hold of his stuff.'

'So you're officially following up on the murder?' I remembered Johnson dismissing a dead gangster as no loss. Despite myself, I was touched.

'Brigadier Evans is taking a personal interest.'

'I'm glad.' I was also surprised, from what I'd seen so far of his wife and son.

'Did you test the rambutan skins in his pocket,' I asked, 'to find out if they had been poisoned? Or if eating rambutan skins could have poisoned him?'

'The man was stabbed, not poisoned. Johnson said he probably ate them before he died.'

'Johnson.'

'Johnson's an idiot but he's not too bad when you get to know him,' Fahey said. 'We were at school together. That's how I got this job. At school Johnson was far too busy having fun to open a book, so I did his papers for him. And he – his father rather – got me this job. I don't know why Evans wanted the Singapore post so badly when he could have had himself sent home, but he sees something in this place and I'm grateful to be here. It's all about the people you know.'

'Is it?'

'Of course. Sorry, I'm talking too much. I'm new to interviewing. Anyway, on the face of it, it looks like a gang feud, nothing to do with us. But the brigadier said look into it, so I thought, with the war over, there wouldn't be any more dead bodies. You know what I mean?'

I did. You expected to be attacked by your enemies but not by your friends. 'Where's the brigadier searching for Botak's warehouses?'

The problem with a small island is that its whole perimeter is a possible port.

'Everywhere. One mile inland from the coast. But it's taking time. They've already found a lot of stuff, tobacco, opium and chocolate—'

'Chocolate?'

'—but Evans isn't satisfied. According to him there must be more. And that's the thing. If you can help us find the man's smuggling warehouses, we'll let you off all charges.'

'Let her off what charges?' Ah Ma demanded, appearing from behind the decorative screen that shielded the servants' entrance.

'Her arrest charges from yesterday.'

'What arrest charges?' Ah Ma advanced on the room.

I was happy to see how well she looked, less happy that she couldn't decide which of us to glare at.

'Some of his friends grabbed Parshanti and me. And then they arrested us for not letting them hug and kiss us.'

'What? You kiss girls, then arrest them if they don't like it? What kind of police are you? Hah!'

'It wasn't me! I didn't do anything! And those men are not my friends. Just colleagues—'

'Sergeant Fahey wrote out the charges,' I said. 'Charges for resisting assault and molestation.'

'No, no. I didn't write anything. I was just scribbling. It wasn't even a charge sheet. I was just trying to frighten her.'

Ah Ma gave him one more deadly look, then picked up his empty glass and stalked out.

'Have we finished?' I asked. 'I have to go to town.'

'I'll give you a lift,' Fahey said. 'They let me take the motor today.'

'No, thank you. I have to call in at a neighbour's first.'

'That's fine. I can wait.'

'Here!' Ah Ma returned with a refilled glass (even ice cubes, I saw) and a plate of her pineapple tarts. 'You, sit and tell me what you're eating in Singapore. Don't scared. My English very good.'

Despite his pleading looks, I left Fahey to her. It served him right for trying to scare me. But I was also very glad he hadn't written us up.

Tailoring to Fit

———◆———

I got dressed quickly. My poor New Year *samfoo* was soaking in a tub of soapy water after yesterday's encounter with drains and policemen. Today I was wearing an old Western-style frock. It had once been dark blue but had faded after many washes into a gentle grey. And what had been a pretty white floral pattern resembled blobs and streaks of bird shit. But it was clean, and I was happy not to be noticed for my clothes.

Though I'd hurried, Fahey was already outside, leaning against the motor-car when I joined him.

Because of Chinese New Year, there were red 'good-luck' papers, decorations and ashes from fireworks and offerings covering the front of the house and drive. Once I'd mocked these customs, but they had been forbidden for two years – three – so it was like a return to innocence at a time when we feared the gods rather than the soldiers. And it was still home. I'd forgotten how I'd longed at one time to escape from this place. When I was studying at the Mission Centre school, dreaming of going to university, I had been afraid that my family meant to marry

163

me off to a suitable husband as soon as one could be found. Now I felt defensive about the lucky chaos all around us, seeing it through the outsider's eyes.

'It's for Chinese New Year,' I said.

'I know,' he said. Of course, he was interested in Asian culture and languages.

Fahey had got away from Ah Ma more quickly than I'd thought possible. Maybe he had a chance of surviving out here after all.

'Can I give you a lift into town?' Fahey asked, as though I hadn't already turned him down.

'I have to call in at a neighbour's,' I said, as I'd said before.

'Would you like a lift there?' Leaving his car, the irritating man walked along with me.

'It's just over there.'

The roadside was still torn up where they'd dragged Botak's body out of the drain and a brief early-morning shower had made mud, which was already turning into clay. I got bogged down and stumbled but Fahey steadied me before I could fall. 'Thank you.' I'd rather walk on rocks than through mud anytime.

Fahey remained outside the gate when I turned through the Mirzas'. I knew he was taking note of its address and condition and would look it up in Le Froy's files once he got back to the police station.

The Chen family mansion had fallen on hard times since the war. In the old days it was painted every year, on an auspiciously chosen date. Now even the holes in the roof were patched with tarpaulin and some of the paintwork was stained with damp and dirt. Appearances took second place to food and safety.

But the Mirza house was still carefully kept up. Much of it looked new, having been rebuilt since the fire that had destroyed part of the extension Mr Mirza had built for his study and his wife's prayer room. Nasima was the only one of her family left now. Most people thought she would move out to stay with relatives, but instead she'd renovated the house. I'd seen her supervising the construction and the painting, talking to workers and suppliers, but this was the first time I'd seen it completed.

Everything was clean, even the steps I was walking up. People who took such good care of their physical surroundings scared me a little because I didn't understand them. There were some girls at the front, planting something in a space cleared of gravel. They ran into the house when they saw me. Nasima's house was always full of the girls she was teaching. They must have announced my arrival because Nasima came out to meet me even before I reached the house.

'I wanted to thank you for the fish,' I said.

'You're very welcome.' She looked over my head. 'Is that man with you?'

'He's a policeman,' I said, without turning. 'He came to ask questions about what happened yesterday.'

'He wasn't the one who came yesterday. Is he waiting for you?'

'No,' I said.

Nasima gave him another look and turned back to the house, 'Come in out of the sun. There's something I want to talk with you about.'

We ended up sitting in her workroom. It was large and airy, her late father's study, with almost as many books as he had owned, but more children's books now. There were mats around low tables with drawings and exercise books.

'I hear Parshanti is getting married and you're going to be her bridesmaid.'

'Unfortunately.' I made a reluctant face, and Nasima laughed.

'Will you be next? That's the Western custom, isn't it? After a wedding, the bridesmaid catches the bouquet and marries the best man?'

'Oh, no,' I said. 'I'm never going to marry. I'll probably get my teaching certificate and teach other people's children.'

One of the little girls came and stared at me. Nasima said something to her I didn't catch and she scuttled away.

'You don't know what you're getting into,' Nasima said. 'Other people's children, you teach them as well as you can, and when you're happy with their progress, they leave and you start from the beginning with new children. It's rewarding but heartbreaking.'

'I don't think I want the responsibility of bringing a child into the world I'm not sure I can care for,' I said.

Somehow it was easy talking to Nasima about such things. We had more in common in some ways than either of us did with Parshanti. We might have become good friends if we'd met when we were younger, but it's harder to let new friends in after the shell of your personality has hardened.

Nasima still hadn't got round to what she wanted to talk to me about. 'You can still get married, though? I remember you had many offers in the old days when we were still girls. My father used to joke with my mother that he wouldn't accept proposals for me and my sister because he wouldn't get the kind of courting gifts for us that he saw your uncle receiving for you.'

Many of the old gangsters who still held nostalgic memories of Big Boss Chen had offered to adopt me or marry me out of respect for my father. They had brought gifts of gold coins, pipe tobacco and home-brewed toddy, which Ah Ma had accepted on my behalf and passed on to the servant girls to take home to their families.

It would be rude to refuse gifts presented out of respect for my father. But Nasima thought it wrong that I had accepted them without marrying any of the donors.

'They weren't really gifts,' I said. 'And not really for me.'

'I know. It's no joke that women have so little say in what concerns us most. My parents never understood each other. I used to find it very sad when I was younger. But, looking back, I believe they were happy.'

I agreed, though I'd not known either of her parents well. Once someone is dead you might as well think of them as having been happy since it won't make any difference to them even if they weren't.

But something about being here, with Nasima not saying why she'd come to Chen Mansion last night and again this morning, made me uncomfortable. A Malay word '*layan*' described Nasima perfectly: it means following the flow without initiating a subject or direction. Was she waiting for me to bring it up?

'Shen Shen said you brought your maid to talk to the police about the woman she saw running into Chen Mansion around the time Botak was killed.'

I saw Nasima's relief.

'Yes. One of my newest girls. She's scared, but I wanted her to tell her story while she remembered it, before her imagination took over.'

'What did she say?'

'That she didn't recognise who it was. And she didn't see you go into your gate, just through the gap in the fence. I suggested she might have seen you at another time and got mixed up, but she was quite sure of the time. She had asked my permission to go outside by herself to pick *kacang botol* for cooking so I told her to go ahead.' Nasima nodded. 'I believe she's right about the timing. I remember being pleased when she came to me because she was getting more independent.'

The *kacang botol* or winged-bean plants grew in profusion in the scrubland between our houses and the jungle wilderness beyond. They were popular weeds because the whole plant – leaves, flowers, roots and bean pods – could be eaten. I'd often collected them.

'They're growing a lot this year,' my mouth said, while my brain wondered why Nasima Mirza was trying to make trouble for me with the police. I remembered Shen Shen's warnings about her. I'd thought we were friends. I'd believed Nasima didn't hold me responsible for the deaths of her father and her little sister. But maybe it had been an act, just as I was acting now.

The girl Nasima had sent away came back with another I recognised as Rosmah, the girl who'd found Botak's body. Nasima held out a hand and Rosmah went to her and buried her face in her shoulder. But as Nasima kept talking to her the child looked at me uncertainly, then whispered to Nasima.

'Rosmah says she doesn't recognise you,' Nasima said. 'Rosmah's eyes are not so good. She can see colour and movement, but without her spectacles she can't make out details very well. She says you were wearing a different dress that day. She remembers the cloth very well.' Nasima sounded as if she was trying not to be irritated. 'Does anyone else in your house have a *samfoo* like the one you wore yesterday? The . . .' she turned to check with Rosmah '. . . the one with lots of colours and gold squares?'

'Only Little Ling,' I said. The girl, however *goondu*, could never have mistaken Little Ling for me.

Nasima seemed disappointed.

'Can you ask her how big the woman she saw was?' I asked Nasima.

'Who are you thinking of?'

I had Fancy Ang in mind. 'Another Chinese woman came to our house yesterday, taller and larger than me.'

'What was she wearing?' Nasima asked.

It was my turn to look *blur-blur* – that's Singlish for unaware or confused. I'd been so caught up with Botak Beng and the crabs and not waking Uncle Chen, I couldn't for a moment remember what Fancy had been wearing.

'*Aiyoh*, between the two of you . . .' Nasima took a deep breath and tried again, with me this time. 'Was she in Eastern or Western dress?'

'I don't – Western, I think. Yes, Western. A frock with short sleeves.'

'Colour? Come on, Su Lin. Was it red for Chinese New Year?'

'No. Not red. Not white or black either – I would have noticed.'

'So was it purple? Pink? Green? Yellow? What other colours are there?'

I was seeing the side of Nasima that made her so good at working with her girls.

'Blue!' I said. 'Blue with dots.'

'Which blue is closest to the blue of the dress that you can see here?' Nasima held out a children's book with a brightly coloured cover.

I pointed to the blue base of a rocking horse. 'That. With white spots.'

Nasima turned back to Rosmah and asked her about seeing another woman, pointing at the blue of her dress. But Rosmah was shaking her head. She'd not seen the large woman in a blue Western-style frock, just a small woman in a nice *samfoo*. Like Missy Next-door's Chinese New Year *samfoo*.

Maybe wearing a striking new outfit hadn't been such a good idea after all.

Rosmah whispered to Nasima again. I could tell she was repeating what she'd said about hearing the man wanting to marry the woman. Nasima sent her to round up the other girls to get ready to go out.

I took it as my cue to leave and got to my feet.

Nasima stood too. 'If that man attacked you and you pushed him away and he fell into the drain I can understand. It was an accident if he fell into the drain and broke his head. Some men have weak heads. But please don't lie to me that you weren't there.'

'The man didn't die from a broken head. He got stabbed through the heart,' I said.

Nasima bent and selected a neem toothpick from the holder on the table. Holding it daintily between two fingers she mimed stabbing downwards at me.

I took another out of the holder. It was light wood, filed smooth and sharp and smelt of neem oil, cinnamon and fennel. I held it at the level of my own sternum then jerked it upwards towards the back of my left shoulder, as Dr Leask had described.

Nasima put down her toothpick as though she'd suddenly realised how dangerous it was. I laid mine next to it.

'You didn't kill him,' she said.

'No.'

'I believe you.'

'I was there when I saw you. Not before that. I didn't argue with the man or kill him.'

Nasima nodded. She looked into the hall where the children were gathering, excited but on their best behaviour since a (possibly deadly) visitor was present.

'Has the policeman's car gone yet? You don't want him to see you standing at the bus stop and force you into accepting a lift into town.'

I hoped Fahey had gone by now, but it would be like him to wait, out of sight, for me to come out of the house.

'We'll take you in the van,' Nasima said. 'We're going into town to learn to shop.'

I sat in the front with Nasima while the girls piled into the back. Rosmah was clearly intimidated by me and whispered something to Nasima that I couldn't catch.

But Nasima said very clearly to her and all of the little girls, 'Su Lin is not dangerous to you. Even if she is dangerous to people who are dangerous, she is a friend to you because she knows you are under my protection.'

I wasn't sure if this was an assurance to them or a warning to me. Perhaps both.

Harry Palin

———◆———

I might have glimpsed a motor-car tucked in by the side of the road across from the trolley-bus stop, but it was nothing to me. I was just glad things were more or less resolved between Nasima and me. I was taken aback, though, that she would have been fine with me having killed a man, with good reason, as long as I didn't hurt her girls.

'Want a tour of the place?' Harry Palin didn't seem surprised to see me.

I'd found him in the rooms he shared with Leask. This was where Parshanti had wanted to live. I couldn't blame the senior Shankars for vetoing the arrangement, but I found the apartment pleasanter than I'd expected, sparsely but comfortably furnished and clean.

At least, it was after I'd pulled up the blinds.

Harry winced at the light coming in. I wondered how long it had been since he'd left the room. There was a heavy, depressed air about him. Perhaps it was just that he clearly hadn't shaved or combed his hair for a while.

'Parshanti would've had this room.' He pushed open the door to a small, square, sunny room. 'She wasn't going to live in sin with Leasky, you know. I told him he could have it for a study. I'm used to making do with very little space. But he says he's got a desk at the hospital and reads in bed. I think he's still hoping she'll change her mind and move in.'

'She'd be here if she could be . . . Thanks for getting Le Froy that day.'

Harry shrugged. 'Want a beer?'

'No, thanks.'

'Suit yourself.'

'I haven't seen you since . . . I think the last time we really talked you were training to be a pilot with the RAF.'

'I was. I did. We ran out of planes at about the same time we ran out of guns and ammunition, medical and food supplies . . . Still we did what we could in the jungle. It was better than getting interned by the Japs. At least our bugs were fresh. In the prison camp, if you found worms you cooked and ate them because they were your only protein.'

He laughed, but I wasn't sure he was joking. I remembered hearing the PoWs singing as they were marched back to Changi Prison after the day's hard labour. That, more than anything else, was about the British spirit. It was worth keeping.

'How's your family?' I was working around to asking, 'Did you accidentally kill the man you blame for your sister's disappearance?'

'My old man spent some time upcountry, but was transferred back to England before the war broke out. I know he made quite an effort to sign up and get back here to "fight the good fight", as he put it. All to his credit, of course. And to the military's credit that they didn't take him. He died of a heart attack soon after the Germans invaded the Netherlands. He was getting ready to go and fight the Huns. Quite a joke, since he'd spent all his energy before the war trying to persuade his higher-ups that the Germans were cousins to our Royal Family and whatever Hitler did he would never be as bad as the Communists.'

That had been before anyone knew what Hitler would do.

'He must have been worried about you and Dee-Dee.'

'He'd have expected us to do what we could. Dee-Dee was a little trouper. She kept her chin up and was as brave as anything.'

I couldn't keep up with the small talk. 'Why were you hunting for Botak?' I asked. 'I know it's something to do with Dee-Dee. But a lot of people got lost during the war. I love Dee-Dee, and I'd do anything I could to find her.'

'Yes, yes, of course.' Harry pressed his fingers to his eyes as though he was trying to force unwanted images back into the depths of his brain. 'She loved you. When you came to look after her, I saw her really happy for the first time. She was so proud of her drawings, and writing "B-I-R-D" and "T-R-E-E" all by herself.'

He laughed at the memory, then looked at me soberly. 'Back then I thought I was living in Hell. I didn't know we were in Heaven. When the Japanese came, I thought, This is what Hell is like. But I was wrong again. This is Hell, knowing I left my sister in the care of a monster. Who knows where she is now or what that woman – or man – did to her before – during–'

I looked away while he wiped his eyes and coughed loudly.

'What actually happened?' I asked.

'That's just it. I don't know. I know she got on the boat and she was on the boat when it reached Darwin. Then she disappeared.'

'Are you sure she was on board when they docked? Could something have happened to her at sea?'

Dee-Dee's strength and impulses were strong and unpredictable. There was no malice in her, no more than there is in any seven-year-old who wants what she wants and won't listen to reason.

'Someone on the boat would have seen or known. And I'd persuaded someone Dee-Dee knew to meet the boat in Gladstone. It took eleven days, going down through Selat Sunda, through the Java Sea and the Torres Strait. Stuart would have seen her if she was still on board – she's hard to miss. And she likes him. She'd have run to him if she'd been there. He spoke to the crew, who said they'd got through without incident. No one fell overboard,' he winced, 'or no one they saw, anyway.'

'What do you think happened to her?'

'I should never have trusted those people, that woman. I thought I could trust her because – well, because Dee-Dee liked her. She doesn't take to many people.'

I knew that. Harry had decided to trust me only after he'd seen his sister liked me. And I'd seen through his surly manners and hostile attitude because of the tenderness with which he treated her.

'That was just before the Japanese arrived? And you're sure she was on board?'

It had been almost impossible to get off the island. 'Someone might have – I don't know – offered her something for her ticket?'

'There weren't tickets. It wasn't quite legitimate. I know she was put into the berth I'd paid for down in the cargo hold with a porthole. It must have been awful but it was less than two weeks and safer than letting her loose on the ship. And it was a tiny cargo ship, not like the Japs would waste a torpedo on it. My friend said she was seen coming on board. She stayed in her quarters without fuss–'

'Really?'

That made him smile. 'Really. I guess the novelty was entertaining. For a while at least. Stuart asked to see her berth, just to make sure. He was getting pretty panicked by then. Someone had clearly been staying down there, but she and all her things had gone.'

'All her things? She took all her things with her?'

The Dee-Dee Palin I remembered couldn't pack up the mess she made in an afternoon, let alone after more than ten days at sea.

'That's how I know someone took her off the boat before Stuart got there,' Harry said. 'I'm the prize fool who sent my baby sister straight into the arms of the devil. Along with paying through the nose and begging the devil to take her!'

'Oh, Harry, but you don't know for sure–'

'I just need to know what happened to her. Everyone says move on, but I don't even know whether I'm moving on from losing a sister or whether she's out there waiting to be found. And if she's alive, what kind of condition she's in.'

It was a frightening picture. Dee-Dee Palin might look like a beautiful young woman but she was no more than a child.

'Harry, don't assume the worst–'

'I gave that woman some spiked sweets for Dee-Dee so she would sleep on the boat. Or in case she panicked.'

Dee-Dee Palin had always had a child's innocent greed for stories and sweets, and a child's inability to distinguish between truth and lies.

'And I assumed that with the Government House people on board she'd be pretty safe.'

'Government House people? I thought you paid Botak to take her out.'

'I did,' Harry said. 'So did they.'

'Tell me.'

Harry sounded as if he was reciting a story he'd told many times before. 'It was just before the invasion. The Japanese were already moving down the northern states. I was at Government House when I heard Botak bargaining with Evans about transporting him and his wife out of Singapore. Evans was just a government official then. He told me to get out but I'd heard enough to do a little blackmailing. Churchill wanted us to stand and fight but Evans was clearly making a run for it. I wouldn't have for myself but this was for Dee-Dee. I was heading upcountry into the jungle and I couldn't take her with me. But I couldn't leave her here, with the Japanese coming.'

I nodded, understanding.

'Dee-Dee loved you. You were always so good with her.'

I remembered his sister's shrieks of joy when she ran to fling her arms around Harry after the shortest absence. He'd been good with her too. Dee-Dee didn't have it in her to pretend.

'I spent just a few months with Dee-Dee. You spent almost your whole life with her. You were good with her too, Harry.

You know she loved you. There was no one she would rather play with.'

'I never had time for her, did I? Yes, I tried to watch out for her, but I was always too busy to play with her and listen to her stories . . . I don't even know what I was busy with. Feeling sorry for myself, probably.

'I even thought of putting a bullet through— I was desperate. I would have gone with her, of course. Instead I got Botak Beng to agree to take Dee-Dee. I raided what was left of the pater's earthly possessions and came up with a big enough bribe.'

'But what was Botak doing there?' The Botak I remembered had stayed well away from officials and government offices. 'Going round all of the British offering escape to the highest bidders? I can't believe that.'

Harry had to laugh. 'No. He was there with a diplomatic package. He was trying to get Evans to sign the receipt, acknowledging delivery, so he could get out of there, but Evans decided that if Botak could get goods and papers in and out, he could do the same with people.'

'Why was Botak delivering diplomatic packages?'

'It was probably safer than official channels. And remember he was already bringing in all kinds of stuff from Australia. He had contacts on the Indonesian islands. The Japs over there weren't as savage as the ones we got here. Apparently they learned Bahasa to work with the locals there and built up farming and fishing – I don't know why I'm blathering on like this. For a while I was hoping he might have dropped off Dee-Dee with a family. Or even that he could tell me she'd jumped ship there. She'd always liked being by the sea and on the beach, but such a long voyage, I don't know. The Evanses said she was on board all right when they arrived in Darwin. It didn't help that the worst Japanese bombing of Darwin took place the day after they docked. It was bombed worse than Pearl Harbor. Between three hundred and four hundred people died, and they never found all the bodies.'

Harry's voice cracked.

'So Brigadier Evans and his wife are sure Dee-Dee arrived in Darwin?' I prompted.

'That's what they say. He wasn't a brigadier then, just an aide, old Blotto Evans. I remember he opened the parcel Botak brought there and then, even though it wasn't addressed to him. I didn't see what was in it but I saw he was disappointed it wasn't anything useful like money or tickets out. That was what he said. And that was when Botak said he could get him passage out if he could pay enough. Him and his wife, he said. When I heard that I knew I had to get him to take Dee-Dee too. I didn't have the kind of money those people were paying but Botak said we could work something out. So we did.'

Harry didn't explain what they'd worked out and I didn't really want to know. I already knew he'd have done anything he could – as would I – for his 'little' sister.

'Botak must have made some arrangement. Or Fancy. She said he'd make sure Dee-Dee got on the boat all right. But neither of them would talk to me. I've been going after them to try to pin down what happened, but they keep avoiding me. Why would they, unless they know I'll kill them for what they've done?'

It didn't seem a good time to point out that one of them was already dead.

'But you spoke to the brigadier and his wife about Dee-Dee being on board when they arrived?'

'Le Froy got me in to see them straight after he got back. They thought he was moving in with them.' Harry laughed. 'The old bitch was in such a state. Worried he'd run off with her precious linens maybe. But he just said I had questions about my sister who'd been on the same boat out as them.

'They weren't too happy about it, kept claiming they didn't know anything, didn't even want to admit they'd been on the boat. Of course they didn't. Winston Churchill said he wanted the British troops here to fight to the last man but the Evanses turned and ran. Mrs Evans kept yelling about getting me shot for treason, but once he saw I knew all about it, I had the name and licence of the Motor Vessel *Neptuna* they'd left on, the brigadier said staying would have been a fool's sacrifice. He was right. We were hopelessly unprepared. No one expected Peninsula Malaya to fall. We blew up the roads and bridges but their soldiers came down through the forest trails on bicycles and they were so fast. Roosevelt promised American aid but none came.

'Then Mrs Evans decided she remembered Dee-Dee after all. She said she hadn't stayed in her cabin. She said she was a flirt and a slut and ran after all the men on board, including Mrs Evans's husband.'

'That's doesn't sound like Dee-Dee,' I said.

'Flirts like Mrs Evans think everyone does it,' Harry said. 'But I keep wondering, did Fancy teach her to behave like that? Around men, I mean. I left Dee-Dee with Fancy because I had to get upcountry. Botak said Fancy was arranging supplies and she'd make sure Dee-Dee got on board, too.

'Now Botak's dead and Fancy's avoiding me. Avoiding Le Froy too. He used to be able to track down anybody but he couldn't get hold of her. She's good at hiding. I'm too visible here, as a European, but I'm going to find her if it's the last thing I do.'

There was craziness in his voice, which scared me. At the same time it seemed that his search for Dee-Dee was his only reason to live.

I had an idea where I could find Fancy Ang, but I wasn't going to say so to Harry. I was afraid he had so much anger inside him that he was just looking for an excuse to kill someone – or himself.

'So that's my cheery story,' he said. 'What are you going to do, now that the world's at peace and Leask and Parshanti are going into the happily-ever-afters together?'

I shrugged. After the kind of stuff he'd been talking about, a teacher-training certificate or a course in journalism seemed hardly worth mentioning. And I wasn't ready to think about where I stood with Le Froy either.

'No plans,' I said. 'Or anyone to plan anything with.'

'You could marry me,' Harry Palin said.

Had I heard him right? For a moment I felt I'd turned into a woman in a French farce who believes every man who says 'Good morning' is passionately proposing to or propositioning her.

Except I could see there was nothing remotely passionate in Harry's sad eyes and he had definitely proposed. How else could you interpret 'you could marry me'?

'What?'

'What I said. If you want to, I mean. No obligation. You know me. I just mean you don't have to be trapped here for ever,' Harry said. 'There's no place in England for me, but with a marriage certificate no one can stop you settling into the old family home if you like. I know I'm not much of a bargain, but once they sort out what the pater left me you'll have a place to stay that no one can kick you out of, and there should be some money too. Plus I won't be around for ever. I don't intend to be here much longer, once I find out what's happened to Dee-Dee. I won't tie you down, I promise. You can study or work or whatever you like.'

I didn't think much of Western courtship rituals. From what I'd read it was a highly irrational business, dependent on falling in love at first sight unless you came backed by family money and connections. Even by those standards this was shocking. 'Why, Harry?'

'The family name and all that. It's like this is my one chance to do some good with it.'

'And something that the establishment types would hate?'

'There's that.' Harry's mouth twitched into a small grin. 'My old man said he'd have done much better to marry a local woman after my mother died.'

Remembering the late Lord Palin's late second wife I had to agree.

'Think of all the pater's important people freaking out over a Chinese Lady Palin! I didn't think anything could cheer me up. You want to think about it?'

'No, thank you,' I said. 'Look, marriage is like any other partnership. As long as the partners are satisfied and want to be together nothing else matters.'

I was channelling my grandmother, I thought. Or maybe my parents. Their lives hadn't ended well but, as far as I knew, they hadn't regretted their marriage.

'Don't bother shocking them with a Chinese wife as a joke. Wait till you find someone worth fighting for, who's as willing to fight for you. Then you can face your establishment folks together. It won't matter what happens because you'll already have won. But, first, let's find out what happened to Dee-Dee.'

Desker Road and Fancy Ang

◆

After leaving Harry Palin, I headed for the place that romantically reckless girls, who reject offers of financially secure marriage, are most often threatened with: Desker Road. It wasn't much more than an alleyway between two- and three-storey shophouses. I stood where it branched off from Serangoon Road and looked down it. I couldn't see very far because it was crowded with paper flowers, seductive pictures and veils that hung on rods jutting into the walkway from the narrow entrances. I knew I was looking for number forty-one. The problem was, I couldn't see any house numbers.

People joke that it's the businesses in places like this that put the 'sin' in 'Singapore'.

Several women eyed me as I passed, but none spoke. They probably guessed I was there looking for a runaway friend or sister rather than for work. Mostly they fanned themselves, chewed their betel or tobacco and picked at their teeth. This clearly wasn't a popular time for clients, which made me feel safer.

Although I'd lived in Singapore all my life, this was the first time I'd been to this area, though I'd heard about it. Like so many wild childish exaggerations, I found this reality drab and dingy. It smelt bad too. People had clearly been relieving their bladders as well as fulfilling their sexual needs.

Here, in the areas around Amoy Street, Carpenter Street, South Bridge Road, Bugis Street and Desker Road, British authority was limited to the road names and the authorised licences that hung on red boards outside official opium shops and brothels. They showed each shop's licence number and stated that the premises were licensed to operate between six in the morning and nine at night. Of course, the businesses were geared towards attracting *ang moh*s with money. The photos were scrawled with English phrases, like 'I love you' and 'I miss you', but they had probably been written by old men rather than the young girls pictured.

I knew it was only after the officially regulated hours that the real business started. Then the hundreds of unlicensed, unofficial 'comfort' establishments would come alive, with cigarette and bottled-beer vendors on the streets. Unlike most areas where you see families crowded around hawker baskets, it was mostly men outside, staring through grille doors at women sitting on the stairs within, pausing, smiling and flirting.

The few men around paid me no attention but I felt nervous. This was unfamiliar territory. I peered at a couple of the printed licences but they were impossible to read through the thick coating of street grime. I saw labourers buying the government-sanctioned opium sold in small triangular bamboo-leaf and white-paper packets red-stamped with 'Monopoly Opium'. Each cost about forty cents, almost half a day's wages, and was enough for about six smokes. That wasn't much for the addicted and chronically sick. A coolie's low wages meant opium was the painkiller of choice. It was also the only distraction and indulgence most could afford.

For those who couldn't afford even that, there was *chandu*, the ashy residue that was collected from the floors of the dens after the smokers had gone. It was less effective, but cheaper.

Venturing down the street, I was aware of how lucky I was to be a visitor, not a prisoner.

I stopped by a hawker's buckets and bought myself some *bandung*, condensed milk stirred with rose syrup. It was deliciously refreshing after the ride to town in a van full of chattering girls. This was the original Indian recipe, and the syrup had been made in the traditional way, by boiling rose petals in sugar water; recently Westerners had imported cordials made with artificial rose flavouring and red colouring, which were served in smart hotels.

'What are you doing here, skinny chicken?'

A couple of women eyed me from a doorway. Though they were wearing their work makeup (heavy) and outfits (low necklines and high slits), they weren't in work mode. The one who'd spoken looked bored rather than hostile.

'I'll treat you to a drink if you can tell me where to find Fancy Ang,' I said to her.

Without being prompted, the hawker ladled *bandung* into two glasses.

'Who's that?'

'How would we know?'

But they took the drinks.

The hawker held out his palm and I dropped another coin into it.

'Don't know where she is,' one said, after she'd finished her drink. 'If I see her, I'll let her know you looking for her.'

The other nodded, and they strolled off, arm in arm.

That was pretty much what I'd expected. I walked on in the same direction, taking my time. Was this getting me any closer to finding Fancy Ang?

'Cooee! Cooee!'

Yes. The woman I'd last seen with the now dead Botak was waving at me from a nearby alley.

'Su Lin, girl! Why are you here? Did she send you to find me?' Fancy demanded, 'What does she want? How did you find me? Never mind. Don't talk so much. Come, come with me!'

She didn't mention the girls and I didn't see them again but I guessed their *bandung* had been worth the two cents it cost me.

I followed Fancy as she turned into an even narrower alley carved between the back entrances of two shophouse blocks. Here the air was thick with the smell of flowers and spices. There were no signs, only small wooden tables – rather, three-legged wooden stools – supporting trays with cups of tea and mint leaves. Women sitting in the doorways offered them to passers-by, who at this hour didn't go inside. At their backs, narrow staircases led upwards. The women looked like dolls, all dressed up with their painted faces and colourful jewellery. This was the oldest profession for women, and those on duty now looked to be older women who hadn't landed the more lucrative late shifts or who were working even the lean hours in hopes of picking up a little extra. They worked to survive or had been sent here so their families wouldn't starve. There was nothing to be ashamed of.

This was a world apart from the rest of Singapore. Migrant workers came for an hour's respite from their hard labour and harder lives.

Fancy turned in at the base of one of the staircases. A young country girl wearing an old evening dress was sitting on a stool biting her nails. She had two long thick plaits and didn't look up till Fancy snapped, 'Lily, sit up properly! If you can't do anything useful at least don't scare people away!'

Fancy barely slowed as she delivered this, and I followed her up the steps. We passed a first landing with two doors opening off it, a low bed in each, then continued up to a second landing. It looked like Fancy lived and worked here. It was a small, densely cluttered room with a skylight and a small window over the single bed. There were photos of Fancy on the walls with men and women, always posing flirtatiously, cigarette held between dark nails and darker lips.

An altar had old photographs of Botak and some people who must have been Fancy's ancestors, the usual glass of water, incense sticks and fruit. There was also a small cup of coffee and a thimbleful of orange liquid. My grandmother had an altar like that. Most homes did. Whenever she ate, she first put some food on the altar. Even when there was not much food, she made sure the ancestral spirits always had water.

Nothing was unusual about Fancy's except that the fruit on the altar was three yellow rambutans.

'Where did those come from?' I asked, at the same time as Fancy said, 'Did she send you?'

I assumed she meant Ah Ma. 'No.'

Fancy looked disappointed. 'Then why have you come to bother me?'

'Harry Palin wants to ask you about his sister. I promised I'd try to find you but—'

'That Harry is mad. Of course, *lah*. You know his kind. Maybe he killed his sister himself. I've got nothing to do with him. You get out of here!'

'But I came to find you because I want to find out what happened to Uncle Botak. Who was the woman Botak was talking to just before he died? I don't believe it was you, and I don't think you killed him. But you must have seen the woman he was talking to.'

'What difference does it make who he was talking to? He had a heart attack and died. What's the big deal? Ha ha, I tell you – once one of my girls *kenah* this giant fellow who had a heart attack *mati* on top of her and all the shit—'

'It wasn't a heart attack,' I said. 'Botak was stabbed. He was murdered. It wasn't an accident.'

Fancy, silent for once, although her mouth was still open, processed the information.

'You sure?'

'One hundred per cent sure.'

I felt a stab of fear as she looked at me. There was something in her eyes I didn't understand and didn't like. It occurred to me that if Fancy had killed Botak Beng, she might kill me now. My first thought was that Le Froy would be so angry with me for going there alone. Which made me angry with myself and less scared.

My second thought was that it was none of Le Froy's business where I went, alone or not.

I didn't feel Fancy Ang was really a threat, in that little room. No, she was trying to decide whether to trust me. I decided to distract her.

'No photos of your daughter here? I heard she was very beautiful.' I waved generally in the direction of the altar, and could have kicked myself. Is there a worse way to get someone to trust you than making small talk about their dead daughter? Not likely.

'Yes, she is beautiful – she was very beautiful,' Fancy said. 'Very, very beautiful. If I had her looks, *aiyoh*, I would have been a movie star or a rich tycoon's mistress.'

She leaned in and whispered, although we were alone in the room, 'Her father wasn't my husband. My husband was a farmer, like all the men in my family. Good with pigs and goats, lousy with women. It wasn't the life for me. I ran off with Lieutenant Douglas Stewart. He was a British officer. He wasn't very senior, but more important than any local could be. He called me his "Asian Frances" because Frances was his wife's name. That's how I got my name.'

Of course. 'Frances' became 'Fancy' in her pronunciation.

'He had a wife?'

'Somewhere.' Fancy dismissed the woman. 'Not here. Kim was our daughter. So beautiful . . .' She pulled out an old photograph.

Many children of mixed race are beautiful – look at my friend Parshanti Shankar with her Indian-Scottish bloodlines. But Kim Stewart had her mother's broad face and hips, and even so young, she was gawky, slightly cross-eyed and taller than many adult local men.

I realised I'd seen little Kim Stewart in the old days. She was one of the officers' children who'd been brought to play with Dee-Dee Palin when I was looking after her. Kim must have been about nine then, but Dee-Dee Palin, still seven years old in her head, was happy to play with anybody.

Only a mother could have called her beautiful. I felt a surge of tenderness for Fancy.

'What happened to Kim?' I asked.

'My daughter was killed by the Japanese fire bombs before the Occupation,' Fancy said. 'We thought – actually, Botak said – cremation is a good way to go. With fire, you go straight to the gods. Like when we burn offerings.'

I've noticed that – after the initial shock – people who were on good terms with loved ones they'd lost were better at getting on with their lives than those who weren't. There's less guilt and regret entangled in the loss.

Still, I was surprised Fancy wasn't more grieved by her daughter's death. An only child, as far as I knew.

I was also surprised that Kim Stewart had no place on Fancy's altar.

Maybe Fancy was one of those who believed that having a child die before you was even worse luck than never having had them? But, even so, wouldn't you want to give that child something to eat in the afterlife?

'I was thinking of coming to talk to you.' Fancy had reached a decision. 'I know that Botak Beng was a good friend of your family, especially of your father. Everybody knows that Botak was Big Boss Chen's right-hand man. And, of course, I was very close to Big Boss Chen. That's why I feel I owe it to them to warn you.' She looked at me with challenging eyes: do you really want to hear secrets about what your father did with me? I knew Fancy had always claimed she and my father had been lovers – at least to everyone who hadn't known my father well.

'Botak Beng had known he was sick for some time. He was coughing all night and couldn't sleep. In the morning he coughed blood. He knew he would die soon and wanted to leave his conscience clean because he didn't want to be tortured in the afterlife. He also wanted all of his children properly taken care of. Botak Beng had three wives with fourteen children between them. He had already made sure his older children had enough money to eat and go to school. But he had one more baby coming he needed to look after.'

She looked at me meaningfully. I looked back blankly. 'She's pregnant. Your sister-in-law is pregnant. She's having his baby.'

'I don't have a sister-in-law. Shen Shen's my aunty by marriage. And she's not pregnant.'

There are far more complicated – and precise – Chinese terms to describe the familial relationship between me and the woman who had married my father's younger brother, but the English term 'aunty' made everything simpler.

Fancy looked at me as if I was a child throwing a tantrum to avoid going to bed . . . but who might actually be sick.

'Why are you lying to me? Everybody knows she has a baby coming.'

I believed her. I should have guessed when I'd heard Shen Shen vomiting and when she kept accusing me (joking, she said) of being pregnant. I'd been vomiting too but I knew I wasn't pregnant.

'I didn't know you and Shen Shen were such good friends.'

'Somebody like me? Women need me because I know their men better than they do.' She laughed as if we were sharing a joke. She was wearing a calculating look now.

Shen Shen had always talked about Fancy as though she was untouchable. But, as I was learning, there were many sides to Shen Shen.

I needed to get away and think. But first, since I was here . . . 'What about Harry Palin?' I asked. 'Can't you just tell him that you got his sister safely onto the boat to Australia? He knows you didn't go on it, so that's all he wants from you.'

Fancy turned away. 'I don't deal with his kind,' she said.

But I'd caught a glimpse of . . . was it guilt? Her face wasn't used to relaxing into honesty so it was gone as soon as it came. 'Don't tell him you saw me.'

'He knows.'

We both spun around. It wasn't Harry, though. It was Le Froy.

'You can't blame Palin. He's afraid his sister was sold into prostitution somewhere and all he's hoping to find is proof that she's dead. Can't you help him? Please?'

Fancy's struggle showed on her face. She glanced at the altar where Botak's photograph stood, as though looking for guidance. 'That girl, his sister—' She stopped. She walked over to Le Froy and leaned in close to him, taking his hand. 'I would rather help you. I can teach you to do things that will make all women want you, not just crooked little cripples.'

The look on Le Froy's face almost made me laugh.

He pulled away his hand away and wiped it on his trousers. 'Come, Su Lin. Let's go.'

'Don't pretend to be so high and mighty. Why don't you tell her why you're really back in Singapore? Tell her about the drug money you're after.'

'What?' I asked.

'Come on.' Le Froy propelled me from the room in front of him. I fell over the girl, Lily, who had been crouched on the landing just outside the doorway, listening, and Le Froy tripped over me.

All the way down those dim steps, we heard Fancy laughing.

'You were following me?'

'Actually I was following someone who was following you. Rather painfully obvious, he was. I only moved to get him out of trouble.'

'Harry,' I guessed.

'Harry,' Le Froy agreed.

Cemetery

———◆———

It had started raining while I was in Fancy's room and I was glad to see Le Froy's borrowed car on the road just beyond the alley with someone in the front seat.

'You were following me?' I asked him, as I climbed into the back seat.

'I was here. I saw you. That's not following.'

Harry was steaming with fury. Most of all at being handcuffed to the steering wheel of the car while Le Froy went after me.

'I told him which staircase you went up. I'm not bad at tracking.'

'Tracking wild pigs maybe,' Le Froy told him. 'A couple of protectors were watching you. Some of their women must have complained. Better me than them, if you don't want your ribs broken.' He unlocked Harry's cuffs and started the car.

'So what did that woman say?' Harry asked me. 'You found her, right? Did she say anything about Dee-Dee?'

Talking to Fancy had given me an idea about Dee-Dee's fate, but I needed to think more about it and do some digging before

I put it to him. 'Nothing new,' I said. 'Where are we going?'

'Home?' Le Froy said.

I needed to think over what Fancy had told me. This was Chen family business, nothing to do with Le Froy or Harry. But I didn't want to go back to Chen Mansion where I would see Shen Shen. I didn't want that until I'd worked out what I thought of her.

'I want to go to the cemetery to pay my respects.' I wasn't going to worry about Le Froy and Harry. 'You can drop me anywhere in town. I'll book a car to take me.'

'Which cemetery?' Le Froy said, at the same time as Harry asked, 'What the hell for?'

'The Bukit Brown cemetery. The family graves are there and I didn't go to pay my respects on the tomb-sweeping day.'

Shen Shen had said she'd dealt with the Third Day visit, but at least I could see my parents' gravestone and tell them I was all right.

'Then let's do that,' Le Froy said. 'Harry? Where can we drop you off?'

Harry complained that he hadn't anywhere else to go. He reminded me of Little Ling – or his sister Dee-Dee. Maybe it wasn't just brain fever that was wrong with Dee-Dee – she was simply behaving like a Palin. I'd have to remember to tell Harry, but he wouldn't appreciate it at the moment.

Le Froy drove us out to the cemetery in silence. It was a long way. The cemeteries were far out of the city, to keep evil spirits at a distance. I'd always felt at home in the graveyard. My parents weren't really there. Ah Ma and I had put up a stone for them but their bodies had been burned because of infection.

OVIDIA YU

I didn't know how I felt about Le Froy being there. It was not a part of my life he'd ever seen. And Harry? Harry fitted in even less, but somehow that didn't matter. Not because I was closer to him but because it mattered less to me what he thought. I didn't want to consider why that was so.

'This way . . .'

It wasn't easy navigating the paths, which were still soggy and slippery from rain. I struggled and so, I suspected, did Le Froy.

I hadn't been to visit the family graves for the last three years. The Japanese *kempetai* hadn't approved of anyone going anywhere and we didn't want to add ourselves to the hungry ghosts wandering around the cemetery. There was also the matter of not wanting the Japanese to see where the family graves were. There had been stories of them plundering the bodies of the dead.

But when we arrived, it was as if the last three years and seven months were there before us: the graves hadn't been cleared at all. I'm not talking about a few dead leaves and some grass tendrils: thorny shrubs had grown over the headstones, almost completely obscuring them.

'Shen Shen said she came to clear our graves. Maybe she only did her own family's.'

'Well, one person couldn't do much.'

'I have to do something,' I said. I felt suddenly tearful. 'Just my parents' stone.'

'I'll do it,' Harry said. 'Your ancestors are already dead so it won't give them a heart attack to wonder which *ang moh* you've taken up with.'

'There's a *parang* in the boot,' Le Froy said. Then, to me, when Harry had headed back to the car with the keys, 'You'll be doing him a favour.'

'Do I have to chant prayers or rake the soil in a pattern or anything?'

'Of course not. Don't be silly.'

'Hey, a snake!'

A banded coral snake fell from the bunch of greenery Harry had yanked up. It flipped and flashed its black underside to intimidate us. Harry raised the *parang* but—

'No! Please don't!'

'Why? Is it one of your ancestors?'

It might have been.

'This one is poisonous,' I said. 'And it eats other snakes.'

'Enemy of my enemy. Got it,' Harry said.

Le Froy found a rock to sit on, and we watched Harry from there.

'He's a good boy,' Le Froy said.

'A good man.'

'Of course.'

'I'm going to look at the graves of Shen Shen's family,' I said.

Their section was at the other side of the Chinese cemetery. It was even worse over there. Someone had vandalised and trashed the memorial stones set up for Shen Shen's parents, brothers and sister Mimi. There was even red paint splashed on them, paint simulating blood being a common loan-shark threat, but what loan shark would follow someone into the afterworld?

'Whew. Someone was angry.' Le Froy had followed me. 'Should we do something?'

'No.' I turned to face him. 'I don't need your help here. I want you to tell me why you're really back in Singapore.'

Le Froy glanced back at Harry, a football field away from us.

He was working hard. Birds were swooping in the sky above him, catching post-rain bugs, and a few daring ones were following him, picking through the weeds he tossed aside for grubs. I saw Harry talking to them, throwing bunches of earthy rooted plants at them, making them flutter up in alarm. Harry started whistling as he chopped and cut.

'I came to investigate the missing Opium Fund money,' Le Froy said.

I nodded to show I'd heard him and also that it wasn't enough of an answer.

'There's some confusion as to whether it's really missing. Or just a bureaucratic slip. They can't declare it's been stolen when there isn't any evidence as to who received it at this end.'

'Can we walk? It's easier than standing.'

'Yes. I'm finding that out.'

I would have sat on the ground, but not in the graveyard. 'What was the money for?'

'The money was sent to be used for the defence of Singapore, but the Opium Fund was originally set up to pay for the treatment and recovery of addicts.'

'I've never heard of such a fund.'

'Probably because no one could agree on how the money was to be spent. In the meantime the original fund was invested, reinvested and reinvested . . . Then someone persuaded the powers that be that a percentage should be converted to share scrips and sent out via their special courier network to fund the defence of Singapore.'

'Sorry – what are share scrips?' I had to ask, even though it meant interrupting him. I don't like showing ignorance, but I like remaining ignorant even less.

Le Froy paused and frowned. I knew he was coming up with an explanation basic enough to be understood while covering the part the scrips played.

'You understand representative money? Right now one ounce of gold is worth thirty-five American dollars, meaning their paper money represents value that can be exchanged for a certain quantity of American gold reserves. The share scrips represent value within the banking community that can be exchanged for most major currencies.'

'So they are like bank cheques?'

'But not made out to any recipient. The scrips serve as international currency. This suited the bank, because they didn't have to come up with the money themselves. We know that the share scrips arrived before the fall of Singapore, but too little too late.'

Le Froy looked at me as though he was waiting for questions.

'Botak was in your special courier network, wasn't he? Is that why you were looking for him? You think he stole the share scrips? Can they be used as money?'

'The money tied to the share scrips is held in sterling securities in London. So, yes and no. They wouldn't be much use to you here, but back in Britain? In the right – discreet – hands, it could be the making of a fortune.'

eed to claim them in Britain? They would be no
ne like Botak?'

'They wouldn't do him any good out here. But anyone he sold them to could make a huge profit in the UK or anywhere in Europe.'

'So you're here to hunt for the missing share scrips? I knew it!'

Le Froy looked surprised. 'Knew what?'

'That you had a real reason for coming back. So many people were trying to work out what it was.'

However ridiculous I thought her, I wasn't going to mention Parshanti's crazy ideas. For sure I was never going to admit that, in my most private mind, the space I didn't even allow myself into, it might have looked like the perfect fairy-tale ending. And like a fairy tale, it didn't exist.

'It had to be an unofficial investigation, for obvious reasons,' Le Froy said. 'They were torn between not wanting a scandal and not wanting to set a precedent of allowing funds to vanish without trace.'

'So where are the share scrips?'

Le Froy shrugged. 'Who knows? At the bottom of the ocean, maybe. But not in the hands of those who would have stolen them.'

'Whose money is it, really?'

'The Opium Fund was set up by politicians to force the colonial authorities to signal the Empire's willingness to end its dependence on opium revenue. The thirty million dollars set aside—'

'Thirty million?'

Le Froy nodded. 'Came from Singapore's opium-trade surplus. It was locked in an investment fund giving four per cent interest, an annual income of one million four hundred and sixty thousand dollars.'

I was good at calculations. But the figure froze my brain.

'It's not that much money. Less than a quarter of the opium profits Singapore earned them.'

'How much are the missing share scrips worth? Just approximately?'

'We're talking in the neighbourhood of nine million dollars.'

'You're missing nine million dollars? That would make someone look bad, especially if it's just an administrative oversight.'

'You see why it can't be made public? It's not real till you acknowledge it officially. Actually, they didn't realise it was missing until they tried to close the war fund accounts.'

'And you were sent over to investigate what happened to the opium money?'

'They probably thought it was a good way to get me out from under their feet.'

I could tell he was lying. 'You volunteered, didn't you?'

He laughed: an admission. 'Given I'd spent the past five years demanding they send assistance and financial aid to Singapore, my name came up. Of course, now there's no urgent need for arms and ammunition to defend the island it's agreed that if or when the money is found, it goes into rebuilding Singapore's public-health infrastructure.'

'That's good of you.'

'It couldn't be an official search because the funds were never officially sent. I agreed to come back and see what I could find out.'

He'd always been good at going undercover and infiltrating levels of our society of which most British administrators remained blissfully unaware. But he must have lost touch after almost three years in prison and returning to England.

Also, thanks to the Japanese, we locals had become better at hiding things. We've always been good at surface obedience and keeping our overlords – whoever they might be – happy. And for the most part the authorities are content with that, especially the mid-level administrators, who only want to earn a living. So, as long as you don't rock the boat you can do whatever you like.

'I hope to God we find them. I'll be able to say I did one good thing even with this.' He thumped his fist against the leg that ended in his prosthetic foot.

I could have said something encouraging and uplifting but I just nodded. I was grinning inside. Even if Le Froy hadn't noticed he'd said, 'We find them,' I had.

'Where have you looked so far?' I asked. 'It might be something completely innocent, like an official received the delivery and locked it away. Even if the Japanese found the share scrips and knew what they were, they wouldn't have been able to convert them into money. Have you searched Government House?'

'Government House, all the offices, the residences of all the officials here at the time. Evans's place, especially.'

'Why especially?'

'He requested, lobbied for, demanded this posting. Triggered my alarm bells. But he doesn't seem to have done anything, apart from handing my department to his idiot stepson. I had my cleaners search their place. If the share scrips were there they would have found them. But we got zero, zilch, *nada*. The only strange thing there was that the Evanses were burning offerings for several weeks after they'd arrived. Ashes in the metal prayer bins at Government House? The servants said it was the brigadier, his wife and her son doing the burning. Who knows? Maybe they made a pact when they left that they'd come back and give thanks if they survived.'

'What were they burning?'

'Books, apparently. Many, many books, cut from their covers. They brought me some of the ashes. Huge chunks of the *Encyclopaedia Britannica*.'

'I think he's finished.' Harry, sweaty and shirtless, was waving at us. 'We'd better go back.'

'I'm sorry,' Le Froy said quietly.

'What for? Why?'

'My insufferable British egotism. I grew up taking the Empire for granted. I came out east with an insufferable faith in my ability and right to rule the world. It wasn't just a right either. I believed it was my calling.'

'You can't blame yourself for your education,' I said. 'You came out here and saw for yourself. Maybe Brigadier Evans will too, in time.'

'If he can. He's a man who regards himself as the embodiment of the Empire and therefore expects his every whim to be taken as revealed truth by the "blasted natives".'

I heard a bitterness in him that hadn't been there when we'd worked together at the Detective Shack. I wondered if Le Froy was thinking of Brigadier Evans or someone else.

'But you came back not as part of the Empire,' I said. 'And with luck you'll be funding our public-health system. Come on – Harry looks desperate.'

Actually, Harry looked great, flushed with exercise and glowing. 'I'm done in. In more ways than one. Sorry for whining. Can we go back to town? I'm going to die if I don't get a cold drink. Look, I did a pretty decent job, even if I say so myself.'

'Great job!' I said, and meant it. 'Where did you get all those scars on your back? Was that from the war?'

'The benefits of home and school discipline. Survive it, and nothing that comes after is too bad,' Harry said. 'Not even war.'

By the time they dropped me off, Harry was snoring gently in the back seat. The physical work had done him good, I thought.

I let Le Froy take me right up the driveway to the house. If Shen Shen wanted to make something of it, I had a few questions for her too. But no one jumped out at me when I passed the charcoal bins. The kitchen light was on and I found Uncle Chen and Little Ling sitting on stools behind the kitchen, watching drowsy chickens in the coop. Ever since Uncle Chen had slid in the boards that separated an incubating hen from the others, Little Ling had been looking forward to the new chicks.

'Did you bring anything for me?' Little Ling asked.

'Sorry, no.'

She pouted, then said, 'We think they're going to hatch soon,' and went back to watching chickens.

Uncle Chen shook his head at me. Won't be hatching yet. 'I won't ask you where you've been,' he said.

'And I won't ask what you're doing sitting out here in the dark.'

We smiled at each other. It was like the old days when he used to sneak me sweets so I could 'practise' not telling Ah Ma that I'd had a treat.

'Shen Shen?'

He shrugged. 'She had a call and had to go to town urgently. Won't say what it's all about. Says she doesn't want to worry us.'

'Shen Shen is trying to be too clever,' Ah Ma said, from the kitchen. 'She thinks it's so easy to do business. You undercut people, others undercut you. Have some barley water?'

'Yes, please, Ah Ma.' I was still thirsty though we'd stopped by a roadside stall for coconut water.

I wondered if I should tell her I'd been to see Fancy, and what Fancy had let slip about Shen Shen's coming baby. Should I tell her I'd been to the cemetery and nothing had been done to clear our family's gravestones? Or about the red paint that had been splashed on Shen Shen's family stones? But Harry had cleared our gravestones and there was no point in worrying her about what had been done to other people's.

Ah Ma and Uncle Chen watched me as I drank my warm barley water. Here in the cosy yellow light of the evening kitchen, everything else seemed petty and irrelevant.

'Is Shen Shen having a baby?' I asked.

'Mustn't say yet,' Ah Ma said. That was as good as 'yes' from her. Ah Ma was one of those who believed it was tempting Fate to celebrate any new arrival until after its birth. And sometimes not even then, in case the gods or spirits saw it as hubris.

'No, *lah*,' Uncle Chen said. 'No more babies coming. Not for this old man.'

Fifth Day:
Chen Mansion

'What time did Shen Shen get home last night?' Exhausted by my day out, I had fallen asleep before I heard Ah Ma's old Armstrong Siddeley tourer return.

'Don't know. Shen Shen has gone to sulk with her superiority complex,' Ah Ma said proudly, in English, as she watched me change into day clothes.

She looked much better this morning and had clearly been up for some time.

'Inferiority complex,' I corrected.

'Superiority,' Ah Ma said. 'Despising people she feels are above her.'

'Okay, not bad.'

'What do you mean, not bad? My English good, okay! Where did you go whole day yesterday?'

I wouldn't mention the grave-clearing because it felt like telling tales on Shen Shen – where had she gone on the Third

Day if not to clear the graves as she'd said? – and I didn't want to do that, especially if she was pregnant. Pregnant women were allowed to get away with things because their primary mission was to keep safe the baby inside them.

I still wasn't sure Shen Shen had a baby coming. Parshanti had tried to teach me to distinguish between pregnant women and those who were just fat but I still wasn't good at it. I was sure Ah Ma knew – but, being Ah Ma, she wouldn't talk about a coming grandchild until she'd held it in her arms. But I was more and more sure that Fancy was right about the pregnancy. In her line of work she would be able to spot it easily. Still, why had Shen Shen been spending so much time with Fancy that she'd noticed, even if she'd not confided in her?

Instead I said, 'Harry Palin is trying to track down his sister. He's very worried about her. She hasn't been seen since Fancy put her on a boat to Australia.'

'Fancy's daughter died just before the Japanese came,' Ah Ma said. She shook out the two pieces of my *samfoo*. She'd taken them into the house for the night even though the cloth was still damp to the touch: if you left clothing outside overnight it might tempt spirits to dress in it and do mischief. 'Still wet. I'll take it outside. It was one of those fire-bombing planes blowing up people's houses. Boom! And then the fire. Next thing you know, the whole house has gone. That's what Fancy said. She put the girl's body to bury with the dead soldiers because the father was one of the soldiers. Also dead.'

I remembered the Japanese fire-bombers. If the explosions didn't kill you, smoke would from the fire after the bombing. At least it was a merciful death compared to what the girls taken alive by the Japanese had suffered.

'That boy Harry should go back to England and marry a nice girl. The weather here is not good for him. Too hot.'

That was impossible for so many reasons. But I couldn't help smiling when I remembered how good Harry had felt, how well he'd slept in the car – after months of insomnia, he'd said – after his work at the cemetery.

'Why are you smiling?' Ah Ma was scrutinising me.

'Nothing. Have you had breakfast? I'm hungry!'

There was leftover lotus root and peanut soup the servants had made yesterday. They had been at their own homes for Chinese New Year but they had come to visit us and Ah Ma had taught them to make the soup, which was traditional for this time of year.

Of course, lotus roots can be cooked at any time and we grew them in our fish pond so they were always available to us, but during Chinese New Year they were especially important: lotus roots signify abundance, and when paired with peanuts that signify wealth, the soup would bring us good fortune all year. Ah Ma trained all of the servants in this and much more, just as she'd taught me. Whether they went on working or ended up running their own families, those girls would cook and manage households better for their time working at Chen Mansion.

Lotus roots were not easy to clean, with their many passages. After they had been scrubbed and peeled, the insides needed to be flushed. The soup had continued simmering all day on a few glowing chunks of charcoal because there wasn't enough space in the refrigerator for the huge pot.

'What did they use for stock?'

'There was no pork or chicken so we used dried anchovies and dried squid from the store shed.' Ah Ma had been up early, cleaning and turning on lamps in dark corners. She wasn't in great shape but she was better than she'd been a couple of days ago.

The Fifth Day of Chinese New Year is when the god of wealth and good fortune comes to visit. Some believe it's not good to leave the house empty on the Fifth Day, in case the god, finding no one at home, gives away all your household wealth to your neighbours. All the lights must to be turned on and you should look through all your jewellery and most precious possessions to value them, thus inviting more to come to you.

It's also the day to ignore and discard your bad luck.

Too bad for us: bad luck came to our house just after eleven o'clock in the morning, delivered by the police.

This time the police motor-car delivered Robert Johnson and Mike Fahey.

'You knew Fancy Ang, didn't you?'

'She's an old friend,' Uncle Chen said. 'Yes, we know her. Why?'

'No, you don't,' Shen Shen said. 'You didn't know her. It was that friend of yours, Botak. He knew her and told you about her.'

'We know who Fancy Ang is,' Ah Ma said. 'She is not a close friend. What did she say about us? Why did she send you here?'

'She's dead,' Johnson said. 'She was killed in her rooms some time last night. What have you got to say about that?'

My first thought was that Harry had bluffed me. He hadn't been as tired as he'd pretended, and once Le Froy had left him in his rooms he'd returned to Desker Road to find Fancy and kill her. After all, Harry believed Fancy had done something to the sister he'd sworn to protect, and the Palin family had already produced at least one murderer, as I remembered from my first encounter with them under the frangipani tree. Whether murderous tendencies were passed on by nature or nurture, Harry Palin had been exposed to both.

Then I woke up to the fact that the police were asking why I'd gone to Desker Road to see Fancy late last night or early that morning.

'I went to see her there yesterday, yes, but in the daytime, not last night. And she was fine when I left.'

I didn't know if mentioning that Le Froy had been there and we'd both seen Fancy alive would help. Likely it would just drag him into this and make things worse.

'What were you doing there?' Uncle Chen demanded. 'You cannot go to places like that! Did the woman take you there?'

'It wasn't me,' I said. 'I wasn't there last night.'

'Another dead body and you on the scene again,' Fahey said. 'You can't keep blaming it on coincidence.'

'Who says I was there?'

Fahey looked at Johnson. The detective chief seemed uncharacteristically subdued. I realised he was intimidated. Chen Mansion was doing it. He'd expected to drag me out of some slum. I was surprised Fahey hadn't warned him. Fahey had been here before and knew what to expect.

Robert Johnson pulled out a scrap of cloth. 'Proof,' he said. 'Proof that you were there and did it. The woman managed to tear off a piece of her attacker's clothes. Fahey here recognised the cloth. Seems some fellows pay quite a bit of attention to what their hookers are wearing.'

I looked to Fahey who was studying the porcelain vases and figurines on the glassed-in teak shelves. He'd triggered this visit (I didn't want to call it an arrest) but was acting as if it hadn't been his idea and he was on a social visit.

Le Froy had told me Mike Fahey was a good man. Well, his good man had just got me into trouble. But the material did look familiar. In fact, it was almost exactly the same as the cloth from Ah Ma's ceremonial batik sarongs that had been cut down to make *samfoo*s for Little Ling and me.

'Same cloth, eh?' Johnson looked intimidated but stubborn. 'Same cloth, same killer. We got you this time, Miss Slippery. We're going to take you in and get you sorted out in a nice cell.'

'No, wait,' I said. I was still trying to wrap my thoughts around the fact that Fancy was dead. 'She can't be dead, I just saw her. And I wasn't even wearing that *samfoo* when I went there.'

'Anyone else have access to your clothing, Miss?' Fahey asked.

'What? No, of course not. I mean, my family here, but—'

'Could we see the outfit this piece of cloth comes from?'

'I get for you,' Ah Ma said quickly. If she was speaking English in front of the police she must be worried too. Or times really were changing.

As Ah Ma left the formal living room where the police had assembled us, it felt as though my last anchor was leaving. It was all superstition, of course. But, more than ever before, I felt as if Death was following me around, killing everyone I encountered. First Botak and now Fancy – not so much every person I met as everyone who irritated me.

Ah Ma returned with the blouse and pants of my Chinese New Year *samfoo*. They were dry but still crumpled from washing.

I held them up and showed the policemen that no piece was missing.

'This can't be your only fancy outfit,' Johnson said, without really looking at it. 'We need to search the place.'

Fahey took the blouse from me and examined it closely. 'This is the same material.'

'It's very common cloth,' I lied. 'Everybody wears it. Especially for the new year.'

Luckily they didn't know much about batik and accepted that.

'Poor people's cloth,' Johnson said. 'You can see it's all bits and pieces joined together. Falls apart if you so much as look at it.'

Johnson took my poor top from Fahey and yanked at a sleeve. Sure enough, he ripped the stitches. 'Fahey, you're a fool. Look, it's not even the same pattern. It looks the same but it's not. You don't know anything about women and their clothes, do you?'

'This is batik cloth, isn't it?' Fahey took back the blouse. 'You dye the colours over wax. Time-consuming. This wouldn't have been cheap.' He handed it back to me. 'There's no way you would have got the blood out of this. Sorry to have troubled you.'

I barely had time to register this and feel relief when Johnson said, 'We're taking you in for questioning anyway. Don't be a fool, Fahey. We made this bloody trip. We need to log a suspect.'

I thought I was going to be arrested and charged with murder. You wouldn't expect anyone to believe my word against that of a European – a policeman at that. But Fahey surprised me.

'Get over the hangover first,' he told Johnson. Then, to me, 'You may have to come in for a couple more interviews.'

'Now, look here! Who do you think you're talking to? I'm in charge here!'

'Hello?' Le Froy had arrived and let himself in without any of us hearing him. 'What's going on?'

'Nothing to do with you,' Johnson said. 'Police business. We're taking this suspect in. Murder case. None of your business, *Mr* Le Froy.'

'Dr Leask heard the police were coming here, so I thought I'd join the party,' Le Froy said. He came to stand between me and Ah Ma, facing the two policemen. In body language, he was saying he was on our side. 'I thought you might like to have a lawyer on standby.'

'What lawyer?' Johnson sneered.

Le Froy put up his hand. 'I haven't used my law degree since my pre-police days but I still have it.'

'You're full of surprises.' But Johnson seemed uncertain how to proceed. 'Fahey? This was all your stupid idea.'

'We checked a lead. We learned the material found with the victim is a common Chinese New Year fabric popular with locals.'

'Well, see that you write it up and have the report on my desk.' Johnson stormed out.

I couldn't understand why Sergeant Fahey was being so nice. I watched him, waiting for the gag, the big punchline, but nothing happened. In fact, when he saw me looking in his direction, he flashed a small grin, then headed out after Johnson.

Johnson's departure was spoiled by his having to wait in the light drizzle for Fahey to unlock the passenger door of the car for him.

'Can we give anyone a lift into town?' Fahey looked at me. 'Unless there are neighbours with vans going in the same direction, we've got room.'

So he had been hanging around to see Nasima drive me into town. I did want to go as I needed to see Mrs Shankar – I hadn't tried on my bridesmaid's dress – but I was not going to drive in with the police. Besides, Le Froy was there. 'Thanks, we're fine,' I said.

Le Froy stood beside me till their car turned out of the driveway. I don't know if he expected them to grab me and throw me into the back seat at the last minute.

'What did you do to Sergeant Fahey?' I asked Le Froy.

'Why? What did he tell you?'

'Nothing. He was just behaving strangely, that's all.'

Le Froy raised his eyebrows. I remembered that from the old days in the Detective Shack: what seems strange to you may be normal behaviour to someone else. Fitting in, going undercover, isn't about doing what you normally do but what appears normal to those you don't want to notice you.

'Strangely,' I said, 'he didn't say anything rude or vulgar. He was almost nice.'

'Strange,' Le Froy agreed. 'I told him we solved problems together, but I trust you already know that.'

Le Froy was seeing Fahey as an underdog, I realised. Until now it had been our locals he'd supported against the Home Office.

'He's still picking on me,' I said. 'He pointed me out as a suspect.'

'Your fancy *samfoo* was placed at two murder scenes by various witnesses. You can't blame the man for trying to find out more about you,' Le Froy said.

'So Dr Leask dispatched them after me with the cloth, then sent you to the rescue?'

'He heard they were coming here after he sent them the dead woman's effects. It seems there are some bumps in his love life, so he's cheering himself up in the morgue.'

Another thing I was neglecting: Parshanti, and how she was doing, but I was sure her problems didn't measure up to mine.

Le Froy at Chen Mansion

———◆———

'Police demon, why haven't you come after us for so long?' Uncle Chen said, when we went back inside. It was as though Le Froy had just arrived. He had decided to ignore the less pleasant policemen. 'Happy New Year! Have you eaten yet? Come and have a drink!'

I saw Le Froy's shock as he registered how much weight Uncle Chen had lost. He glanced at me, as though wondering if I'd noticed too, and there was anger I didn't understand. But it was gone in the next instant and he turned back to answer Uncle Chen in Hokkien: 'Small Boss Chen, good to see you again. Happy New Year!'

Le Froy and Uncle Chen had had a cordial cat-and-mouse relationship in the old days when Uncle Chen had run a pawn shop and informal (i.e. illegal) money-lending business from his small shophouse in town. He had started selling tools and spare mechanical parts but he and Shen Shen had gone on to stock everything from shoe soles, dress materials, hat trimmings and medicinal roots to dried and canned foods.

Also, once Uncle Chen had become the official head of the Chen family, as my late father Big Boss Chen's only surviving brother, the authorities probably saw him as the focal point of illegal gang activity. Le Froy was one of the few who'd realised my grandmother was really calling the shots.

'You're all wet!' Little Ling said gleefully. 'Your *samfoo* is so wet it's all sticking to you!'

It had started raining in earnest but we hadn't hurried in. The fat warm raindrops made me feel better, as if they were washing away Johnson's accusations. I remembered how much I'd loved playing in the rain when I was Little Ling's age.

'You'd better go and change,' Ah Ma said. 'And dry your hair. Or else you'll be sure to fall sick.'

'I used to go swimming in the *longkang* and dry off in the sun,' I said. 'I'm not going to be ill from getting wet.'

'Can I go swimming in the *longkang*?' Little Ling asked.

'No,' we all said, except Shen Shen, who said, 'Why must you set her a bad example?'

'Were you serious about being a lawyer?' I asked Le Froy. 'When?'

'I got my degree while I was recovering from a gunshot injury, thanks to a case involving a very important judge's son-in-law. The judge was impressed by my knowledge of the law and smoothed the way for me. I took the exams, of course.'

With his memory, they wouldn't have been a problem for him.

'So he helped you because you got his son-in-law off? Was it a murder case?'

'He helped me because I made sure his son-in-law was convicted of murder.'

'Ah. So now you're here as a lawyer instead of a policeman.'

'I'm here as a friend,' Le Froy said. 'I would like to help you with your problems. And I need your help with mine.'

'Sit down, police demon,' Uncle Chen said. 'Drink tea with us. How can we help you?'

'It's about rambutans,' Le Froy said. 'Yellow rambutans.'

We ended up sitting around the worn wooden table in the kitchen, where the stools were more comfortable and Ah Ma could listen in as she fussed over the cooker.

'Rambutans?' I asked.

Le Froy nodded. 'Do you remember the scraps of dried rambutan skin Dr Leask found in Botak Beng's pockets? The ones that looked as if they'd been boiled? How did you know they were yellow? And then at Fancy Ang's place, there were yellow rambutans on her altar. I'm sure you noticed?'

I had. And now I was seeing Ah Ma's back stiffen on learning I'd been at Fancy Ang's place with Le Froy.

'Why are the police worrying about yellow rambutans?' Uncle Chen asked. 'Did the police ask you to find out?'

I knew Le Froy. It was because the official police had dismissed it as irrelevant that he suspected it meant something.

'Not the police. *I'm* trying to find out. I know rambutans are in season. But no matter how I try, I can't find any yellow ones for sale. I just wonder if you know where to find the yellow rambutan trees.'

'Yellow rambutans are mostly harvested from the jungle,' Uncle Chen said. '*Kuning* rambutan are not easy to grow. There's no guarantee they'll come out yellow. I can't remember the last time I saw any. You very seldom see them, these days.'

Yellow rambutans might be seldom seen but I'd seen them in a dead man's mouth and on a dead woman's altar.

'They're supposed to be more cooling than red rambutans,' Ah Ma contributed. 'Some people believe they're more powerful in traditional medicines. But that's the fruit, not the skin. Nobody uses the skin and seeds. They're poisonous. Even goats and monkeys are smart enough not to eat them.'

'Botak's ma used the seeds to make candles and soap,' Uncle Chen remembered. 'She boiled them down into this thick soup and used it when there wasn't any animal fat.'

'Animal fat?' Little Ling asked.

'Yes. When your baba was small his baba would save the pork fat after killing a pig to make soap and candles.'

'Come on,' Shen Shen said to Little Ling. 'Time to wash.'

'I don't want to wash with pork fat!'

As soon as Little Ling had gone I said, 'Tell us what happened to Fancy.'

'Why don't you tell me what you know about her first?' Le Froy suggested.

'We already told the police we haven't had anything to do with her . . .' I started.

To my surprise, Ah Ma came to the table and sat, drying her hands on a tea-towel. 'I already told her we're not renting to her any more. In three months' time her lease finishes and we're selling the block. She must move out before then. She kept trying to bargain and bully. Tried to say that my son wants her to stay and he should make the decision. She also said she can earn more money than any other tenants and if we don't rent to her she will *sabo* and make sure we all go down with her.'

I was shocked. 'You mean you own that building? You own buildings on Desker Road? I thought you didn't like Fancy Ang! I was sure you didn't.'

Le Froy didn't seem surprised. I turned on him. 'You knew? Why didn't you tell me?'

He didn't need to remind me this was my family we were talking about.

'I remember Fancy from the old days, when she went after my boys,' Ah Ma said. 'She went after all the boys. I'm not judging her. She couldn't help it. Like if you're a cobbler, you look at everybody's feet. It's natural. But I kept my boys away from her. She got a better man than she deserved but then she ran away from him. Ended up with that *ang moh* lieutenant and had a daughter. He was also a better man than she deserved. Then the Japanese came. But even before they came, Fancy was running around with Japanese officers.'

'You can't blame people for what they did during the war to survive,' Uncle Chen said. 'Staying alive was the only important thing.'

'Fancy was talking to Shen Shen about the rental properties,' Ah Ma said, lowering her voice with one eye on the kitchen door. 'Shen Shen has been talking to me about how we don't have to do anything except rent to Fancy for her girls to use the rooms. Much less trouble than gambling – for that you need a big space for a big number of people who get into fights. These will be quiet, private spaces.'

I knew Shen Shen had been trying to talk Ah Ma into some new business, though they'd never discussed it in front of me. That's the problem with these old houses built for maximum ventilation. Wind carries words.

I'd heard her saying things like, 'It's going to happen anyway. And somebody is going to get the money. Why not us?'

I could understand Shen Shen's point of view. It should have been mine too – but I couldn't focus on the importance of making money.

'Why did you decide to stop renting to Fancy?' Le Froy asked. 'Is it about the new permits?'

'Shen Shen is very angry about your decision,' Uncle Chen said. 'She's just trying to grow the business. She says you shouldn't judge Fancy for doing the only work she knows how to do.'

'I don't judge her. But it's dangerous for us to rent to her. The government and the Military Authority will use it as an excuse to steal everything we've got. Everything is changing,' Ah Ma said. 'I have to make sure my granddaughters can run the business I leave them. Even if it is worthless. What is the use if we've got this big business and the British change their laws and grab everything? You can't trust the *ang mohs* who are running things. They change the rules, change the laws. If they don't like you, they have you arrested.'

Ah Ma had said this a hundred times before, but this time she was saying it to Le Froy. She was talking to him as though he was one of us.

'So tell us, police demon, what happened to Fancy Ang?'

'Fair enough,' Le Froy said. 'Fancy had a visitor yesterday afternoon. She sent all her girls away, saying she had big plans. She was arranging their future. A couple of them stayed to spy, thinking she was bringing in men to marry them off. Rich old men, they said. They wanted to see how ugly and how old the men were. But they saw her letting a Chinese woman in.'

He looked at me.

'It wasn't me,' I said. 'I was with you all of yesterday afternoon.'

Neither Ah Ma nor Uncle Chen looked shocked by this. I was beginning to feel like the class ignoramus.

'They didn't get a good look at her face, and remember nothing about her other than her *samfoo*. Very striking material, they said. Colourful, with gold highlights.'

I saw why Johnson and Fahey had paid us that visit.

'That's really all there is. No one saw anything until her girls found her this morning. It would have been reported earlier, except Chief Detective Johnson didn't get in to work till almost eleven and the others aren't authorised to go out without his permission.'

'Leask hadn't done the autopsy when he came to me. Stab wounds, blood loss, shock. That was all he would say.'

'But it's Fancy and she's dead,' I said.

'Yes.'

'Does he think the same person killed Botak?'

'A bit messier. It looks like Botak's death was a lucky strike. This took a few more.'

It was an ugly picture.

'She was here with Botak the other day,' I remembered. 'But she didn't stay long.'

'Why didn't you say so earlier?' Le Froy demanded.

'It had nothing to do with Botak getting killed . . . did it?'

Again I saw Le Froy debate how much to say. He had a mission but no team, which limited his reach unless he could bring in outside help.

'I think Botak might have agreed to transport something out for Brigadier Evans. Evans would have felt safe going to him because Botak transported it in for him three years ago. I believe that's what the brigadier has his people searching for. The usual warehouses near ports and along rivers have already been searched. But I have a feeling they're not going to find anything other than food and drugs if the brigadier paid for special transport. Can you think where Botak might have stored his most important, most secret cargo?'

'How big? How much space?' Uncle Chen asked.

'Not so big.' Le Froy gestured a two-foot-square cube. 'Mostly papers.'

'He used to keep all his most valuable goods at his ma's place because she guarded them better than any men he hired,' Ah Ma said. 'But she's dead. Nobody lives at that old place now.'

'Where is the old place?' Le Froy asked.

After he left, I was glad Le Froy hadn't brought up the subject of me going to study in the UK. It wasn't simply what Ah Ma would say about it. I needed to think it through, whether I really wanted to do it and where it would lead, and it was hard to think about it clearly when Le Froy was around.

I'd always wanted to go to England. It was our Promised Land, where all the stories in our English readers were set. The only problem came when I realised that once I was in England I wouldn't be walking among daffodils with my poet brother, like Dorothy Wordsworth, or wandering the moors like Cathy Earnshaw with my Heathcliff. I would be stared at as an oddity.

The new year so far had left me exhausted. Luckily there was still some leftover soup on the stove and Shen Shen cooked some rice so we had a simple dinner.

'There's a funny taste,' I said.

'They didn't remove the peanut skins but it gives quite a nice rich colour,' Ah Ma said. She took a mouthful. 'It tasted all right earlier. Maybe I boiled it too long.'

'It tastes a bit like medicinal soup,' I said. 'There's bitterness.'

'Your friend that Muslim girl brought some soup for you,' Shen Shen said. 'I wanted to return her pot to her so I just added it to what we had.'

Two soups might each be delicious on their own but still not work together as one. Sometimes I wondered how Shen Shen could be so dense.

'Why are you staring at my stomach?' she asked.

'Was I? Sorry.' I still couldn't tell.

I was glad the servants would be back soon. I'd barely managed to finish the washing-up before I crawled onto my mattress. Ah Ma was already asleep in her day clothes. I wondered if Nasima had poisoned us with her soup, as Shen Shen always said she would. I was too tired to think about it or to unroll my mattress. I lay down on the floor, half in the corridor and half in Ah Ma's bedroom, and sank into unconsciousness.

Bad Luck?

———◆———

'Hello? Hello – is anybody in? It's Nasima. Hello?'

I considered staying where I was and saying nothing. Then I realised I couldn't move. I was comfortable on the floor and it made sense to stay there. I must have vomited because there were stomach contents on the floor around me.

'I brought you all some food,' Nasima said.

The thought of more food made my stomach lurch. I moaned softly.

I felt rather than heard Nasima's footsteps come down the dim hallway, her sudden gasp as she saw me. 'Su Lin!'

She looked around and set the *tingkat* on the floor, then came to kneel beside me. 'Su Lin, what happened to you? Did you fall? Where is everybody?'

'I fell asleep,' I said. Suddenly it seemed very funny. I giggled.

'Did someone attack you? Is your grandmother all right? Where is she? Where's your uncle?'

'I'm all right,' I said, waving at her to stay away. 'Don't come nearer. I don't know if I'm sick. We're all sick. I don't know if we're infectious.'

Nasima ignored me. She knelt by me and I felt her cool fingers against my forehead and neck, then pressed against my wrist. We heard Ah Ma in her room, retching painfully.

'When did this start? What did you eat last?'

'I ate your soup and felt sleepy. Did you poison us? Did you come to finish us off?' That seemed very funny too.

'I came to check why there was a padlock on your gate.' Nasima sat back on her heels. 'I came through the hole in the fence. First I'm going to get you into your bed.' She pushed open the door to Ah Ma's room and peered inside, squinting into the deeper darkness as her eyes adjusted. 'On second thoughts, I'm going to get you into the bathroom. We're going to wash. But first I'm going to send for Dr Shankar. I'll be right back.'

'He doesn't see patients any more,' I told her helpfully, but Nasima had gone. Maybe I'd dreamed she had been there. No. The food containers she'd left against the corridor wall remained, giving off a faintly nauseating smell. I'd thought Nasima was my friend. Why had she poisoned us?

Maybe she'd found out that Botak had died because I wouldn't let him into the house. If he'd come inside, no one could have stabbed him in a drain, right? I'd as good as done it myself. But I couldn't have because I didn't have anything to stab him with.

I'd got Fancy killed too, hadn't I, by leading Harry Palin to her? He must have used the parang he'd had in the cemetery to kill Fancy. How had he managed to kill her at the same time as he was clearing the graves, though? With Le Froy and me watching him?

This triggered another line of thought. Should I go to England with Le Froy? But every single person I spent time with died. My mother, my father . . . Ah Ma might be dead in the bedroom now, for all I knew. And, of course, Botak and Fancy.

I was feeling very sick. I just wanted to curl up and not feel anything. Every thought was a bad one. The air was thick with humidity and negativity.

'I sent word to Dr Shankar.' Nasima was back. 'You're all down with something.'

'My grandmother . . .' I tried to get up and failed miserably.

'She's all right for now, she and your uncle. They're worse than you are, but there's nothing I can do. You probably threw up most of it, but they're completely knocked out.'

I trusted Nasima's medical judgement. I knew she had worked with Dr Shankar during the war, in the hospital as well as carrying messages from PoWs that she'd found in the jungle outside the camps. Prisoners pushed them through the barbed wire begging anyone who found them to post them or put them into a bottle in the sea. That was while Dr Shankar was working at the Changi Prison infirmary. He was one of the few with access to the outside world via a shortwave radio that the Japanese had declared illegal. It seemed a lifetime ago.

I felt a strange sensation of déjà vu, as though I'd lived through all this before and more than once, maybe. I also felt horribly nauseous.

'We're going to move you to the bathroom now. Very slowly.'

Nasima was stronger than she looked.

Then I was sitting on the low bath stool, leaning my forehead against the cool wall tiles as Nasima washed me like a baby. That seemed funny too.

'Goo-goo,' I said.

'Rosmah said she saw you,' Nasima said, 'driving the motor-car out of the gate, putting the chain around the gate and padlocking it, then driving off. I know that girl and I know she's not lying to me. But I also know it wasn't you.'

'I drove off? Where did I go?'

'I wish I knew.'

'Did you know Fancy was involved with smuggling people off the island when the Japanese were coming? She came and offered my father passage for my sister and myself. Only us, because it cost double to transport men, unless he was willing to pay. She would take cash in any denomination, gold or jewellery on condition that she could get it valued first.'

'You didn't trust her? Or you didn't want to leave your father?' The warm water was soothing and comforting and it was wonderful to feel clean again.

Nasima had lost her sister and her father during the war, her mother having died some years earlier. I couldn't imagine living with the awareness that her father and sister might still be alive if she had accepted Fancy's offer.

'Where would we go? This is our home, even if some people don't accept us here. It would be the same or worse somewhere else. And, yes, our father didn't trust her. Her people were smugglers. And to them women are a commodity. He could have been paying to sell us into slavery. But he asked us what we wanted and we said, "To stay."'

Nasima reached for a towel and started to dry me. She had a clean housedress and knickers waiting. And talcum powder. It was bliss.

'You shouldn't have to do this,' I said.

'I've done worse,' Nasima said. 'During the Occupation, I boiled used bandages stripped off dead prisoners, – washed, boiled on a bamboo stick, sun-dried and reused.' As she chatted she half lifted, half slid me towards the living room where she'd unfolded my mattress on the floor.

I could see why she'd been such a help to Dr Shankar. War was a terrible thing, but that didn't mean no good could come of it.

'Are you sorry you didn't go?'

'You mean do I wonder if my little sister might still be alive if I hadn't been such a coward? Of course. But who knows? We might both be alive somewhere, wishing we were dead. We just have to get on with what we have now.'

We heard someone knocking on the side of the open door. Because of the heat, most doors were left standing open during the day, to encourage any breeze. After all, closed doors wouldn't stop anyone determined to enter.

'Dr Shankar!' Nasima said, in relief. 'Thank you for coming. I've got Su Lin. Let me show you where Chen Tai and Mr Chen are.'

Dr Shankar hadn't come alone. Mrs Shankar and Parshanti were by my side, hugging and kissing me. I was glad Nasima had got me cleaned up.

'I had a lot of strange dreams,' I said. 'Am I still dreaming?'

Mrs Shankar darted off in response to a summons I hadn't heard. But Parshanti held both of my hands in hers. 'Tell me. But first let's try to drink some water.'

I drank the china spoons of warm water she fed me, then lay back and told her all about my dreams. How I'd seen everyone

– even Ah Ma and Uncle Chen, Parshanti and Nasima – dancing around in my Chinese New Year *samfoos*.

'Shen Shen made them for all of you, as well as for me. I thought she only made them for Little Ling and me, but she made them for everyone.'

'Where is Shen Shen?'

'I don't know. Did you check Little Ling's room? Nowadays Shen Shen sleeps there instead of with my uncle. You know, I dreamed that Shen Shen was talking to Brigadier Evans and she was also wearing my Chinese New Year *samfoo*. She was dancing with him, the waltz, where they hold hands and spin around. And Robert Johnson was there too, dancing with his mother, Mrs Evans.'

'More water,' Parshanti said.

'Shen Shen told the brigadier that she handles all Botak Beng's deals for him because she was Botak's Singapore wife. She said she handled all the deals for the Chen family too. I shouted, "No, she doesn't," but they couldn't hear me. And then Ah Ma got in my way and told me she couldn't die because she had to save her granddaughter from her mother. I told Ah Ma, "I'm here, I'm all right," but she pushed me away. "Not you! I have to save my granddaughter."

'And then I saw Shen Shen again but she was in the cemetery, pouring paint on gravestones and cursing them.'

Dr Shankar appeared. 'Su Lin, your grandmother and uncle are going to sleep for a while but they should be all right. Do you know where your uncle's wife and daughter are?'

'Going by her dreams, either in the cemetery or with Brigadier Evans,' Parshanti said. 'I don't think she knows.'

'Su Lin.' Dr Shankar came to sit on my other side. 'Would anyone want to get your grandmother out of the way? Anyone who owes her money?'

Ah Ma had been 'lending' money for years to people who could not get loans elsewhere. Many of them worked for her in one way or another. Even if they didn't, she likely owned the properties they lived or worked in. Recently she had told them she would cancel interest for the next three years. The money they paid in would go directly towards reducing their debt. If, after three years, it was paid off, she would return their papers and their properties would be theirs.

'Not now,' I said. 'If they did, they would have killed her a long time ago. Only Uncle Chen is angry with her about money now. He told Ah Ma she was throwing it away on ungrateful people.'

I heard Ah Ma retching in her room.

'That's very good to hear,' Dr Shankar said, and headed in that direction.

'Dr and Mrs Shankar will be staying the night here, so I'll go home and check on my girls. I'll see you again tomorrow,' Nasima said. 'Your friend Parshanti will be with you.'

'Poor Parshanti has problems,' I said. That felt hilarious and I said it again. 'My poor pal Parshanti has a pack of petty problems.'

Nasima put a hand on my shoulder and pushed me onto my back. 'Try to sleep it off,' she said.

'My pretty pal Parshanti . . .' I grinned at Parshanti, who had come over on hearing her name.

'Ssh. Try to sleep, Su.'

'No, really, it's true. She loves him and he loves her but she doesn't want to marry him just because everyone wants her to marry him.'

'Ssh! Su!' Parshanti said. 'Sorry,' she said to Nasima.

'Don't be silly,' Nasima said to her. 'No relationship is ever going to be perfect if you're not willing to work on it together. But if you're both willing to commit to it, there's nothing in this life more worth fighting for.'

The passion in her voice and face surprised me. I thought I'd never seen her looking so beautiful and so tragic. If I'd been any kind of artist I would have wanted to paint or photograph her exactly as she was right then.

Parshanti stared at her.

'You're talking about yourself, aren't you?' I heard myself saying happily. And I didn't stop there. 'I know it's not my business. It must be the food poisoning or the medicine acting on my head.'

Nasima laughed at me. 'It's probably the medicine in your system. You sound like you're drunk!'

'If this is how it feels when you're smoking opium, no wonder people smoke it. But whoever you're in love with, he's a fool if he doesn't love you back. You're so beautiful and wise and kind. He's a fool not to choose you.'

'Yes, he was a fool,' Nasima said. Even in the darkened room I saw the gleam of tears in her eyes. 'A sweet, noble, brave fool of a hero. The only thing I regret is not dying with him. But I kept hoping he would be found. By the time I knew for certain he was dead, I had to stay alive for him, so someone would remember him.'

'So as long as it's heartbreak and not death Parshanti's worried about, she should go ahead,' I said, and giggled.

'If you weren't already half dead I'd kill you,' Parshanti said. 'Sorry,' she told Nasima. 'My pa says there's drugs in her system. She might be seeing monsters and murderers so we're lucky she's just talking rubbish.'

'We're always facing death.' Nasima smiled at me, not seeming at all offended. 'That's one good lesson the war taught us. May we never forget it. I'll see you tomorrow.'

I saw Parshanti stand up and give Nasima a hug as she passed her. It was a good sign. It seemed hilarious. I laughed at them and they laughed too, but they also seemed to be crying.

Our Old Selves

———◆———

I floated on the shoreline of sleep for most of the night, occasionally drifting into dreams that surprised me with how obvious the solution was to my dilemma, only I could never remember the answer when I woke.

Every time I surfaced, though, it seemed someone was sitting by my side with water, telling me to go back to sleep. Dr Shankar was there most of the time too, back to his old self, prescribing more liquids, testing, probing and questioning. One of the others usually sent him away, saying, 'Wait until she's feeling better.'

Best of all I felt safe, in a way I hadn't in a long, long time.

Mrs Shankar had taken over the household, scolding everyone, but she was gentle with Ah Ma and me. It was Mrs Shankar who helped Ah Ma walk out to the living room because she insisted on seeing me herself.

'When are you going to give this girl her own room and own bed, Aunty?' I heard Mrs Shankar ask Ah Ma, as she walked her back to her bedroom.

I could tell Dr Shankar was more worried about Uncle Chen than he wanted to say. He'd been the worst affected, and it had taken him longest to come round. Dr Shankar had wanted to take Ah Ma and Uncle Chen into the hospital but Dr Leask persuaded him that we were probably better off in Chen Mansion under his care.

'They're short on beds, short on staff, short on medicine, short on functioning equipment. Plus you aren't on the staff there and, I swear to you, there's no one on the staff in the military or public hospital that's up to your standard. I'm probably their best guy right now and, well, between the two of us, who would you trust your loved ones to?'

Dr Shankar looked flattered and doubtful. 'Are you trying to tell me my daughter's not safe with you?'

It was meant to be a joke but it fell flat. Neither Parshanti nor Dr Leask laughed and Mrs Shankar muttered something in her Scottish dialect, which made her husband slink away to check on his other patients. It was so comforting having Mrs Shankar scolding and fussing over me, just as she had when I was a child visiting Parshanti.

And I was very glad to have some time with Parshanti, but it was difficult to talk to her about her getting married when Dr Leask and her parents were around.

'Would you like to try to eat something?' Mrs Shankar suggested.

She and her husband had been into town and returned carrying so many bags and bundles you'd think they were moving into Chen Mansion. Only it was mostly Mrs Shankar's food with a few of Dr Shankar's preparations.

'I don't know,' I said. 'I'm hungry but I can't keep anything down.'

'*Aiyoh*, I know *lah*, my girl told me,' Mrs Shankar said in Singlish and English. 'I was thinking it sounded like something in your water supply so I made a batch of *makan* to keep you going.'

'*Makan*, in Singlish, covers all manner of food from raw peanuts to elaborate multi-course meals. From what Mrs Shankar handed to Nasima, she'd inclined towards the latter.

'Hello, dear,' this to Nasima, who was standing protectively beside the camp bed they'd brought in for me. 'The food's not halal but there's no pork in anything so please help yourself.'

'I think someone is trying to poison them,' Nasima said.

Mrs Shankar stopped in the middle of unwrapping something. Her mouth stayed open for a moment before she looked down at the covered bowl she was holding. 'This is just kidney beans with onions and tomatoes. It's to go with the white rice I also brought. I'm sure it's safe.'

'Ssh.' Dr Shankar took the bowl from her and put it down. 'Why do you say that?' he asked Nasima. He didn't seem surprised. Just curious.

'Well, someone's been drugging them,' she said. 'The slurred speech, clumsiness, fatigue ... If it was from an infection I would expect a high fever but they have no fever.'

I giggled. 'That's why, when I got food poisoning and couldn't eat anything, I actually got better. Food poisoning saved me.'

'Yes, it did,' Dr Shankar said, with a smile. 'There are other possible explanations but I doubt you're drunk.' I saw him look questioningly at his wife.

'No sign of her or the child,' she said. 'I checked with the hospital, with the police, no reports of any accidents.' She smiled at me. 'Le Froy's been following up on a lot of things, but he'll be coming over to see you as soon as he can. He's been so worried and all the more determined to get to the bottom of this awful business.'

'What awful business?'

'I'll wait till Le Froy gets here,' Dr Shankar said.

They helped me to Ah Ma's room so I could lie beside her on her bed for a while. Being together did us both good. Though still feeble, Ah Ma took my hand in hers and held it tight.

'No word about Shen Shen?'

'No, Ah Ma.'

'I meant well, you know. I thought I was doing her family a favour by marrying her to your uncle.'

I knew Ah Ma had written off Shen Shen's family's debts after the marriage. After her family had been wiped out during the Occupation, Ah Ma had bought her family's farm. 'She thinks her family sold her to Uncle Chen in exchange for their farm. We own the farm but we shouldn't own her.'

'Shen Shen told you that?' I couldn't believe it.

'I heard her telling Little Ling.' Ah Ma shifted on the bed. 'She was talking to me through Little Ling. I told her, I don't mind her saying anything to me, but don't get my granddaughter involved. But you know Shen Shen. She said she was only talking to her daughter. Can't she say what she likes to her?'

'Why is she so angry with us?' I asked.

'I don't know. After your father found his wife, I wanted my second son to marry a good Chinese girl. And Shen Shen's family owed us money so I thought it would make everyone happy. I did this to your uncle.'

'Don't blame yourself. I think Shen Shen started getting angry with us when you wouldn't throw me out of the house.'

Ah Ma squeezed my fingers tight. 'She was testing me. You are my son's child. I will never tell you to go.'

Le Froy's car came up the drive at just after two that afternoon. He ran up the front steps and into the living room faster than I thought any man could, whether on one or two feet.

It was so good to see him again. After the blur of sickness and nightmares I'd begun to think I'd only imagined he was back. He was also very angry. It wasn't directed at anyone in the room: it was anger as energy, the only thing keeping him going. Apart from that, I thought Le Froy looked, if anything, worse than I did. I suspected he hadn't been to bed at all since I'd last seen him.

He limped into the house and sat down next to my camp bed with concern in his eyes but without a word. His exhaustion was almost palpable. I wanted to get up and offer him the bed. He reached over to lay a hand on my shoulder and I knew everything was going to be all right.

Mrs Shankar came into the living room. Seeing him, she turned without a word and made for the kitchen. I knew she was going to fetch coffee.

'How?' Dr Shankar said.

'Alive,' Le Froy said.

I'd known them long enough to interpret the exchange as:

Dr Shankar: How are things with you?

Le Froy: I'm alive. What else can I say?

Le Froy was massaging his calf just above his ankle. That must be where the prosthesis was attached. 'Not necessarily a good thing.'

I'd been tempted to use my withered leg as an excuse to step out of this but now I smacked myself mentally and told myself to get on with it. If the man could carry on with a foot missing I could manage with my crooked leg. And I'd had a lifetime to get used to my handicap whereas Le Froy was still adapting to his.

'Is it bothering you? Can I have a look?' Dr Shankar had noticed too. He started towards Le Froy then stopped, looking at me.

'Would you like me to leave the room?' I raised an arm but couldn't get to my feet. I was absurdly reminded of the old women sitting in rows weeping and moaning in pain as their servants unwrapped and washed their bound feet. The exquisite three-inch 'golden lotus' and four-inch 'silver lotus' were hideously blistered flesh and deformed bones hidden within their tiny decorative shoes. That was why men were never allowed to see the actual process, even though in their day no respectable man would have married a woman with healthy feet.

'Never mind,' Le Froy said. He might have been speaking to either of us and perhaps he was. 'The release needs to be easier,' he said. 'Getting it off – not to mention out of the trouser leg – I might have to figure out a song-and-dance act to keep people occupied while I'm doing it. But no matter.'

'It needs to be secure,' Dr Shankar said. 'No matter what other purpose it serves, it must function as a support.' Then he looked at me. 'I could fit you with a brace, Su Lin. You're not likely to grow much taller than you are now. If we use it to stabilise your hip it would give your back further support.'

For years, Dr Shankar had been coming up with various leg braces and other gadgets designed to help me walk with more stability. I'd always avoided them. I looked weird enough as I was, without any additional contraptions. But I appreciated his attempts even as I shook my head. 'Thank you, Uncle. But no need.'

Dr Shankar turned back to Le Froy, 'If I could just make sure it's not fixed too tight . . .'

'Not now.' Le Froy waved him off. 'Too much to do. I just wanted to see your patient for myself, but I should be away.'

'You should try roller skates,' I said. 'You told me a roller skate would help me go faster.' Like everything around me now, this seemed hilarious.

'Roller skates,' Le Froy said. His face was still drawn from the pain but he laughed, too, and winked at me. 'Maybe we should both get on roller skates.'

'Don't laugh,' said Dr Shankar. 'Such things may well come to pass.' But he accepted that neither of us was interested in contraptions offering hope we couldn't afford. (It wasn't the contraptions: if I'd thought anything might work I'd have found a way. I just couldn't afford to risk hoping for anything.)

Now that we needed him, some of Dr Shankar's old self was returning. Once the friendliest and most dedicated of doctors, he hadn't reopened his practice after the war ended. He occasionally treated an old patient, but as a favour more than as a doctor. I hoped he would reopen his pharmacy and photo print shop again soon. After the Japanese Occupation, I was sure locals and *ang mohs* alike would go to him for treatment. He'd been treating so many people for free during the war when they'd had no other recourse.

But I could also understand Dr Shankar's prickly detachment. After all, what difference had it made that the British were back? There was still little food and little hope. We were just bowing to different masters.

But now it seemed the old Dr Shankar was resurfacing. 'Any sign of Chen's wife?'

'Not yet. How are the others doing?'

'The old lady's going to be all right. She's strong. We'll have to wait till she flushes it out of her system but she should get her balance and coordination back. This one's going to be all right too, as you can see.' He smiled at me.

I grinned back at him.

'Seeds of morning glory,' Dr Shankar said. 'Poisonous. Deadly if taken in sufficient quantities, and in this case combined with rat poison. You'd have thought it would finish them off but instead the poisons counteracted and neutralised each other. We were very, very lucky. Overkill turned into underkill.'

That struck me as hilarious. 'Underkill! Because Ah Ma told us morning-glory seeds were very poisonous. She was only warning Shen Shen not to let Little Ling eat them.'

'Also hallucinogenic.'

'Yes. Leask said you wanted to tell me something?' Le Froy asked Dr Shankar.

'Ah. You've been asking around about the dead woman – Leask's latest project?'

'Fancy Ang, yes?'

'I just thought you might be interested. She approached me several times, before and after the war, about getting her opium prescriptions. She offered me the company of her lady friends as perks.'

'You?' I asked. 'What did you do?' Fancy wasn't easy to shake off.

'I pretended not to understand. It's easier and less tiring to be stupid than to be moral. And I know that she was peddling so called "treatments" for sexually transmitted diseases at exorbitant prices. All snake oil, of course. It's charlatans like her who give pharmacists, herbalists and traditional medicine practitioners a bad name. But people still went to her because they believed she knew the facts of life. Rubbish!'

'I've heard about that,' Le Froy said.

'She came to me just a week ago. Said if I changed my mind to send a runner to her any time. And wanted to know whether anyone from this household,' Dr Shankar jerked his head to indicate Chen Mansion, 'had come to me for assistance in terminating a pregnancy. I wouldn't have told her if I had, of course. I didn't answer her. Saying no would have been as much a betrayal of privacy as yes.'

'Shen Shen,' I said. 'Fancy told me Shen Shen was pregnant, but I didn't know whether to believe her.'

'Where is she?' Le Froy asked.

'We'd all like to know,' Dr Shankar said. 'I have quite a few questions for her myself.'

'Eat,' Mrs Shankar said. She was carrying a tray with *roti* and a wonderful-smelling curry. Behind her, Parshanti had brought mugs of local-style coffee – I could smell the roasted beans from where I was.

'Enough for everybody,' Mrs Shankar said.

Suddenly I was starving.

'Remember to drink water,' Dr Shankar said. 'Coffee isn't enough to hydrate you.'

Sixth Day:
Two Places At Once

———◆———

It was the morning of the Sixth Day of Chinese New Year, and what a year it had been so far.

Some believe the Sixth Day is when the god of sanitation runs checks for his annual reports, so people clean and put flowers in their bathrooms and WCs. I've always found this one harder to believe than the others. After all, back in the days when all these customs started, did they even have WCs? Weren't they all squatting over holes dug in the ground or buckets designated for collecting manure to be used as fertiliser?

Anyway, it's the day we're supposed to make sure our bathrooms and WCs are clean, so that the report that goes up to Heaven is positive. It's also the day we throw away old clothes and worn-out equipment as 'waste'.

I loved our modern sewage system. We had a seated flush WC installed just off Uncle Chen and Shen Shen's room, and there were the squatting cubicles between the kitchen and vegetable gardens that the rest of us used. I would give them a token clean.

Ah Ma was still in bed with shaky legs and poor balance but she was well enough to give orders. 'You must scrub! Don't just splash water!'

Dr Shankar believed that she and my uncle had been being given low doses of rat poison for some time. The culprit had expected the poison to accumulate in their systems but luckily their bodies had managed to expel it, until the last massive dose.

I'd been so afraid Ah Ma was succumbing to old age that finding out she'd been poisoned was almost a relief. Even Uncle Chen was feeling much better. As for me, taking twenty-four hours off had really helped. I just wished I could have done that without being sick.

There wasn't much to be done in the WCs, if the sanitation god didn't mind a faint smell of bleach. Mrs Shankar, our visiting angel, had been at work there too. But I'd needed to get out of the house to think.

The worst wasn't over, even if we had all recovered. Where were Shen Shen and Little Ling? Had my family been poisoned?

What had happened had been possible only because Shen Shen had insisted on sending all the servants away from the house for New Year. Could she really have been planning to poison us all along? I couldn't see any other explanation. How long had she been planning it? And why?

Or perhaps Shen Shen and Little Ling had been kidnapped by some monster who'd poisoned us all.

'Well, you're the one talking nonsense now!'

I heard Parshanti snapping at Leask before I saw them. They'd started quarrelling again, once they were satisfied none of us was going to die.

'Su Lin! Su, we're back. Where are you?'

'Out here.'

Parshanti charged through the house. 'I was just thinking, could any of your father's gangster friends be involved? Someone might be angry with him and taking it out on your family.'

'I don't think so.'

'Or maybe someone killed Botak for wanting to break with your family.'

'Then it wouldn't make sense for them to try to kill Su Lin and her family as well, would it?' Dr Leask appeared, laden with bags.

'Laundry and lunch,' Parshanti explained. 'Ma wanted to make sure there wasn't a germ left alive. Can you believe this fool told me he saw you in town this morning? I told him he was seeing things!'

'I just said I saw someone who looked like you with the brigadier,' Leask said. 'Le Froy's bringing round someone to interview you.'

'No, he's not! He just said he'll be coming round to talk to her, and bringing someone,' Parshanti barked.

'That's what I said.'

'No, you said "interview".'

Parshanti was just picking at Leask. But I couldn't entirely blame her. As Dr Shankar had once said, 'Leask should have been one of those university dons, one of those academics writing papers on things no one else understands. Lots of brains but no idea how to watch out for himself or get along with others.'

Le Froy turned up, at his side the girl with plaits I'd seen outside Fancy's room. And Fahey.

'This is Lily,' Le Froy said. 'You wanted to see her?'

'Why did you bring him?'

Fahey looked awkward. I knew I was being rude, but when you've been throwing up as much as I had, it's hard to be polite about things you don't want around you – even *ang moh* policemen.

'He located the girl,' Le Froy said.

'I'm here officially,' Fahey said. 'She's under my care until we send her home.'

Lily looked more curious than frightened. I guessed she hadn't been in Fancy's business for long.

'One week,' Lily said, when I asked how long she had been in Singapore. 'I wanted to see the big city, but I don't like it. Aunty Fancy said she would give me money if I worked for her but she didn't.'

'What work did you do for her?'

The girl shrugged. 'She was too busy to tell me what to do. She kept saying, "Wait, wait, wait until I have time," and then she went and died.'

'Was this the woman you saw going into Fancy's rooms?' Fahey asked Lily. Lily nodded. 'And him!' She pointed at Le Froy.

So that was why he was here. I gave Le Froy a dirty look. I had almost got hold of what I was trying to work out and didn't need to be distracted by more time-wasting at the Detective

Shack. But Le Froy was watching Fahey talk to Lily so I watched them too.

'On the day that Fancy died? Was this the woman who went to see her and argued with her?'

Lily shook her head.

This was putting a different complexion on things.

'Can you tell me about the woman you saw that day?' I asked Lily.

'Tell you what?'

'Everything you can remember about Fancy and about the woman you heard arguing with her. You're going home, right? If you tell me enough things I will give you some money to take back to your family.'

Fancy had told Lily her own daughter had died, so she needed a girl to watch her door in the daytime. She promised that Lily wouldn't have to entertain men unless she wanted to earn more money, and Fancy would show her how to do that later. Fancy sold love potions, pregnancy potions and anti-pregnancy potions from her rooms. She made them up out of powders she got from the pharmacy and weeds she sent Lily to pick, but she told her customers that all her brews and teas were based on traditional cures. Fancy said the worse her treatments tasted, the more women believed they worked. Women needed to suffer before they allowed themselves to feel better. Men were the opposite. They didn't want anything bitter or unpleasant. They wanted you to do all the work, then give them a pill to swallow and be cured. Fancy said she wasn't cheating people because her medicines worked. If your body believes it will be cured, it cures itself.

Fancy had made pills for men – for things like bed problems and baldness – but not many. Most of her customers were women.

'The woman who argued with Fancy the day she died, had you seen her before?'

Lily had seen the woman the day after she'd arrived. Fancy called her 'Mrs Chen' when she was in the room with her. But once she'd left she called her 'that CB'.

I was glad Le Froy seemed to understand 'CB' and I didn't need to explain it. 'CB' in Singlish could either mean *'chio bu'*, attractive female, or – more likely in this context – be an offensive reference to a certain area of the female anatomy.

'Mrs Chen' had to be Shen Shen. I kept my mouth shut, not wanting to interrupt Lily's flow. Parshanti, who'd come in and sat next to me, gave a little gasp and slipped out of the room.

Le Froy was listening intently, his face impassive. Fahey was scribbling in his notebook. Real notes this time, I hoped. I wondered if Le Froy would warn him that 'CB' was a vulgarity referring to a part of the female anatomy that wouldn't reward enquiries.

The first time Mrs Chen had gone to see Fancy she had been polite. She asked for the medicine Fancy gave her girls to take so that they wouldn't have babies. Fancy asked why, since her husband had already stopped trying to give her another baby.

'*Wah*, Mrs Chen so angry with her! She shouted at Fancy and told her she doesn't know anything and it was none of her business! Then, after Mrs Chen left, I told Fancy my mother said you can boil rambutan skins, especially the yellow ones, to make medicine to get rid of babies. Fancy got very excited and rushed off.'

'When was this?' Le Froy interrupted. 'Why did Fancy get excited? About the yellow rambutan skins causing miscarriages?'

'That was the Third Day of Chinese New Year,' Lily said. 'I remember because that day we had a lot of customers walking around outside. Fancy wouldn't let them in because it would be bad luck. Mrs Chen shouldn't have come. Fancy told me not to let her in, but Mrs Chen banged on the door until I opened it for her.'

Just like Botak had done at our place later.

So that was where Shen Shen had gone instead of the cemetery. She'd gone to ask Fancy for something to get rid of a baby. But why?

'Do you know where Fancy went when she rushed off?'

Lily shrugged. 'She never took me with her. She never took me anywhere. I don't like living in Singapore. But I think she went to see the big *botak* man.'

'What's his name?' Fahey asked.

'Don't know. Fancy called him Botak. He came and gave her some packets and she paid him. And he also brought her yellow rambutans. She told him she would use them for her medicines but we just ate them. Very sweet. Fancy was very smart.'

'Do you think Fancy was pregnant?' Fahey asked.

Lily's storytelling had made her confident enough to scoff at him: 'No, *lah*! She was only sad she wouldn't hold her grandbabies.'

Grandbabies? With her only daughter dead?

Parshanti reappeared with orangeade for a delighted Lily – I was surprised she'd found it in our house – and tea for the rest of us.

'Do you know how Fancy's daughter died?'

Lily helped herself to the pineapple tarts Parshanti put before her. I saw Mrs Shankar and Ah Ma had also slipped into the room to listen. Parshanti must have gone to get them.

'Japanese fire-bombs. But that was early in the war and she got over it. I don't know how. My ma lost my sister ten years ago and she's not over it. Oh! I remember – Fancy said she was going to talk to the baby's father—'

'Wait,' Parshanti whispered to me. 'I think I missed something. What baby is she talking about?'

'The baby Fancy thought Shen Shen was having.'

'What?'

'Ssh – listen.'

'–because a man wouldn't want to bring up a baby on his own,' Lily said, 'but maybe he would pay Fancy if she took care of it for him. That was why Fancy had to see him fast, because she knew he had other wives upcountry and if she didn't get in with her offer fast, he would send the baby to one of them. And increase their monthly allowance.'

'Smuggling is a high-paying profession,' Le Froy observed.

'Makes you reconsider your choices,' Fahey said.

'You want to know a secret?' Lily asked.

Of course we all did. Ah Ma edged her stool closer.

'Fancy had a hold on Mr Botak too. He had someone's little girl staying with him. She found some sweets he'd hidden and ate them all and got sick. He couldn't wake her up so he called Fancy and she couldn't wake her up. Every time he tried to cheat her, she threatened to tell the girl's brother.' Lily laughed.

'That's interesting. What exactly did she say?' Le Froy asked.

'Fancy called her that stupid, stupid girl. She had told her that if she was a good girl Fancy would give her lots of sweets and she promised not to touch anything. Botak had hidden the tin of sweets and didn't know how she found them. Fancy said she was dead before the bombs came down but people like to blame the Japanese for everything so she blamed the Japanese.'

Fancy's daughter Kim was supposed to have died in the Japanese bombing.

But Dee-Dee Palin had loved sweets more than anything.

I felt sick. I knew Lily was talking about Dee-Dee, who might have been slow in some ways but had a sharp slyness and could sense when people were hiding things from her. She'd reminded me of a squirrel or feral dog in how she trusted people to feed her but suspected them of hiding food from her. I knew how cunning she could be when it came to getting what she wanted, and what she wanted most of the time was sweets.

Telling Dee-Dee she would have sweets if she was a good girl but she mustn't touch them otherwise was asking for trouble. Once she found them, she would have eaten them all.

It hadn't been Botak or Fancy who had killed Dee-Dee. It had been the soporific sweets that Harry had prepared so lovingly to protect her on the uncomfortable boat ride she'd never taken.

A fire-bombing just before the invasion was the perfect cover-up. So why hadn't they told Harry his sister had died in the bombing? He would have understood – who could predict where the bombs would fall? – and wouldn't have gone after them. Most likely he would also have vanished quietly and for ever.

I owed them for that at least.

'The ticket issued in the name of Deborah Palin was used,'

I said. 'All Fancy's daughter had to do then was disappear once she got to Australia.'

'That's the name Fancy warned me to watch out for!' Lily said. 'Anyone wanting to see her, just send them up. There's a bell on a string in her room that goes down to where I sit. I pull it once if a woman is coming up to see her, twice if it's a man. But if it's that man Palin I'm supposed to pull it, keep pulling it, and not let him in. That was so that even if I didn't stop him because I'm useless, Fancy had time to go down into one of the girls' rooms and escape. There are planks linking the windows between the houses, you see, so customers can get out if there's an emergency like police or wives or fire.'

'Really,' Fahey said, making a note on a different piece of paper. He seemed to follow Lily's Singapore English without too much trouble.

'She was very proud of the links. Had to get someone to bash through the walls. And after all her work getting it done, the stupid building owner says Fancy's got to move out of all her rooms there.'

I looked at the stupid building owner, whose aghast expression showed she was having trouble following this. The stupid building owner's friend was whispering explanations to her with gestures indicating passage through walls of adjoining units.

'I told Fancy she should get the owner to pay her back for making the passages.'

'Pay her back? You know how much it will cost to repair the walls?' Ah Ma burst out, even though Mrs Shankar was trying to hush her. 'Stupid girl!'

'That's what Fancy said,' Lily said. 'These tarts are very nice. I wish I knew how to make them. Did that man Palin kill Fancy? She said he was like a madman. Nothing could stop him.'

I had seen Harry being obsessed so I believed her. But he must have had some idea. Bombs and fires had been tearing Singapore apart when Dee-Dee disappeared . . . I understood now why Fancy had avoided Harry. I wondered what he had done about it.

'I need to talk to Harry,' I said.

Le Froy nodded.

I would tell Harry that Dee-Dee had died in her sleep, had already been dead when the fire started. That she hadn't felt a thing.

Break-ups and Breakthroughs

———◆———

'We're breaking up,' Parshanti said. 'It's the only thing to do.'
'Breaking up meaning you're not going through with the big wedding?'

'Breaking up meaning no wedding. No big wedding, no small wedding,' Parshanti said.

'What? Why? When did you decide this? Did you both decide it?'

Parshanti and I were sitting in the kitchen after doing the washing-up. Fahey and Le Froy had gone off with Lily, Fahey saying he needed to get her statement typed out and Le Froy that he would track down Harry so I could talk to him.

Of course, Le Froy could just have told Harry what we'd learned – guessed – about his sister, but he seemed glad not to have to. And I did want to talk to Harry.

'Harry Palin is a sweet boy,' I said.

'Harry? What's Harry got to do with anything? I'm talking about me and Leasky! I know he's nice and my parents like him but that's not enough reason to marry someone, is it?'

* * *

Parshanti's parents and Dr Leask had brought Uncle Chen and Ah Ma into the military hospital for some tests, what Dr Leask described as 'a mere precaution' and Dr Shankar called 'covering our arses'. I wasn't really worried about them. Ah Ma was more upset by the doctors' insistence on throwing out any leftovers more than a day old, and Uncle Chen was already looking better and stronger than he had in a long time. This wasn't surprising since it seemed Shen Shen had been dosing him with her concoctions for some time.

If anything, I was concerned for Little Ling. At least she was with her mother, wherever they were.

As for Shen Shen, I didn't know what to think of her. Part of me, the part that had always taken her for granted as a stocky fixture in Uncle Chen's life, still didn't believe she could have done anything to him.

'My ma won't believe it's not just that I don't want a big wedding. She keeps suggesting things like booking a hall instead of having it in church. She doesn't understand!'

'I don't either,' I said carefully. 'I want to. I thought you were so good together. I thought you two were as good as married.'

'I thought so too,' Parshanti said. 'And we were. We were great together. But we don't know each other under "normal" circumstances. Without a war on, and a bunch of people trying to kill us, I don't know that we have anything in common.'

'So get to know each other again. As your normal real-life selves.'

Parshanti rolled her eyes, stretched her arms dramatically and moaned.

'What?'

'I don't think our normal selves like each other. At all. Remember before the war I always thought Leasky was such a twerp and a scaredy cat? And he said he thought I was the most beautiful girl he'd ever seen when he first set eyes on me, and that I was vain and spoiled and a flirt.'

'You're angry with him for saying that?'

'He was right.'

I still didn't see they had a problem. 'So the best you can hope for is another war and then another so you can go on fighting together?'

'Ha ha, very funny. No. I never ever want to live through all that again.'

'Shanti, sweetie, do you think maybe you're worried that if you end up together you'll never be able to forget "all that"?'

She shook her head hard, as though she were trying to shake off the thought, which made me think I might be right. 'Any sign of Shen Shen and Little Ling?'

I accepted the change of subject. 'Not yet. But Fahey's got someone watching the causeway and the port.'

'Why's he being so helpful, do you think?'

'She tried to poison us. She's a murder suspect!'

'Are you sure? I think he likes you, and he's not bad-looking. You know, I remember Mrs Evans talking about meeting Miss Palin on the boat out. She said she wasn't pretty, clearly passing for white, and too stuck-up to talk to them. I thought it was just Mrs Evans being Mrs Evans, but it doesn't sound like Dee-Dee Palin, does it?'

No, it didn't.

* * *

'I thought I saw you at the gates of Government House this morning, but you ignored me and went straight in, so I guess it wasn't you,' Harry said. 'At least I hope it wasn't. Le Froy said you had something important to tell me and you'd have told me then, wouldn't you?'

His attempt to joke just highlighted his apprehension.

'It's just a speculation. About Dee-Dee.'

When Harry arrived, Leask and Parshanti had left us together to talk while they went elsewhere to quarrel.

'She's dead, isn't she?'

'I think so.'

'So there's still no proof . . .'

'I believe it was Fancy's daughter who got on the boat to Australia as Deborah Palin. That was why Fancy kept forgetting to be a bereaved mother and didn't even have an altar spot for her daughter. Her daughter wasn't dead.'

'You think they killed Dee-Dee? Her and Botak Beng?'

'No. I think they were telling the truth about the bombing. They just lied about which girl died.'

'But it's still speculation . . .'

'Sergeant Fahey dug up the story of the bombing and even found a child's drawing on a plank on the site. One of the volunteer firemen sent it in. He thought if any of the child's family had survived they might want it. I think it was Dee-Dee, Harry.'

Harry's eyes were fixed. I couldn't tell what he was seeing.

'Harry, dear Harry, you said you could kill yourself with a clear conscience once you knew what had happened to Dee-Dee. Please don't . . .'

'I've said a lot of stupid things, haven't I?' Harry smiled. 'Don't worry. I won't end it all without saying goodbye.'

'We don't know for sure—'

'I think I've known for some time,' Harry said. 'I've been trying to work off my guilt by being angry with everyone else.'

'Harry, you have nothing to feel guilty about!'

'All the times I got impatient with her? Handing her over to Fancy instead of seeing her safely onto the boat myself?'

'You barely got out in time. You think staying and getting killed or interned would have helped her?'

'I'm guilty because part of me is glad to know she's dead. And out of my hands. I didn't kill Fancy or Botak, though that ass Johnson's been trying to get me to confess to it.'

'You're just glad Dee-Dee won't be alone or frightened any more. And she would be glad you're going on with your life.'

'It feels like she's given me a second chance.'

I knew what he meant. I'd been given a second chance too. Sometimes accepting what we're given can be more difficult than working for what we need.

But one big thing was still bothering me.

'Harry, you said you thought you saw me going into Government House this morning—'

'I know it wasn't you. Sorry, I've got to be by myself for a bit.'

'Please wait, Harry,' I said. 'Give me ten minutes. Where are Leask and Parshanti?'

'Probably in the bamboo groves making love.'

'In the bamboo groves?'

'What's wrong with that?'

'Snakes,' I said.

'Snakes?'

Now he was looking at me as if I was the crazy one. 'Birds and rats like bamboo clumps. Meaning that snakes that like to eat birds and rats will be in the bamboo too.'

'Only you could turn a racy comment into a nature lesson,' Harry said, but he sounded calmer. 'I think they're in the kitchen with your grandmother. You want me to get them?'

'What's she doing in the kitchen? She's supposed to be resting!'

I heaved myself to my feet but Harry pushed me gently back into my chair. 'So are you. I'll send them to you and keep an eye on Madam Chen.'

'No, I need you to come back with them,' I said.

Harry swept me a courtly bow, 'Your wish is my command,' and went in search of the others.

'What's wrong?' Parshanti looked concerned. 'How are you feeling?'

'I'm fine. Harry, you said you thought you saw me outside Government House this morning.'

'Yeah. At the delivery entrance. Across from the Indian barber's. I know it couldn't have been you, but it looked like that new outfit of yours – I couldn't understand why you were ignoring me. I thought maybe you were hiding from someone so I shut up and followed you. Just in case. But you – I mean she who wasn't you – didn't seem in trouble. You – she – went into Government House.'

'You hear that, Leasky?' Parshanti put in. 'I'm not saying all Chinese girls look alike, I wouldn't dare! But maybe Su Lin has a doppelgänger.'

'That's where I thought I saw you with the brigadier and Johnson this morning, but some people made me keep quiet about it,' Leask said.

'Oh, shut your mouth,' Parshanti said, but without heat.

'In the exact same place I saw that bald guy last week, with the brigadier and Johnson. And the next day he ends up on my autopsy table,' Dr Leask said.

We stared at him.

'Not that I'm saying you'll end up on my autopsy table tomorrow,' Dr Leask said quickly.

'Why didn't you tell me?' Parshanti demanded.

'You were angry with me about . . . I can't remember exactly what about, but something.'

'What were they doing,' I asked, 'the brigadier and Botak?'

'It's the delivery entrance,' Dr Leask said. 'They were making a delivery.'

'Of what?'

'Wooden crates with stuff inside. The bald man was putting boxes in the back of a small van. Dark green, I think.'

'Go and find Le Froy and tell him.'

'What? Why? That was days ago!'

'Tell him what exactly?' Harry asked.

'That someone looking like me – or wearing a *samfoo* like mine—'

'Maybe that's it,' Dr Leask said.

'—was talking to the brigadier and Johnson.'

'Her *samfoo*,' Parshanti said. 'The problem is, do you pick a man who doesn't notice clothes or a man who notices only clothes?'

'Parshanti, Dr Leask, can you two fight later? You have the rest of your lives not to live together. Right now I need your help,' I said.

Dr Leask looked at Parshanti, then back at me. 'Go ahead,' they both said.

'You weren't wearing that outfit today,' Harry said thoughtfully. 'How many of these things are there?'

I thought of Ah Ma's three ceremonial batik sarongs, how she said she could have made three *samfoo* sets with them. Maybe Shen Shen had been more skilful at pattern-cutting than we'd known.

'If whoever was in that *samfoo* is the person who killed Botak and Fancy, do you think she's going to kill Brigadier Evans?' Parshanti wondered.

'I don't see why. But just in case could you let Le Froy know? And about seeing Botak Beng loading the brigadier's boxes last week. Fahey's fine, but don't say anything if Johnson's there.'

'Fahey's fine,' Parshanti agreed.

'It's just that Fahey has official pull right now.'

'Come on,' Parshanti said. 'I'll drive and drop you off. Then I've got to collect my ma.'

'You can drive now?' I asked.

'She's a better driver than I am,' Dr Leask said, with enough pride to make Parshanti look embarrassed.

'Well, you're a better shot. He does non-kill shots,' she added to me. 'It's a doctor thing. He shoots not to kill.'

'Non-kill shots can save more lives than kill shots or not shooting,' Dr Leask said.

'When you two have finished the love talk, I'll be waiting

outside,' Harry said. 'See what I've had to put up with?' He leaned over to give me a quick hug. 'Thank you for telling me. And think about the other thing, yes?'

After they'd left I went through Shen Shen's things. She was a hoarder, so there were clothes, trinkets, so many small things. But I couldn't see any patterns of preference or taste or even value. They were just collected.

I looked around the room where Shen Shen had been sleeping with Little Ling. There was a rolled-up mattress, much like the one I slept on in a corner of Ah Ma's room. Originally it had been meant for whichever of the servant girls was on duty to watch Little Ling through the night. But though I searched carefully, even shaking out her clothes and bedding, I found nothing. Yet I felt more convinced than ever that something in the house could point me to where she had gone.

Was I invading her privacy? Well, yes, but she had violated my stomach.

And I wasn't finding anything. Instead I was charging around turning over rocks, like a hungry monkey searching for grubs. There had to be a better way to do it.

If I was right and Shen Shen had been planning this, slowly poisoning Uncle Chen for months, there had to be some evidence. Where would she have put it in this house, where there was so little privacy?

Not in the room she shared with Uncle Chen. Not in Little Ling's room, where the servants took turns to play with the little girl. And not in the kitchen where they looked into everything all the time.

I walked out to the kitchen, and to the charcoal bins where I had so often seen Shen Shen squatting on her wooden stool. You would think this was the last place to hide anything of importance with all the dust and dirt.

This was Madam Small Boss's area, which the servants avoided.

I went to Shen Shen's corner and planted myself on her stool. There was nothing to see, except the wood pile to my left and the charcoal bins in front of me. But on my right was the planking of the side wall of the kitchen. I knocked and shook. A foot or two of the planks had been sawn through and lifted out easily.

Inside I found a storage nook. On the other side of this wall was the kitchen's dry pantry. Clearly, one of the cupboards had been placed facing the hole in the wooden wall. When I checked inside the kitchen it was invisible, behind the tall shelves that held our bins of rice, sweet potatoes, dried mushrooms and other produce.

It was pretty brilliant, I thought. And she might have been using it for years. Outside it was all but invisible, once you stacked a basket of charcoal chips in front of it.

Four wooden shelves had been slotted into the sturdy cupboard. There was quite a lot of room in it, enough space to store a small suitcase or two, if you slid out the shelves, or maybe four sacks of rice lying flat. But there wasn't anything much in there now. I stuck my hand in to feel around, because it was dark, and I touched something soft. When I pulled it out I saw it was my new Chinese New Year *samfoo*, with brown patches on it.

But that was impossible because I knew exactly where my *samfoo* was: hanging up to air at the window of my room. When

I shook it out, I saw this one was almost identical but not exactly. It wasn't as carefully finished as the one Shen Shen had made for me. The hems were coarsely tacked down in a hurry and the buttons hadn't been sewn on. Instead little safety pins were clipped to the collar: they had clearly been used instead. And a piece was missing: the sleeve had been torn from the shoulder as though someone had grabbed at it just before they were stabbed – then had spurted blood over the rest of the fabric. That was what the brown stuff was.

Underneath I found a stalk with three dried-up rambutans and letters addressed to Miss Chen Su Lin. Five were from Le Froy . . . and two from the London School of Economics. All the envelopes had been torn open. It looked as if the letters had been taken out and stuffed back in. That made sense: Shen Shen couldn't read English. I took out one of Le Froy's letters and unfolded it.

> . . . you are quite right not to respond to my previous letters.
> They were the fevered rantings of an old fool. My only
> excuse is that when death cracks open the door, all dregs
> of sense exit before the last breath. Finding myself alive I
> beg you will ignore and forget my rash declarations. Please
> know I will always be a friend to you and yours. As the
> greatest favour, write a line to say you are alive and well
> and I will bother you no further.

Of course, I then had to find and read the rash declarations I was supposed to ignore and forget.

I'd not allowed myself to hope for anything beyond the chance to see him and work with him again. Now it was an exquisite agony reading the words he'd already cancelled. And knowing he believed I'd ignored him.

If Shen Shen had been in front of me I would have killed her. But that would have to wait. Right now I had other things to work on. I tucked Le Froy's letters into my *samfoo* pocket, left the rest in their hiding place and brought the stalk of dried rambutans to show Uncle Chen.

'Botak believed the yellow rambutans were more powerful than red. His mother always made him eat them against overheating. Even after she died, if Botak heard me cough he would bring me yellow rambutans,' Uncle Chen said. 'Where did you get those?'

'Botak must have had a yellow rambutan tree somewhere. Uncle, can you remember how to get to Botak's ma's old place?'

'It's not there any more.'

'But do you think you can find where it used to be?'

'From Kallang Road I can find it. But it's so far – why do you want to go there? Nobody lives there now.'

'But Uncle Botak was still living there, right?'

'He had caretakers to *jaga* the place. A couple of the old fishermen. But after he died his new woman came and sacked them. She had all the keys to his house, the storage sheds and the lorry so they had to believe her. They came to ask me if I could help them because Botak always said if anything happened to him they could have the small boat. But I said, "Why come to me? What can I do?"'

I suspected I knew why the old men had come to see Uncle Chen. 'I think Shen Shen might have gone there. I'm worried that she might try to do something about the baby she's having.'

'Shen Shen isn't having a baby,' Uncle Chen said.

'Yes, she is.'

'No,' Uncle Chen said.

'Hello, Su Lin.' Mrs Shankar had returned with Parshanti. 'I know we're not having a big wedding – or any wedding – but I was hoping I could get you to try on your bridesmaid's dress before I put in the finishing touches. I swore to Mrs Evans I'm fully booked so you would be making an honest woman of me.'

'So kind of you, Mrs Shankar, but not now, sorry. Could you stay with Ah Ma while Parshanti drives me and Uncle Chen somewhere? Please? It's really important.'

'Of course. Where are you going?'

'I don't know. I'm hoping Uncle Chen can find it.'

Where was the old tree hideout?

———◆———

'You aren't going to drive all over the island looking for some deranged poisoner?' Mrs Shankar said.

'We're not,' Parshanti said. 'We're looking for yellow rambutan trees. We're just going for a drive. What's the problem? I'm sorry I can't just stay home applying cold compresses, like you do.'

So it wasn't just Dr Leask Parshanti was snappy with. I hope he knew that.

'I don't want you to. I'm so proud of you, my brave, independent, beautiful, clever daughter. But that doesn't mean I'll ever stop thinking of you as my baby.'

Parshanti made a face, which her mother noticed. This would usually have made Mrs Shankar push harder but . . .

'You were the most beautiful bonny baby in the world. If I had my way I would have had you stay that way for ever. But it wouldn't have been right. Not for you, not for us. And look at you now. The most beautiful young woman I've seen on either side of the world.'

Mrs Shankar had become enough of an Asian mother never to praise her daughter's looks or anything else about her in case the demons or neighbours heard and called down hubris. I could feel Parshanti's shock at hearing her mother call her beautiful.

'I love how you've grown up. I just want to say this to you while your father's not around. I know how it feels, first love and the first stage of love. It's wonderful, new and magic. But you don't want to stay there all your lives. What your father and I have together now is so much better than that early romantic infatuation. I'm not just saying it, darling girl. The best I can wish for you – for you both – is that you somehow come to find someone you can love and bond with in the same way.'

'I loved him when we were in the jungle,' Parshanti said, in a small voice. 'But it's not the same.'

'If you're talking about love and not sex,' Mrs Shankar said.

I got a jolt when I heard Mrs Shankar say that word and I suspected the same thing happened to Parshanti. Neither of us said anything, and Mrs Shankar continued, although I suspect she knew exactly what she'd done to us. We were really listening to her now. She wasn't just delivering the usual this-is-something-we-don't-talk-about-girls speech.

'Love is companionship. Love is being able to talk to each other and to prefer talking to each other than to your friends. You may not share the same interests but you have enough respect for each other to listen when the other wants to talk. That's what your father and I have.' She looked at Parshanti. 'It was different when we first met, of course. It's always different. We were different. And the kind of love you read about in books and poetry – it does exist, don't let anyone tell you different. And when you feel it, when you share it with someone who is worthy of it, worthy of you, who feels the same way, it's the most wonderful thing in the world. It doesn't last in that form. But that's not a bad thing. Because it gets much, much better as you grow to know each other well. I promise you that.

'I won't stand in your way, whatever you decide to do. I'm going to worry, I know I am, no matter what you say or I say to myself. But that's my problem, not yours. And I'm sure that your Dr Leask will wait. As long as it isn't him you're running away from, I think it's good that you find out what you really want before you commit yourself. But, oh, my darling, I just want you to be safe. I want to lock you up in a little box with cotton padding and keep everyone else away from you, even Dr Leask. And you don't have to tell me that's wrong. That's why I'm fighting all my instincts to say this. Now go, before I change my mind.'

We set off in the Shankars' little Morris, with Uncle Chen in the back seat.

'The brigadier wasn't in town. He took the day off. So did Johnson,' Parshanti said. 'Leasky and Harry didn't want to talk to Fahey without seeing Le Froy first so they went to hunt him down. He wasn't in his rooms or at the station. Ma was talking about wanting to see you so I thought I'd bring her.'

'I'm glad you did.' I was relieved that Mrs Shankar was staying with Ah Ma while Parshanti and I took Uncle Chen on what might be a wild-goose chase.

Parshanti was a good driver, although I would have been more comfortable if she'd kept her eyes and attention on the road.

'Mrs Evans was so furious when Ma and I said we were going out and she had to leave. Can you believe she wanted to wait for us in the shop? She said her husband controlled the whole island of Singapore so she could sit wherever she wanted. Ma said she couldn't leave her inside with other clients' half-finished dresses and she would put a stool on the five-foot way outside if she wanted to sit and wait there. We had to take an arm each and pull her out. While Ma was locking the door she was yelling that she was going to have her husband and son arrest us and put us in jail or expel us from Singapore or shut us down and have the house taken away—'

'Oh dear. Do you think that's why Johnson and the brigadier weren't around?'

'No. They were gone before Mrs Evans had her tantrum. Whatever happens, it was worth it. I didn't know my ma still had such spunk in her! By the way, where are we going? You said all the way down East Coast Road, and then?'

'Uncle Chen will direct us.'

Uncle Chen was sitting quietly in the back seat, taking in the sights. I hoped he wasn't getting car sick.

Parshanti glanced back at him. 'Uncle?'

'Go straight until Kallang Road. Then turn left until the river.'

'Thank you, Uncle.' Then, quietly to me, 'Now I know the where, why?'

'I'm thinking the Evanses took something delivered to Government House and left it hidden in Singapore when they ran away,' I said. 'That's why they came back to Singapore and got themselves into a position where they could retrieve it.'

'I'm guessing that's what Le Froy came back for.' Parshanti gave me a sympathetic look. 'I'm sorry, Su. I was so sure he was here to—'

'Shanti, please! Eyes on the road! I think the brigadier passed it to Botak to transport to Indonesia or even Australia. Somewhere he would be able to collect it and bring it back to the UK with no questions. It must have been the boxes Dr Leask saw them with on the Third Day. The brigadier must have paid Botak extra to work on the Third Day and keep it secret. He couldn't send it through official channels in case Customs or anyone else checked. But after Botak had hidden the brigadier's stuff, he was killed before he could send it out.'

'Is that why the brigadier and Johnson are cracking down on smugglers and breaking into all those warehouses? It's something illegal, isn't it?'

'I don't know. Yet.'

So often whether or not something is illegal depends on whose hands it's in.

Kallang was where the yellow rambutan tree of Botak's story was, where Botak, Uncle Chen and my father had been boys together just starting out on their lives.

Thanks to the widening Kallang river, there was anchorage for sea planes and plenty of docking space for boats coming down the central river or up from the sea. It was the perfect location for anyone working with transport or smuggling. There were spots where boats could come right up to docks that stood off the rough but serviceable roads and, apart from the fencing surrounding the airport, there was little security.

'Not Kallang airport. Near Kallang airport.' Uncle Chen came to life as we approached. 'Don't turn here, go straight.'

Kallang airport had been hailed as 'the finest airport in the British

Empire' when it was built. Famous pilot Amelia Earhart had described it as 'an aviation miracle of the East'. But we drove past it down an increasingly narrow road into more and more *ulu* surroundings. As the wilderness grew thicker on the roadside, Uncle Chen became more confident. 'Botak always said he could only live near the sea,' he said. 'You know all this, including the airport, used to be his family's land. The government took it to build the airport.'

Even if Botak's family had been compensated, I could see why he felt entitled to make what he could of what he had left.

I could already smell the sea. There's no place in Singapore that's more than a few miles from the coast. True Singaporeans, whether born on the island or not, feel most at ease within sight and smell of the sea. As we continued along the road that followed the river to the coast, I couldn't help feeling that things might work out. After all, we hadn't expected to survive the war, but we had. We might survive this too.

'After this milestone.' Uncle Chen, with his head stuck out the window, seemed to be sniffing out our destination, like a tracking dog. 'Here. Turn right down this lane.'

There were a couple of *attap* houses near the turn-off but they looked deserted.

'Are you sure?' Parshanti sounded apprehensive as she changed down to the lowest gear. 'There's not much road.'

'Just keep going,' Uncle Chen said.

We ended up in front of a row of shacks that looked like a double row of workers' quarters standing back to back. They seemed deserted.

'Here,' Uncle Chen said. 'This is the place. This is where Botak started his operations.'

'These aren't *attap* roofs,' Parshanti said. 'They're all weatherproofed with zinc and tarpaulin. The mess on top is just for show. This is amazing!'

The rambutan trees in a small clearing were heavy with green fruit. I wondered if they were going to be red or yellow. Uncle Chen laughed at me for asking. 'Just like Botak – he spent his life trying to get yellow rambutan trees for his mother.'

I laid my hand on the trunk of a nearby tree. Some people believe in tree spirits that communicate with them. I don't know that trees would want to communicate with us even if they could. When you think about their life span compared to ours, it would be like us trying to communicate with mosquitoes, which move so much faster through life than we do and kill us with malaria.

That was when I felt the nail sticking out of the trunk. At first I was angry that someone had done that to a living tree. Then I noticed the curling strip of fruit skin it held to the trunk. It had dried almost to the colour of the bark, which was probably how it had been missed. Now that I looked I saw holes left in the bark by other nails, and on the ground, remnants of fruit skin that had been torn off. Though wrinkled and brown, I could tell by the characteristic fine hairs that they had been yellow rambutan skins, nailed to the tree trunk to dry. Just like the bit I had found in Botak's mouth.

I looked up. Through the thick leaves I could see the unripe green rambutans in bunches. Around the base of the tree lay the seeds and skins of fruit that had been eaten and discarded. The work of monkeys, squirrels and fruit bats, I guessed.

Why would someone have stuck rambutan skins to the tree trunk to dry? I pulled out the nail, to release the dried skin without tearing it. It was longer than I'd expected, more a metal skewer than a nail . . . Much like the skewer that had killed Botak Beng.

The place felt bereft and abandoned, as if it knew that its owner had recently died. There was no overpowering smell, no blood, but after you have shopped in the meat section of a wet market you develop a sense for recent death – recent violent death. And that was what I sensed here. Something changed about the air. As though traumatised wisps of spirit had not yet departed. If you have light waves and sound waves I don't see why there shouldn't be spirit waves. We haven't the technology to measure them yet. But it's only the Western world that refuses to believe in anything you can't measure.

I also saw this was the perfect location to store shipments in transit. But I was disappointed. I'd hoped to find Shen Shen and Little Ling here, that she would explain everything so that we could go home as one family again.

'Maybe we should leave it for the police or Le Froy to go through,' Parshanti said. 'We should have enough petrol to drive back to town and let them know where this hideout they've all been looking for is. But first I really have to pee.'

I looked around. 'Maybe there's a WC inside the house.'

'Don't be silly,' Parshanti said. 'After two years in primary forest, this is like the Savoy or the Ritz.'

Uncle Chen and I leaned against the car to wait for her. 'I'm sorry I didn't let Botak in to see you,' I said again.

Uncle Chen shook his head. 'We cannot know what would have happened. Botak was happy in this place. This is where I want to remember him. Thank you for bringing me back here.

This is where I can remember who I am.' He nodded to a trail beyond the storehouse. 'Botak's ma had her house somewhere up there. She was always so fierce. It was her who introduced your mother to your father.'

'No, *lah*. I know my mother ran away from her family in Japan.'

'How do you think she came to Singapore? Botak learned to transport things from his ma, who transported people. We were all working for her then. Same principle. As long as you pay, they deliver. Your Ah Ma never forgave her for that. She never talked to Mrs Ho again after your pa got married.'

So my father and mother had been together in this place? I didn't believe in ghosts but I wished I did.

Three sampans – small, flat-bottomed wooden boats – had been tipped up against a log to dry, still draped with their nets and giving off the smell of good sea salt. Their long sculling oars were there too, although two were fitted with outboard motors. I guessed these were the boats that had been promised to Botak's men. But Shen Shen had never been good at letting others benefit from what was of no use to her.

'There's something back there,' Parshanti said, as she ran towards us. She was tense and excited. 'Come and see.'

She'd found Botak's mother's house.

There was no one inside. But though it looked empty, it didn't feel empty enough. There's something about the way dust settles on uninhabited space. You sense it even if not with a conscious part of your mind. It's a signal that this is a safe space, without predators lurking. But this place didn't feel safe, even though it seemed no one had been there for a while.

'Someone's been here recently,' Parshanti said. 'More recently than before Botak died. No bugs in the water in the pail there.'

Botak's house was dirty in the way only a man living with occasional visits from a woman can make it: a few clean surfaces but rubbish and cockroaches under cupboards. There was a Singer treadle sewing-machine with scraps of familiar fabric around it. This was where Shen Shen had sewn the batik *samfoo*s, mine, Little Ling's, who knew how many?

And there was more.

In what had once been the kitchen, I found a thick sludge in the bottom of a cast-iron pot. This was where Shen Shen had been boiling down the dried yellow rambutan skins and crushing the seeds to extract the poison.

She couldn't have done it at home without someone seeing what she was up to. Anywhere in town or out in the wilderness, there was nowhere she could have worked unseen and safely . . . except here, in the home of a man who thought she was keeping secret her visits to him because of her husband.

Shen Shen could have done whatever she liked here while Botak was out arranging his deliveries.

Botak must have found the concoction that Shen Shen was brewing, seen the yellow rambutan skins drying outside and concluded that she was trying to abort the baby – his baby – she was carrying. He had grabbed a handful of the dried skin and rushed to make things right.

Actually, she had been poisoning her husband and his family.

This place was making me feel very uncomfortable.

I wasn't up to poking around derelict buildings and invading a dead man's privacy. Besides, the storehouse was where Botak would have put the brigadier's secret cargo. And I had to let Le Froy know as soon as possible.

'We should go back to the car and get out of here,' I said.

'Wait! Just look at this,' Parshanti insisted.

Beyond the little house there was a concealed van – it was very clever: it was covered with an enormous netting dome on a bamboo frame. Branches stuck through the netting and creepers were growing over it. A lever, with a rope attached to it, tilted it onto one edge, like a giant fish trap.

Parshanti hauled on the rope to reveal the little green van. The back doors were open and we saw crates inside. 'Just as Leasky described it,' Parshanti said.

Only, like the van doors, the crates had been opened. I suspected that had happened after Botak's death.

'It's books,' Uncle Chen said. 'Why would the brigadier pay Botak to transport books? And cigarettes. *Wah lau eh* – Marlboro American luxury cigarettes.'

Wah lau eh, in Singlish, literally means 'Oh, father' or 'Oh, male ancestor' and means much the same as 'Oh, God!' in English, which shows how Asian patriarchs are worshipped and Western deities aren't.

I slid a volume out of the packaging. It was a copy of the *Encyclopaedia Britannica* volume 13, its hard covers taped tightly shut around its pages. I opened it with some difficulty and found it contained more than just information. It wouldn't have made any difference to Botak, who could barely write his name. For him it would just have been another job.

The place was making me more and more uncomfortable. When you looked more closely, there were signs that someone was using the land while deliberately maintaining its abandoned appearance. I couldn't see any ripe or rotting fruit, meaning it had been harvested before the birds, bats and monkeys got to it, and I saw a stack of green coconuts in the shade of a group of rambutan trees.

I walked over to them and shook one. It was a firm, hard fruit and I heard the slosh of water within that told me its kernel wouldn't be ripe enough for coconut oil or milk. I wondered why Botak had harvested them before they ripened to brown and dropped naturally. Had he meant to sell them for their water? Or had he meant to drink it himself? Given how much more you could make from a mature fruit and its husk, coconut water was usually an indulgence for children . . . and for pregnant women.

Some people believe that drinking coconut water makes fairer, more beautiful babies, their skin white and smooth like the coconut flesh, with thicker, stronger hair, tough and lasting like the coconut husk. But I've also heard it can make your baby's head as big and hard as a coconut so I'm not sure I would take the risk.

'We should go now,' I said. 'Quickly.' I had a bad feeling.

'I hear a car coming,' Uncle Chen said.

'We should get back to ours,' Parshanti said. 'It's our only way out of here.'

Confrontation

———◆———

The car making its way down the narrow track towards ours was an official vehicle. For one wild, hopeful moment I thought it might be Sergeant Fahey with Le Froy come to investigate.

Then I saw Brigadier Evans and Robert Johnson getting out of it.

'There she is!' Johnson said, pointing at me. 'Give her the money and get this over with!'

The brigadier huffed and stared at me. 'That's not her.'

'Of course it is – what else would she be doing here?' Fahey came towards me. 'Hey, no other people, we said. What are they doing here? And you,' he squinted at me, then at Parshanti, 'you're not her. You're the ones who made fun of me and broke my nose.'

Behind them, Mrs Evans climbed out of the car. 'You! I told you I'll have you and your mother arrested and your shop closed down.'

'Stay in the car with the child, Drusilla!'

The child?

I saw Little Ling in the car. And in that instant I understood Shen Shen. At least, I thought I did.

'You took her child?' I headed towards the car. 'You took Shen Shen's baby and made her do all those terrible things?'

'Su Lin! Su Lin!' Seeing me, Little Ling started to get out of the car.

'Stay away from her!'

I wasn't the only one shocked when a figure appeared from what had seemed to be a dead tree. Shen Shen pushed aside the curtain of shrubbery, which was as cunningly made as the van camouflage, and went to stand next to Brigadier Evans.

'Get back into the car and stay there,' Shen Shen ordered Little Ling. 'At once! Or I will *hantam* you!'

'This is the right girl,' Johnson said. 'Okay, we're here. Where are the goods, sweetie?'

'Where is my money?' Shen Shen folded her arms.

'This is extortion,' Brigadier Evans said. 'You know very well it's our property that we paid to have transported—'

Johnson looked at what appeared to be *attap*-roofed shacks. 'I could order the men to come and search the place.'

Shen Shen sneered at him: 'And let everybody know what you're smuggling out? Anyway, it's no use. It's not there. You pay me and . . .' she turned to look at us '. . . and you shoot these people. Then I'll tell you where Botak stored your cargo.'

'Miss,' said Brigadier Evans, 'we don't go around shooting people.'

'Why not? You want them to tell everybody what they saw you taking?'

Uncle Chen was gaping at his wife. 'Why?'

'You think I didn't see you all sneaking around, poking your noses into my business?' she snarled. 'Everything I've got your family must steal from me. I have as much right as anybody else to a good man. Not a useless lump like you, who thinks that having a daughter is as good as having a son.'

'You can't mean that. Of course Little Ling is good enough!' said her father.

Could Shen Shen even turn on her daughter? The precious child who bonded her for ever to Uncle Chen and his family?

'If Little Ling had been a boy, I would be respected by my husband, my husband's family, everyone!'

Shen Shen was crazy. Or maybe I was, for not having seen it till now.

'Is that why you had an affair with Botak Beng?' I asked. 'You wanted him to give you a son?'

'I never meant to have an affair with Beng. Stupid, smelly old man. But he thought I was there because of him, and it was the best way to make him believe it.'

Shen Shen smirked. 'It wasn't so bad. At least he knew how to treat a woman nicely. He gave me jade and gold jewellery and imported sweets and liquor. He said a beautiful girl should have beautiful things.'

Botak Beng had said something like that to me, too, when I was twelve or thirteen years old. It had made me uncomfortable and I'd given Ah Ma the little jade gourd he had bestowed on me and avoided him from then on. I hadn't known it was one of his standard lines. But perhaps he had made Shen Shen feel pampered and special for the first time in her life.

'All you stupid people don't know how powerful Botak was.

Even he didn't know. He was the only one who had all the smuggling and shipping connections. He was allowed to get away with his smuggling because he shipped things for the British and even helped the Japs. He was just making money, no politics because he was useful to them, and he survived by bringing in supplies. Compared to him, this husband of mine was weak and getting weaker. I deserved better.

'Botak Beng kept saying he could never work with Small Boss Chen again because he had betrayed him, no matter what Small Boss Chen said. How it was different in the old days under Big Boss Chen. He was living in the past, just like the rest of you.'

'Ah Ma and Uncle Chen aren't living in the past,' I said. 'I thought you were angry with them for wanting to legalise all the family business and properties because it would bring in less money.'

'Their brains are in the past. They think that by sucking up to the British things will go back to how they used to be. They won't. Can't you get that into your thick skull? Once I get the money I will set up in business for myself. I will take over Fancy's business. I can run it a hundred times better than she did.'

'And when you got pregnant with Botak's baby you wanted a son to cement your standing within the Chen family. But Uncle Chen would know he wasn't the father so you tried to poison him by boiling dried rambutan skins and seeds to extract poison from them.'

'I was doing your family a favour, exchanging a useless old man for a new grandson. My son wouldn't be useless, like you people. Botak was a stupid old fool. He wanted to make me his official mistress. He was mad! I wasn't going to exchange my place in the Chen family for his dirty hut.'

'Fancy thought you were trying to abort the baby so she went to tell Botak. She thought he would throw you over, maybe turn to her. Instead he went to see Uncle Chen to claim responsibility for the baby. Fancy, in a panic, rushed after him but didn't manage to stop him before he reached the house.'

'Fancy was trying to steal him. That's why she went and told him nonsense about me. Hah! Fat chance! He pushed her away and rushed back here. But then he found my rambutan skins. I couldn't tell him I was trying to poison his friend so I let him think Fancy was right.'

I thought I heard the sound of a car engine approaching. I saw Brigadier Evans look round too, and beside me, Parshanti tensed. But the engine died away. Just some vehicle on the main road, too far off to do us any good. Parshanti took a small step away from me, towards the thick undergrowth.

'You were here that day?' I asked Shen Shen. I couldn't have cared less where she'd been, but the longer I kept her talking the longer we stayed alive.

'Of course I was. I was here all along. You think I want to go and see your ancestors in the cemetery? Hah! If they could see you now they would tell you to die! The bald old fool locked me up here. He told me he would settle things with Small Boss. That I'd never have to go back to Chen Mansion, that I could live here with him for ever. Look at this place! I ask you, who'd want to live here?'

Botak's set-up could have been improved, but it was no worse than the pig farm Shen Shen had grown up on – and was certainly far better than the conditions we'd all been living in during the war.

'I started boiling yellow rambutan skins when I became pregnant. Yes, my first thought was to get rid of the baby. Because my useless husband would tell his *kaypoh* mother that it wasn't his. But the medicine didn't work. When my husband drank some of my medicinal tea and started vomiting so badly, though, I thought if he died before the baby was born nobody could say it wasn't his. It would seem like a last gift from the gods. Even your Ah Ma would be happy to have the grandson she had wanted for so long. And I would make sure she threw you out of the house before I let her see him.'

As Shen Shen talked I thought I saw movement on the side of the road, but I couldn't make it out. She turned to see what I was looking at, and so did the brigadier.

'But then you got greedy, didn't you?' I said. I realised Parshanti was no longer next to me.

Shen Shen turned back to me.

'You thought, why not get rid of Ah Ma too? Why not get it all for you and your children? Whether it's a boy or a girl, if it's born into the Chen family, you won't have to worry about your own future.'

'Why not? Look at you,' Shen Shen said. 'Useless ugly cripple, living like a rich man's wife because you're the old woman's granddaughter. You don't deserve to live like that. You're as guilty of all this as me.'

'As I.' I couldn't stop myself.

'What?'

'As guilty as I, not as guilty as me. Because you're really saying "as guilty as I am". You can't say "as guilty as me am".'

A bird or small animal screeched nearby. Shen Shen looked

at me in disbelief. I didn't blame her. I was feeling pretty absurd. All I could think was that maybe some of her drugs or Dr Shankar's medications were still acting on me.

Or I had come to realise I had nothing to lose now.

That's the great thing about having nothing to hope for. There's nothing more that anyone can threaten you with.

'You've got no business talking to me like that! You with your dirty Japanese blood, you're even lower class than me! Why don't you just go off with your *ang moh pai kar*? Or go and kill yourself! You're no better than your mother. Worse! At least she came from a good family.'

'Uncle Botak told you he was going to show Uncle Chen the yellow rambutan skins you were using to get rid of his baby. That's why you killed him.'

The anger I felt surprised me with its vehemence.

All the things I'd been feeling about Uncle Chen recently – irritation, impatience, suspicion – dissolved like ice cubes in a wok of hot oil, melting with barely a splutter and evaporating immediately into nothing.

'It was all that *goblock* Fancy's fault,' Shen Shen said. 'She thinks I want to get rid of a baby. So what does she do? She rushes off to tell Botak. I never asked her to keep my secrets. I never told her any secrets. She imagines crazy things and thinks if she tells enough people it becomes true.'

'Botak thought he was the father of your baby.'

Shen Shen shrugged. 'I don't know what that fool thought.'

'That's why he came to tell Uncle Chen he'd be responsible for you and the baby. He was loyal to my pa and Uncle Chen but he believed Uncle Chen was dying and needed his help.

He wouldn't have taken Fancy's word for that – it was you who told him, wasn't it?'

I saw I'd guessed right. Not because Shen Shen looked guilty but because she looked pleased. Triumphant, even.

'You all think you're so smart and that I'm so stupid. You don't know I'm the one who's running everything.'

'What did you tell Botak? That Uncle Chen was dying or dead and you were trying to keep the business running but needed a man to help you?'

'I told him your uncle said I could trust him.' Shen Shen smirked. 'Stupid fool. As big a fool as your uncle. So sentimental, talking about how he'd do anything for your uncle. At first he wouldn't even touch me. No matter what I did he kept crying and swearing he couldn't touch Small Boss Chen's wife.'

'Why?'

'Why wouldn't he touch me? Some honour thing. I had to tell him your uncle couldn't have babies. That Little Ling wasn't his daughter. But he needed a son to run the business so I had to give him one in any way I could. I had to beg him on your uncle's behalf–'

'Little Ling isn't Uncle Chen's daughter?'

'Of course she is, *lah*. But what use is a daughter? I need a son! Your useless uncle can't even give me one! You're as stupid as those men!'

'When Botak was at the house, you sent Fancy to fetch him, didn't you? Because what would get him out of there? Telling him you were outside waiting to talk to him. Did she help you kill him?'

'Don't be stupid. Of course not. She'd caused enough trouble already. Why would I ask for more? Botak took out the rambutan skins he'd stolen from me and said, "This is to kill our baby, right? It cannot kill a grown-up. I can put it into my mouth and eat it." He put it into his mouth and chewed! Mad, *lah*! I said, "If you want to die, then go ahead!"

Brigadier Evans was glancing around again, trying to see if someone else was nearby. I wasn't imagining things: I saw the wisdom of Le Froy (or whoever it was) parking their car out of sight and walking the last stretch.

'Why are you standing around talking when you could shoot them? Robert? Do something!' Mrs Evans screeched.

'I wasn't trying to kill your uncle and grandma,' Shen Shen said. 'I just wanted to keep them unwell so I could run the business. People don't take me seriously unless I say I'm giving them orders from Chen Tai or Small Boss Chen. The only one I was really trying to kill was you. I always gave you extra poison. But you're like a devil, impossible to kill.'

My body, with its violent vomiting spasms, had protected me from the poison Shen Shen was feeding us.

'Why did you kill Fancy, Shen Shen?'

'She tried to blackmail me!' Shen Shen laughed. 'And she was telling everybody lies about me. That woman had gossip coming out of her mouth like diarrhoea! She was so scared, she grabbed my sleeve so hard she tore it and she was swearing, right to the end, that she'd never said a word about me to anybody. Hah! That one is going straight to Hell for lying.'

The idea of a murderess declaring how much a liar deserved to go to Hell invited discussion. But just then I was too concerned with not becoming her next kill.

I saw Shen Shen pulling something long and thin, with the

gleam of metal, from a pouch strapped around her waist. It was one of the metal skewers we used for grilling meat over charcoal. As Dr Leask had said, it was long and thin. Gripped firmly, it would drive through chicken meat and bone, but it was sharp and powerful enough to stab a man through the heart. It was the murder weapon that had killed Botak and Fancy.

And from the way in which Shen Shen was holding it she was ready to add me to the list.

I was suddenly scared. I'd thought I was ready to die, wanting to get away from everything here, but now I had unfinished business.

I wanted to avenge Botak Beng. I might not have liked him, but he'd been a loyal friend to my late father and my uncle. He'd tried to be a good man by his way of reasoning. And he'd been killed because he'd wanted to do right by Shen Shen. I thought of what she'd tried to do to Ah Ma and Uncle Chen and rage rose inside me. It was like a red tide flooding into my brain and filling me with a giant charge of reckless energy.

I roared – and saw the shock on Shen Shen's face. 'You devil!' I yelled at her, 'You shameless she-devil! You are the one who deserves to die!'

I grabbed at the green coconuts. They'd been harvested recently enough that their stems were still securely attached.

Shen Shen laughed at me. She laughed like her sister Mimi, I thought. I hadn't noticed till now. Shen Shen never laughed much. Maybe she was as mad as her sister had been. Poor Mimi had made a name for herself as Mimi Hoshi or 'Mimi Bright Star: the Mata Hari of the East' during the Japanese Occupation. But she'd ended up murdered under a cannonball tree. I hadn't killed her, but I'd certainly wished her out of existence – as I did Shen Shen right now.

As Shen Shen came towards me and drew back her arm to strike, I swung both coconuts, one at the arm coming towards my chest, the other at her head. I could hear someone shouting but it was as though everything was moving in slow motion.

Then I was lying on the ground on my back with Shen Shen lying across me and there was blood everywhere. From the angle at which she was holding it and the way she was swearing I guessed her right wrist was broken. A bump was swelling on her left temple. I had scored with both coconuts. She would have an ugly bruise, but I hoped no damage had been done to—

'I hope the baby will be all right,' I said.

That made her scream and spit at me. She couldn't do much else with her useless wrist. I tried to squirm out from under her weight but—

Suddenly I heard a loud bang just above my head. My eardrum was buzzing as Shen Shen slumped on me, a deadweight.

Stunned, I saw that the hand holding the gun that had just been fired was attached to Brigadier Evans.

'I think you shot the wrong one, old man,' Robert Johnson said.

The Cavalry Arrives

———◆———

'Hold your hands up,' Johnson said to me. Then, to his stepfather, 'Do you want to shoot her too? Or shall I do it?'

Brigadier Evans ignored him. He was focused on Shen Shen as I wriggled out from beneath her body. 'That's the blackmailing slut who's been making all the trouble,' he said. 'I should have done this right at the start. Would have spared us a few of your mother's episodes.'

He picked up the modern, hygienic, deadly metal skewer Shen Shen had been holding. Then he stepped back and looked at me again. I saw his eyes narrow.

'She's Le Froy's little sidepiece,' Evans said, as Johnson held his gun pointed at my face. 'Use this. It makes better sense, see? That blackmailing wildcat had just stabbed this one when you shot her. We won't even have to hide the bodies.'

He took Johnson's gun from him and passed him the skewer, then smiled at me. 'I'll tell your sweet Tommy his ladyfriend said goodbye.' He went on, 'Quick, Rob. Finish her off. Use the skewer. Then you can tell everyone you shot the other after she'd stabbed this one, but it was too late.'

Johnson hefted the skewer. 'Can't I just shoot her?'

I didn't appreciate it at the time, but later I realised he'd probably saved my life by being squeamish about stabbing.

Brigadier Evans wasn't good under pressure, 'Will you just do it, you fool? Do something!'

Still, Johnson dithered. Pulling a trigger was clearly his preferred way of connecting with women. But then Shen Shen started convulsing.

I'd thought she was dead but she was choking and coughing up blood and her arms and legs were twitching, as if she was having a seizure. She wouldn't cause them any problems but she triggered panic in Johnson. He was jittering with excitement, snorting and swinging the skewer between me and Uncle Chen and . . . Where was Parshanti? I'd not noticed her go. I hoped she'd managed to get a safe distance away and would stay there.

But then I heard shouting, 'Brigadier Evans! Sir! Brigadier Evans! Sir!'

Sergeant Fahey had sprung out of the shrubbery and was coming at a run, yelling, 'Sir! Sir! Sir!' as he came. He could have run faster if he hadn't been wasting his breath on shouting.

Behind him, more slowly but keeping up a good pace, was Le Froy.

'You men are useless!' stormed Mrs Evans. 'Give me that gun, quick, quick!'

She grabbed her son's weapon from her husband. 'Shoot first. You can always talk things out later.'

'My dear,' Brigadier Evans said.

I couldn't tell whether 'my dear' meant he was telling her to stop or go ahead. I doubt anything he said would have made a difference. The men in her life were clearly used to being ordered around. They both stood back, giving her a clear shot.

Fahey, less than ten feet away, was still much too far to do any good. Le Froy was nowhere to be seen. He must have fallen. I hoped he wasn't hurt, that they wouldn't hurt him—

Mrs Evans walked up to me and raised the pistol to my face. 'I'm not a very good shot, so I need you to keep still,' she said.

I thought of closing my eyes, but why miss my last moments on earth? So I had a great view when the prosthetic foot and ankle brace came spinning through the air, like a boomerang, and whacked Mrs Evans on the side of her head.

Maybe I would rethink the leg brace Dr Shankar was always trying to press on me.

'You useless dolts! Do something!' Mrs Evans shouted, from her position on the ground. 'Robert!'

But if Johnson or the brigadier killed me now there were too many eyes on them for even the brigadier to cover it up. Unless he was going to kill Le Froy and Fahey too.

Parshanti had come out of the bushes and picked up the gun that had spun out of Mrs Evans's hand. Also the prosthesis.

Uncle Chen, ignoring and ignored by everyone else, had gone to the car and was sitting with his arms around Little Ling, shielding her from the sight of her mother on the ground.

Fahey was sprinting over to me. 'Where are you hurt? How bad?'

'Not my blood.' I looked around him for Le Froy.

Fahey stood between his boss and me. 'Sir.' He was panting.

I checked on Shen Shen but it was too late for her. Her eyes and mouth were wide open and she looked angry and surprised as well as dead. I didn't feel anything. I would mourn her unborn child later, but for now there was nothing beyond wondering which level of Hell she would end up in: among the murderers, the greedy or the betrayers of family . . .

Then Le Froy was at my side. 'Are you all right?'

'Yes. The scrips – inside encyclopaedias – taped shut.'

He seemed not to hear me. Shen Shen's blood was all over me and he was pulling at the worst-stained cloth, looking for wounds. 'Where did she get you?'

'She didn't. Brigadier Evans killed her. I think he meant to kill me but—'

'Thank goodness he can't tell you Chinese apart,' Le Froy said.

But it wasn't over yet.

'You might as well come around, Fahey,' Johnson said, 'It's going to happen with or without you. Jake Evans has it all under control.'

'Three locals and a renegade crippled troublemaker,' Brigadier Evans said, 'against the word of the island's governor and the chief detective. Who are people going to believe?'

'Oh, stop talking so much and just get rid of them!' Mrs Evans urged. 'Finish them off. Find the cargo and get us out of here!'

Brigadier Evans blinked. I believe in the excitement of the melee he'd forgotten what had brought them there.

'My dear, the man's an Englishman, not a native,' her husband said, 'and the girl understands English. Look, Le Froy, no one wants any trouble. This is all a misunderstanding. We can work something out. You want your post back, I believe. I'll just speak to some people. You may need to show you're able to get around all right on that thing, but with the number of chaps sporting fake arms and legs, these days, I doubt that's going to hold you back.'

Parshanti offered Le Froy his leather and metal projectile prosthesis but he shook his head: not now.

'You're such a fool!' Mrs Evans said. 'You think you can buy him off with a posting? He knows we've got the nine million dollars' worth of share scrips. As long as he's alive we'll never be rid of him. Look, no one is going to pay any attention to anything the locals say. And this crippled lunatic is even worse. They'll thank us for getting rid of him and saving them years of pension. Where's my gun?'

Parshanti held it up but didn't hand it over.

'You! You stinking mongrel slut!'

Parshanti smiled at her.

'How dare you mock me? You! Sergeant!' Mrs Evans shouted at Fahey. 'I order you to shoot her! And her! And him!'

I'd almost forgotten Fahey was there – he'd been so silent for so long. Did Mrs Evans consider him more amenable to long-term bribery than Le Froy? And was he?

'It's an order, Fahey,' Johnson said. 'It's going to happen with you or without you. You can be rich or dead. Your choice.'

I saw Fahey decide he would obey not the order he'd just received but that which his superior officer should have given.

'Obey your orders, you fool!' Mrs Evans shouted.

'Brigadier John Jacob Evans and Mrs Evans, I am detaining you under–'

'You insolent young fool!' Mrs Evans screamed at him, 'Do something, Jake! Don't just stand there!'

OVIDIA YU

But Brigadier Evans shook his head. 'My sister warned me not to marry you,' he said. 'She was talking about money missing from the Sunday school subscription fund and your son bullying his classmates but I told her I would make sure you had enough money and wouldn't need to penny-pinch. But it will never be enough, will it?'

Mrs Evans howled, like a pregnant sow blocked from her sweet-potato mash. She turned on Le Froy. 'This is all because of you and that sly little hussy of yours. If you'd been reasonable it wouldn't have come to this. We could all be rich and comfortable and away from this hellish island. You've only yourself to thank.'

'I thank you too, madam,' Le Froy said gallantly. 'This is a much better case to put before the Home Office than a story of missing mail packets.'

'Sir?' Fahey said.

'It's confidential!' Brigadier Evans said. 'Watch it, man. Internal security. The Official Secrets Act could get you sued to high Heaven and back.'

'A story, then. Just before the war, a member of staff at Government House – for the sake of argument we'll call him Evans – received share scrips worth millions in one of the last diplomatic parcels Botak brought in. Remember, there was a war on and there was need for money everywhere. The first thing the clerks and administrators learned was not to investigate too closely. So what if something wasn't strictly by the rules? One thing everyone had learned – painfully – was that the rules that punished you could not be relied on to protect you. Evans signed for it but failed to put it into the system. There were daily bombings and fires, and any disappearance wasn't likely to trigger immediate alarms in any of the issuing departments. So he kept it. Share scrips that could be converted into over nine million dollars. But they were under heavy fire and barely managed to get passage out of Singapore. Rather than carry the scrips with them, he and his wife hid them. I'm guessing it was her idea to put them into the hollowed-out centres of books, just as she concealed her love letters in the hollowed-out copies of improving works her husband was unlikely to look into.' Le Froy nodded to Mrs Evans.

'Yes, we found your letters. We read only enough to confirm they weren't what we were looking for. When you got back to Singapore, you found the share scrips intact in Government House. But you had to get them out of Singapore, didn't you? That's when you transferred them to copies of the *Encyclopaedia Britannica*. The Government House servants thought you were burning offerings to give thanks for surviving the war. But you were gutting the volumes and taping the scrips in the hollowed-out pages.

'Botak was a safe bet to get them out of Singapore for you. He always used small, competent teams, each responsible for their short trips. None of their members could have betrayed him even if they'd wanted to because they didn't know enough. Only Botak – and Botak's wife in each distributing location – knew what was going on. It was only when Botak died, without having sent out that last shipment, that things fell apart for you.'

'None of this is going to count,' Mrs Evans said. 'We're English. That's what matters.'

We heard the sound of another vehicle coming down the narrow winding track.

'What's going to happen to the share scrips?' Brigadier Evans asked Le Froy. 'We can make a deal.'

'As governor you might use the money to institute a fund for rebuilding Singapore's public-health infrastructure.'

'As governor?'

'Fully documented and audited.' Le Froy looked at Fahey, who nodded.

'A lot of work for nothing!' Mrs Evans said.

'No prosecution?' Evans looked at Shen Shen's body.

'You saved the state a trial and an execution.'

They shook on it just before the vehicles pulled up and more policemen appeared at the top of the slope down which Fahey and Le Froy had come, open mouths and confused eyes taking it all in, then spotting Johnson and reporting to him.

Leask and Harry spilled out of the last vehicle and headed towards us.

'Is the fun over? Dash it, I always miss the best parts!' Harry said.

Leask was holding Parshanti, who had run to him and thrown herself into his arms. 'No,' he said, his cheek resting on her hair. 'This is the best part.'

'I kept thinking I had to get through this alive because if I didn't, the last thing I said to you was "You're a gormless idiot,"' Parshanti said.

'So I'm not a gormless idiot?'

'You are. But I didn't want it to be the last thing I said to you. Let's get married.'

They'd be all right, I decided, as long as we could arrange regular crises to remind them to appreciate each other.

But I had my own story to get on with. 'Thanks for saving my life,' I said to Le Froy, who had reattached his foot and was stamping tentatively on it. 'You're not an old fool. I just found your letters and I'm not going to ignore them unless you tell me to in person. What you said about feeling like half of you was amputated? I felt it and I love you too.'

I hadn't meant to say more than that I'd found his letters, but the rest just followed. I shut my eyes and wished Mrs Evans had fired that bullet. For one agonising moment, three seconds, maybe, of silence, my humiliation was so powerful that I could have willed myself to dissolve into the earth and disappear for ever.

'You could say the shock of almost dying is much like a fever,' I said.

'Best not to leave anything unsaid,' Le Froy said. 'And not wish it unsaid if we don't die.'

'You're supposed to say something back,' I heard Parshanti say. 'Like maybe "I love you too"? And it's best not to call each other fools. As I know from experience. Sorry, rude to eavesdrop, I know. But some people just don't know how to do it.'

Yes, I'd wanted the old Parshanti back but not like this. Not now.

It seemed like all the wishes I'd made were coming true . . . and proving how ridiculous I was to have made them.

'Do you mean that?' Le Froy asked. His voice was unexpectedly high. A little shaky even. 'You're talking to this unemployed crippled *ang moh*?'

Suddenly all I wanted was to make sure he knew everything was all right. All right between us, at least. So that if I did get shot in the face and die it wouldn't be the one thing I regretted not saying.

'Yes,' I said. 'It's just a statement of fact. Like you said, when you almost die without saying what you need to say, it all comes out. I wanted to get it said. I don't expect you to do or say anything. We can go on like we were before.'

But I knew nothing was going to be as it was before.

I felt the change swell and grow inside me, close to the surface of my skin, speeding up my heart rate so I could feel it thudding in my throat. I couldn't say any more. I felt as though I'd swallowed a squid, its writhing, twisting tentacles going downwards into my chest and upwards into my brain.

You read in books about 'seeing love' in someone's eyes. I always thought it was fanciful. People imagine what they want to see. But looking at Le Froy now I saw understanding, acceptance, compassion and – yes – amusement. I didn't think it was my imagination. If I was conjuring this up I would have left out the laughter in his eyes. And, no, it was not only in his eyes but in his expression, his posture, his relaxed stance that I read all these things. It was happiness. The same huge, overwhelming happiness I was feeling just to be alive and there with him.

Harry Palin inserted himself between us and put a hand on each of our shoulders. 'We're all going to lose every single person we love. The thing is to try not to lose them before you have to. Su Lin, does this mean you won't be marrying me after all?'

'What?' Le Froy turned to stare at him. 'How long has this been going on?'

'Nothing's been going on,' I said. I smiled at Harry. 'It was very sweet of you to ask, but you will always be my brother from a different mother.'

'And a different father too, thank God,' Harry said. He turned to Le Froy. 'So, are you bringing Su Lin back to England with you?'

'I don't think I'll be going back to England,' Le Froy said. 'You only complain about heat and humidity here until you've lived through freezing damp.'

'Bless you, my young lovers. I give you my full approval and blessing. Now excuse me, I have to find out what my other young lovers are doing.'

Harry headed over to Dr Leask and Parshanti as Fahey approached us.

'All for nothing,' Fahey said disconsolately. 'No sign of the brigadier's crates in the storehouses. The whole area's pretty much cleared out already.'

Parshanti must have replaced the camouflage. She and Leask were talking intensely, clearly focused on things that were more important than nine million dollars in share scrips.

'Come,' I said. 'I'll show you the van. And the encyclopaedias.'

Postscript

———◆———

Seventh Day of Chinese New Year: mix seven kinds of vegetable and eat raw fish (for good business), noodles (for longevity), pork, liver and kidney congee for good results in school and at work.

Le Froy joined us for the family meal and he was probably the reason why Ah Ma put extra effort into the preparations. But, despite her best efforts, we couldn't tell her what our plans were. How could we, when we didn't know ourselves? This Chinese New Year had truly brought us new beginnings. For now, being alive was the greatest miracle of all.

Since the missing – misplaced – share scrips had been recovered, the official channels were happy. So was Brigadier Evans, after his wife and stepson had returned to England without him.

'They'll need someone to administer the public-health services financed by the Opium Fund money,' Le Froy said. 'Horrible, thankless task. I pity whoever gets saddled with it.'

'Whoever gets saddled with it will need a good assistant,' I said. 'A good, local assistant.'

* * *

Inevitably people whispered and speculated about what had happened.

Without actually saying anything, Ah Ma allowed them to believe that Chen Tai had had both her former contractor and her son's wife killed for betraying him, and the British authorities were aware of it but had done nothing about it. It did wonders for business, even with the Chen family businesses and properties going legal.

I couldn't feel sorry that Shen Shen was dead. I wished I had been nicer to her, though, and got to know her better before everything started going downhill for her. Then again I might have made things worse. Hers was a horrible, unnecessary death but she'd horribly and unnecessarily caused the death of two others and tried for more, including mine. It's hard not to take something like that personally.

The only thing I felt really bad about was the baby.

'There was no baby,' Dr Shankar said.

'She lost it?'

'She wasn't pregnant.'

Shen Shen hadn't been trying to get rid of a baby. She'd been desperately trying to conceive one.

The Seventh Day of Chinese New Year was also Dr Leask's birthday.

Though their wedding had been postponed indefinitely, he and Parshanti were clearly a couple so the Shankars threw a birthday party for him and we all joined them there.

'Thank you so much for this. You people are my family. Shanti, I'll do all I can to support you in a life you deserve, you and your whole family, to the best of my ability. I don't have anything other than my salary but I'm not a drinking or a gambling man . . .'

The punch might have lubricated his words but I believe he meant them.

Parshanti looked more awkward than overwhelmed.

'That's what you say to us, not to her,' Dr Shankar said. 'Do you love our girl?'

'Pa!' Parshanti said, but no one paid any attention.

'Of course I love her.' Dr Leask looked miserable. 'I just mean I don't love only her, I love all of you. Even before all this,' he made a vague gesture in Parshanti's direction, which she acknowledged with a nod, 'you were like a second family to me. I never was close to mine. After my mother died I was like a leftover no one wanted but that they couldn't throw away. But you welcomed me here, Dr Shankar. You didn't care that it took me three tries to graduate from college. You helped me and taught me everything you could. You made me a better doctor than I could have been otherwise. And, Mrs Shankar . . .' He was unable to continue.

Mrs Shankar's laugh was a little shaky as she wrapped her plump arms around the thin Scotsman, 'Silly boy,' she said. 'I've always had a thing for leftovers. Even if you don't marry our girl you'll always be family. But, whatever she says now, we'll bring her around to seeing what's good for her!'

Acknowledgements

I must thank all the wonderful people who made this book possible.

Starting with Hazel Orme, who I swear does more to make my books readable than I can. Thank you, Hazel.

Thank you also to editorial director Krystyna Green and managing editor Amanda Keats, who guided and encouraged me through the writing process.

Thank you to Andy Bridge whose lovely cover design triggered a minor rewrite to incorporate a clue I saw there.

Also, thank you, thank you, thank you to the whole team at Constable/Little, Brown especially Eleanor Russell, Hannah Wann, Kim Bishop, Chris Sturtivant, Simon McArt, Beth Wright and Francesca Banks.

Finally a big thank-you to my angel agent, Priya Doraswamy, who started all this, and who is the reason I get to write books (still my favourite thing to do) that actually get published (always a thrill).

And thank you for picking up *The Yellow Rambutan Tree Mystery*. I hope you enjoy it in good health.

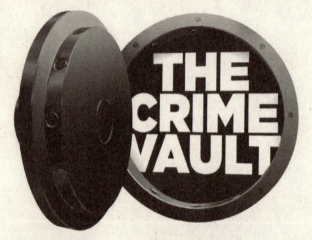